FIRST KISS

Leaning out from his saddle, Phillip pulled Lucy to his chest. "You tempt me, Lucy, as no other woman ever could. And still I wonder— "

He did not finish what he was about to say, and Lucy, held powerless in his embrace, could only stare, her heart pounding madly, as he lowered his head toward hers.

She was not sure what to expect at the touch of his lips to hers, but certainly it was not to feel a shockwave course through the length of her body or to feel her head, suddenly giddy, start to spin. Nor should she have expected to be struck suddenly and most unaccountably with a slow-mounting fever, like a hot wind that scattered her thoughts and rendered her delirious.

Faith, it was true— everything she had ever read or imagined about the first embrace between lovers. She could not doubt the evidence of her own senses. His was the sort of kiss she had always dreamed about . . . the kind one only experienced with one's own true love.

ZEBRA'S REGENCY ROMANCES
DAZZLE AND DELIGHT

A Noble Deception

Sara Blayne

ZEBRA BOOKS
KENSINGTON PUBLISHING CORP.

ZEBRA BOOKS are published by

Kensington Publishing Corp.
850 Third Avenue
New York, NY 10022

First Printing: December, 1995

Printed in the United States of America

To Sharon, the very best of friends and agents, with thanks for always being there with a helping hand.

One

The tower room at Lathrop could not have been said to offer congenial surrounds. Designed originally for defense, it was stark and barren, its octagonal fastness radiating narrow arched windows about its circumference. These, however, while affording an unobstructed view of the Yorkshire hill country for several miles in three directions and the North Sea in one, were deeply recessed, allowing only a feeble light to infiltrate the gloomy interior. They also lacked the benefit of either leaded panes or wooden shutters and so did little to keep out the draught. The wind moaned through the apertures and prowled along the walls like the lost and lonely spirits of the dead who were said to haunt the place. Furthermore, the walls of stone were a cold, drab grey, as normally was the floor. The latter at present had the temporary benefit of two colorful hand-stitched quilts spread out over it to lend it a somewhat more cozy appearance. Because it was seldom visited and never used, the room was dank and musty and boasted cobwebs suspended like gossamer drapes across the windows and from ceiling to wall. It doubtlessly would have boasted other, even less appealing evidence of its disused state had not Florence, the next to the oldest of the Earl of Bancroft's four daughters, refused to step foot across the threshold until the floor had been properly swept.

"It smells of mice, and very likely there are rats lurking in the rubble," she had declared with a distinct shudder. "You cannot expect me to go where there are rats, Lucy, when you know how I abhor them."

"Don't listen to her, Lucy," protested Francine, who, at fourteen, was three years younger than Florence and a devout tomboy. "The fact that it is so utterly loathsome is precisely what makes the tower room a perfect setting. The first reading of *The Lord of Lathrop* deserves nothing less."

"Then it will be read without me to hear it," pronounced Florence in dire tones. "Which would probably suit you perfectly well, Francie. Everyone knows *you're* not afraid of anything, except, perhaps, being made to behave in a manner proper for a female of refinement. No matter how little you might like it, Francine Elizabeth Powell, you *are* a girl, and the sooner you cease to play the tomboy, the better our parents will like it."

"The sooner you cease to play the gaby," retorted Francine, screwing her unfashionably tanned face up at her elder sister, who, with her perfectly coiffed curls and flawless complexion, was the acknowledged beauty of the family, "the better *I* shall like it."

It was at this juncture that Josephine, the last addition to the earl's brood of young hopefuls, a delicate-looking child of eleven, chose to intervene before her sisters could resort to more vituperative name-calling. "Is it really so much to ask, Francie? I daresay we cannot all be without sensibilities like you and Lucy. I confess I cannot like the thought of having rats crawling over my feet any better than Flo. And it is not a very large room, after all—is it, Lucy?" she asked, turning, as they all did sooner or later, to the one person upon whom they could always depend to settle a dispute or resolve a seemingly insurmountable problem. "I doubt it will take more than a few minutes to sweep it out."

Lucille Emily Powell, who had never quite forgiven her parents for naming her after her godmother—never mind that Lady Barrington would die childless, thus leaving her tidy fortune to her one and only godchild—and who preferred to think of herself as Lucinda Evalina, a much more appropriate name for a budding young writer of Gothic romance, quelled her impatience at the inevitable delay. It was only two hours and twenty minutes before the girls would have to report back to the schoolroom to attack the conjugation of French verbs, which was little enough time to give a proper rendering of her latest novella. She could not evoke the proper mood if she were forced to hurry through the pages. Still, she knew from experience that it was better to take the path of least resistance and save time than to try fruitlessly to budge an immovable obstacle.

"Jo is right, Francie," she had said after only a few moments of reflection. "It isn't a very large room, and it won't take long to make it more habitable for Flo if we all apply ourselves to the task. And as for the setting, I think the cobwebs will be sufficient for the mood. Now, let's waste no more time arguing."

In spite of Francie's complaint that Flo always got her way, the girls had set off in good order to fetch brooms from the storage room, fully four flights of stairs beneath the turret, after which they attacked the dirt and rubble on the floor with enthusiasm enough to raise a cloud of dust.

It was consequently with no little relief that Lucy found herself at last some twenty minutes later sitting cross-legged on a quilt spread over the freshly swept floor, the pages of her novella open on her lap, as she began in a properly somber tone to read the opening lines of *The Lord of Lathrop, or The Watcher in the Tower* to her sisters, crouched in various attitudes around her.

In the flickering light of the candle, which Francie had chosen for effect in lieu of the steadier, less eerie glow of a lantern, the girls presented a charming picture of young femininity. All of the Powell progeny, who, counting the thirteen-year-old twins, Timothy and Thomas, and the eighteen-year-old heir, William Michael, numbered seven in all, were blessed with their mother's fair hair and blue eyes. All, that was, save for Lucy.

She, to her disgust, had been cursed with flaming red hair and gray-green eyes reminiscent of her father's Irish grandmother. Added to these attributes was a generous sprinkling of the much dreaded freckles which so often accompanied the complexion of a true redhead. Her mother, who saw what Lucy did not, that her eldest daughter was a classic Irish beauty who would turn heads wherever she went, consoled her with the thought that she had what her brothers and sisters did not— an originality of looks which were distinctively hers alone.

It was Dutch comfort to one who must bear the cross of being called "red-crested," "flame-top,""red-tufted," and "carrot thatch." She tried to think of herself as Titian, but knew in her heart she was closer to rubiginous than chestnut. At least her eyes might have been the color of emeralds. It was so much more poetic, after all, than the nondescript green of the sea on an overcast day. Try as she might, however, she could not fool herself into believing they were not more green than hazel or more grey than jade. What she did not take into account and what anyone who came into her sphere could not but find intriguing was their peculiar propensity for changing from grey to green or back again with the vagaries of her mood, her dress, or the light.

At nineteen, she was convinced that there would never be a Theodore of Otranto in her life, or even the ghostly specter of a Lord of Lathrop, who had died for love of his lost Lucinda; and rather than settle for a marriage of forsaken dreams with one who wanted her only for her fortune, she had determined to live the life of a free spirit. She would live alone and write chilling tales of Gothic horror, mystery, and love triumphant.

Picking up the journal, she began to read her latest endeavor aloud in properly somber tones. An hour passed, then two, while the girls listened with rapt expressions.

"As the mists rolled away, banished by the quickening dawn," Lucy recited, coming to the end of the story, "Roanna shrank in horror from the Usurper's ghastly remains. Lord Faxon lay bloodied and broken among the ruins of the fallen tower— the very same tower in which twenty years before he had foully murdered the beautiful Lucinda and thus condemned the Lord of Lathrop to a lingering death.

It was as if the castle itself had risen up to right the wrongs of the true heirs of Lathrop, thought Roanna with a shudder as Florian enfolded her tenderly in his arms. And, indeed, among the crumbled walls of the

*ruined castle, she had at last found the iron coffer in
which were the documents proving Florian's lost birthright.*

*Lathrop was his now, and she was soon to be his
bride. Surely the spirits of the Lord of Lathrop and his
beloved Lucinda had found their peace at last."*

Lucy sighed as her voice trailed away into silence. Carefully, she closed her journal.

"Well?" she demanded, gazing expectantly at the
rapt faces around her.

"It was *won*derful," breathed Francine, who had
hung on every word of descriptive horror. "I'm
positively covered with goose bumps."

"Do you really think one grows faint at the mer-
est kiss?" Florence breathed, her lovely eyes distant
and dreamy.

"One must," Lucy replied, "if it is from the one
person one is destined to love. All the world knows
that. Unfortunately, it is doubtful that I shall ever
experience for myself that sublimest of passion. It
would be marvelous, indeed, if I were destined for
a great love. Who could possibly be interested in
someone with red hair and freckles?"

"Why, anyone," Josephine affirmed with all the
innocence of extreme youth. "I think you are
beautiful."

"You think Pugsy is beautiful," Francie pointed
out, Pugsy being their mama's pampered pet pug,
to whom their papa was fond of referring to as
"The Abomination."

"For shame, Francie!" exclaimed Florence,
greatly incensed. "How *can* you be so positively
insensible of Lucy's feelings? She cannot help it
that she is a throwback to Great-grandmama. It
might just as easily have been any one of us."

"It should have been you," Francie said unrepentantly, "if there were any justice in the world."

"Well, I, for one, should be happy to have Lucy's glorious hair," Josephine declared in her gentle manner. "And her eyes are wondrously mysterious, like the mists on the moors. I think it would be marvelous if you were *not* destined for love, Lucy."

"Do you, dearest?" Lucy smiled, her arm going about Josephine's shoulders. "And *I* think I am fortunate to have a sister like you."

"Very likely that is why Lady Barrington has asked her nephew, the duke, to pay his addresses," Josephine persisted. "One look at you, and I know he will fall head over ears in love with you."

"I'm afraid you are bound to be disappointed if that is what you are expecting," Florence interjected. "The Duke of Lathrop has no need of Lucy's fortune. He is already rich as Croesus. And besides being extremely well to look upon, he is the *Nonpareil*, a man who sets the fashion for everyone else. He can have his pick of practically any of the eligible females in the realm. It is doubtful he will notice someone like Lucy, who has never even been to London."

"Well, and whose fault is that?" demanded Francie, bridling at her older sister's air of superiority. "She would have made her come-out if you hadn't contracted the mumps."

"Oh, so now I am to be blamed for something that could not be helped, is that it?" demanded Florence, who had never really forgiven herself for having caused Lucy to miss her first Season in London.

"Of course you are not," Lucy asserted. "This is all a pointless discussion, in any event. The Duke of Lathrop is coming only to please his aunt. He has no interest in me and never could have. And nor could *I* in him. If ever I should lose my heart to someone, it will not be to the duke, who has everything he could possibly wish and consequently cannot possibly need anything from me, apart from a chatelaine for his houses and a brood mare to bear his heir."

"Really, Lucy," Florence objected, blushing profusely, "the children. That is hardly a subject for delicately bred females."

"It is, nevertheless, the truth," Lucy insisted. "I shall only love a man of great passion who has known suffering— a Theodore of Otranto or a Florian. And since I am not likely ever to encounter such a one, it is inconceivable that I shall ever marry. I could never settle for anything less than true love."

Josephine frowned, troubled at her best-loved sister's declaration. "Is *that* why Papa married Mama?" she asked, which earned everyone's immediate attention. "Because he wished a brood mare to give him Will?"

"No, dear. Of course it was not," Lucy was quick to answer. "Papa's case was quite different. Papa fell in love with Mama long before he was ever an earl. He was only ten, you see. And she was even younger. But they always knew that one day they would grow up and marry. But enough of that. It's time we were going. Miss Gladden will be looking for you in the school— "

She was interrupted by Francie's harsh whisper, which was enough to make the girls' hair stand on end. "Faith, what was *that*?"

"What was what?" Florence demanded testily. "I don't hear anything."

"That noise," Francie whispered thrillingly, "like the rattle of chains."

"Oh, really," Florence exploded. "Next, I suppose you will claim it is the ghost of Lathrop, come to drive us from his castle."

"Tell her to stop." Josephine gripped Lucy's hand with cold fingers. "Please, Lucy. She's making me afraid."

"Don't be such a goose," Lucy gently chided, squeezing the child's hand. "It was only a made-up story. There isn't really any Lord of Lathrop. At least not a dead one that haunts ruined castles."

"*Sh-h-h!*" Francie's hand shot up in warning. "There it is again!"

The girls drew close together, their faces suddenly pale. For the space of several heartbeats the castle tower remained steeped in silence. Then all of them heard it— a distinctly metallic clank issuing seemingly from the walls themselves.

"There!" Francie exclaimed in triumph. "I told you."

"It's the ghost of Lord Faxon," Florence moaned, pressing a hand to her breast. "I know it. He's coming for us!"

"Oh, but that would be everything that is marvelous," Francie ejaculated, her eyes leaping with anticipation. "I have always wanted to see a ghost."

"*Hush*, Francie," Lucy ordered, glancing significantly at Josephine's strained features. "It is no such thing. There isn't a Lord Faxon. He's only a product of my imagination."

"But you heard it. We all did," Florence insisted. "It will be all your fault if we are about to be flung from the parapets. It was you who insisted we come here." The sudden onset of a low, anguished wail, distinct and separate from the wind, washed

the last vestiges of color from Florence's face. She
swayed and clutched at Lucy's arm. "Faith, I shall
swoon, I know I shall."

It might be expected that the sight of Florence
on the point of going into a faint would be sufficient to elicit sympathy from her older sister. And,
indeed, perhaps it would have done— had not Lucy
detected in the wake of that dreadful moan another sound, faint and quickly stifled. Her features
suddenly grim, she straightened.

"If you do anything so utterly foolish, Florence
Anne Marie Powell, I promise we shall leave you
here," she warned in dire accents. "So I suggest
you get a grip on yourself. Francie, you and
Florence will gather up the quilts. After which you
will conduct Josephine down the turret stairs in
an orderly manner."

"But are you not coming with us?" Josephine's
grip tightened convulsively on her sister's hand.
"Lucy, you cannot mean to stay here?"

Lucy's face softened at the fear in the child's
voice.

"Softly, dearest." Gently she disengaged her
hand. "You go with Francie and Flo. I promise I
shall not be in the least danger. No ghost, real or
imaginary, is going to frighten me from Lathrop
Tower."

"It isn't fair," Francie was quick to protest. "I
want to stay, too. Why should you have all the fun?"

"Because I depend on you, Francie, not to do
anything foolish. With you to look after your sisters, I shan't worry."

Mollified somewhat by the faith Lucy placed in
her, Francie grudgingly took up the quilt and the
candle. "Oh, very well. I suppose it will be no use

to argue. But if you are not down in fifteen minutes, I shall tell Father where you are," she warned.

"I doubt that I shall be that long," Lucy assured them. "Now go. I shall be along directly."

No sooner had her sisters vanished round the curve in the staircase than Lucy hid herself in the shadows beyond the arched portal.

She had not long to wait. Scarcely a minute passed before she was rewarded with a low rumble, like heavy stone sliding over stone. For a moment she thought her eyes were deceiving her as a head appeared to thrust itself out of the center of the floor, followed by a pair of masculine shoulders.

"They're gone," announced a youthful voice in accents of glee. "Oh, how I should have liked to see their faces when you let out with that shriek, Tom. I daresay they will run all the way home without stopping to catch their breath."

Pulling himself through the trapdoor— for so Lucy had seen it to be— the young culprit scrambled quickly to his feet. He was joined by a second grinning cohort, who was an exact duplicate of the first. Though their fair hair was undeniably straight and demonstrated a lamentable tendency to fall haphazardly over the forehead, they both had their fair share of the Powell good looks. They were, in fact, Lucy's young brothers, Timothy and Thomas.

"That was a piece of luck, overhearing Francie tell Flo they were coming to Lathrop to read one of Lucy's stories," exulted Timothy. "I daresay not even Lucy knows about the secret passage."

"Faith, it is the ghost of Lord Faxon, come to fling us from the parapets," chortled Tom, imitating his sister Florence with the perfection of long practice.

"I think I shall swoon," moaned Timothy, the back of one hand lifted dramatically to his forehead. Both boys bent over, doubled with laughter.

The little devils! thought Lucy, who could not conceive of a punishment dire enough for the manner in which they had frightened their little sister Josephine.

"Oh, but it was rich," gasped Timothy, flopping down on the floor, his back to the wall. "It almost pays Flo back for telling Father we filched some of his snuff."

Tom, leaning his elbows against a window ledge, peered out over the downs, where the moorland of purple heather met the green dales of Bancroft Beck, the purling stream flashing silver among the bordering trees, and beyond, set on a hill in a sea of green, Greensward, the home of the Earls of Bancroft.

"Except that we daren't tell who it was that did it," he said, trying to catch sight of his sisters on the lane. "Lucy would never show us how she hooked 'Old Slippery' if she knew. And I mean to land him before Papa sends us off to school in the fall."

"I'll wager it was what she calls her 'Lathrop Fly,'" opined Timothy, who, like his twin, was an avid fisherman. "Lord, I'd love to lay my hands on it. Nobody can tie a fly like Lucy. Not even Papa."

"Nobody can tell a story like her, either," said Tom reflectively. "She almost had *me* believing in this ghost of Lathrop before she was through. I could have sworn there was someone else in the secret passage behind us. It gives me the shivers to think of it."

At this unprecedented announcement, Timothy cocked a disbelieving eye at his brother.

"Egads, Tom," he exclaimed in disgust. "Think what you're saying. You're beginning to sound like one of the girls."

"Am not!" declared Tom, bridling with anger.

"Are too," came Timothy back at him.

"Say that again and I'll show you who's a girl," Tom declared, rolling his fists in the air in the manner of a pugilist. "I'll bloody well draw your cork for you."

"You couldn't land me a facer if I had one hand tied behind my back," Timothy taunted him. A grin split his face as he leaped to his feet and, fists up, began circling his brother. "C'mon, girlie-boy. Come and take your medicine."

Lucy, who had been witness to innumerable such scenes, was unmoved at the possibility that one or both of her little brothers was about to come away with his nose bloodied. If nothing else, they deserved whatever minor damage they might inflict on one another. What she really wished was to teach them a lesson for having heartlessly frightened their youngest sister merely to get even with their older one. She might not agree with what Florence had done— she, herself, was never one to bear tales, especially to Papa— but nor could she condone practical jokes that did not at least spare the innocent. It was time the boys learned that they could not carry on their childish vendettas with impunity.

Suddenly a slow smile curved her lips as the germ of an idea began to take root in her mind.

Withdrawing noiselessly out of sight behind the newel post, she reached up and quickly removed the pins from her hair, allowing the thick tresses

to fall, unfettered, about her shoulders. It was not
enough. Wishing more of an effect, she shook out
the curls, ruffling them into a wild, unruly mass.
Then, gathering handfuls of fine grey dust from
the floor, she made a grimace of distaste, briefly
wondered if she had lost her wits, and thickly powdered her hair with the dreadful stuff. At last, still
not satisfied, she powdered her face as well. She
considered adding a veil of cobwebs for the finishing touch, only to immediately discard the notion. The very possibility that the webs might still
hoard one or two of their loathsome architects was
simply too awful to contemplate— even for one
who was reputed to be utterly lacking in sensibilities.

Judging that she had rendered herself suffi-
ciently unsightly, she at last retraced her steps to
the top of the stairs.

The twins, by this time, had abandoned the
manly art of fisticuffs for a rough and tumble on
the tower floor. Lucy, observing that Timothy had
torn his cuffs and that Tom's nankeens now
sported a hole in the knee where before there had
been none, suppressed a sigh. Their mama might
be a countess now, and the wife of a nobleman
with a more than comfortable fortune, but she had
grown up a parson's daughter who followed the
tenant that children, even those fortunate enough
to lack for nothing, should not be allowed to grow
up wastrels and care-for-naughts. The twins' torn
shirt and unmentionables would undoubtedly find
their way into the girls' mending baskets.

Deciding that it would be worth sewing on a patch
or two if it meant the boys were made to learn their
lesson, Lucy covered her face with loose strands of
hair and stepped across the threshold. She waited.

* * *

Timothy clamped an armlock on his brother and was on the point of demanding a cry for uncle when a sudden gust of wind fluttered Lucy's pale gown.

Timothy, his attention caught, froze. His jaw dropped at sight of the ghastly figure. Tom, feeling his brother's grip go lax, took advantage of the moment to reverse the hold. He flipped Timothy over on his back and almost had him pinned before he, too, caught sight of the specter bridling with seeming displeasure.

"Who-o-o?" it moaned in the anguished tone of a tormented soul. "Who-o-o dares trespass in the tower of doo-o-om?"

What came next occurred with comical swiftness.

Timothy, in his haste to make good his escape, knocked Tom asprawl almost at the feet of the ghost and dove past him for the staircase. In a panic, Tom scrambled to his feet and bolted after him.

Neither saw the tall, ghostly figure loom out of the darkness behind their tormentress and, towering over her, reach out for her with long, grasping fingers.

Two

It was all Lucy could do to stifle her gasps of laughter as she listened to the boys' frantic dash down the staircase. The little scapegraces deserved to be half scared out of their wits after the way they had frightened their little sister. From the sounds of their headlong flight, she doubted they would stop before they reached Greensward.

While she was congratulating herself on not feeling even the smallest twinge of conscience for having turned the tables on the twins, she failed to note the faint sound of a footfall at her back or to detect the towering figure draped in black that loomed out of the darkness of the secret passageway. A hand reached out for her, unawares. It occurred to her suddenly and somewhat belatedly that she was in for a terrible scolding from her mama when she made an appearance looking as if she had been dumped headfirst into a dustbin.

Abruptly she bent over. The hand stretching out to her closed on a fistful of air. Violently, she shook out her thick mane of hair, raising such a cloud of dust that she straightened, eyes streaming and one finger pressed above her upper lip against the irresistible tickle in her nose.

"Ah-aH-*AH—* " she gasped. Steely fingers gripped her shoulder from behind, and, *"Choo!"*

burst from her in something between a shriek and a sneeze.

"God bless you," commented a dry masculine voice.

The fingers loosed their grip as Lucy spun around to gape at what she instantly perceived, from his curly-brimmed beaver and his many-caped greatcoat of unrelieved black, to be a gentleman of fashion.

"The devil!" she gasped.

A single arrogant eyebrow shot upward in what was unmistakably a handsome forehead. "Well, not exactly," he mused whimsically, "though there might be more than a few who would agree with you."

Lucy clapped a hand over her mouth as it occurred to her exactly what she had blurted. "Oh, botheration," she exclaimed testily. "I suppose now I must beg your pardon, but you did startle me. Did no one ever tell you it was bad manners to sneak up on a person?"

"Undoubtedly, at one time or another." An almost indecently broad shoulder lifted carelessly in a shrug. "I am noted, however, for my deplorable manners. And now perhaps *you* will answer a question for me: Are you not in the least concerned to be talking to a total stranger in what can only be described as forbidding circumstances? I might be an unscrupulous villain who would not think twice about knocking you in the head and dragging you off to the dungeons. Er— there are dungeons in the castle, are there not?"

"I should not be at all surprised," Lucy agreed, eyeing him with undisguised skepticism. Certainly his aspect was sinister enough, the eyes little more than a glitter in the shadow of his hat brim and his lip curled in a smile that was distinctly cynical. Still, it was not exactly fear that he inspired in her, but an odd sort of tingling sensation along her spine, which she suspected was more on the order of excitement. And how not, when he was undoubtedly the most intriguing-looking man she had ever encountered before, and certainly the most handsome, from what she could tell in the uncertain light?

She could not but approve of the high, intelligent forehead, she decided, even if the bold slash of the black eyebrows and the drooping eyelids beneath them did give it an undeniably arrogant cast. And she had always had a preference for long, straight noses and lean, stubborn jaws. They, like the wide, sensitive mouth with what would seem to be its habitual, sardonic expression, were so distinctly indicative of reckless, passionate natures. Obviously he was a man of feeling, probably one who had experienced an exquisite anguish of some sort, which, having blighted his youth and destroyed his illusions, had left him a brooding and cynical Man of the World.

There was no denying that the masculine creases that appeared in either cheek when he affected a smile, ironic though it might be, appealed to her highly developed sense of what a romantical hero (or perhaps the villain, she added judiciously to herself) should be. Indeed, with his raven hair and dark, looming presence, he might have been Florian, stepped straight out of the pages of *The Lord of Lathrop*.

A reluctant grin tugged at the corners of her mouth. "You are roasting me, are you not?"

"The way you were roasting those two young thatchgallows, who fled so precipitately just now?"

A gleam of amusement flickered across the strong, arrogant features. "Is it your usual practice to powder your hair with dust? That would be a pity, you know. I suspect without its earthy camouflage it must shine in the sunlight, rather like a glorious halo of fire."

"It is, in fact, the bane of my existence," confided Lucy, who was used to rather less complimentary metaphors for her unruly mane— things involving carrots, foxtails, or red hens being the most common. Made thus aware of the totally disreputable appearance she presented, she blushed to the roots of her fiery tresses. "And, no, I do not in the norm affect a powdered appearance, as you must very well know. *If* it is any of your concern, I was intent on teaching my brothers a much needed lesson. And, now, sir, perhaps you would not think me too forward were I to inquire who you are and what you are doing here?"

"On the contrary, it would seem only reasonable," replied the gentleman, "especially in light of the fact that you obviously consider me encroaching as well as impertinent. The truth is, however, that I have a perfectly legitimate reason for being here."

Lucy stared at him dubiously. "Which is?" she prodded, when it seemed he did not intend to elaborate.

"Which is what?" queried the gentleman, who had been returning her stare with a most peculiarly arrested expression.

Lucy's brow wrinkled in a frown. "Your perfectly legitimate reason for being here," she reminded him, torn between irritation and sudden concern that she might be in the presence of a Bedlamite.

"Quite so," replied the gentleman, upon which he hesitated noticeably. "My name is . . . Carmichael. Phillip Carmichael. And I am, as it happens, the— er— duke's agent," he said at last, slowly, as if measuring his words. "I am here at Lathrop's request to look over the castle and determine the feasibility of restoring it to at least a semblance of its former glory. It seems His Grace is contemplating matrimony . . ."

"Matrimony?" gulped Lucy, feeling the blood suddenly drain from her cheeks.

"I believe that is what I said," Carmichael replied, one eyebrow elevated. "He would quite naturally wish Lathrop Castle rendered comfortable for his future bride."

"Naturally?" Lucy echoed, her mind spinning with alarm. "On the contrary, it is not in the least natural. Why should he wish any such thing *now*, when there has not been a Duke of Lathrop in residence for over fifty years?" It seemed all too plausibly clear to her why he might wish it and *whom* he might have in mind to marry, and all to please Lady Barrington, his aunt. Well, she would not have it. If she could not marry for love, she would rather remain a free and independent spinster for life.

In her agitation, Lucy turned and paced a step before coming back again. Consequently, she did not see the wry glimmer of a smile flicker briefly across Carmichael's lips. "I fear I cannot speak for His Grace," replied that worthy, leaning a shoulder against a window embrasure as he watched her. "It has occurred to me, however, that it is quite possible the female he has chosen for his future duchess may reside in the area. It would seem to fit in with his decision to restore the family seat, after all. It is not inconceivable that his intent is to do all in his power to ensure his bride's future happiness by making it possible for her to remain near her family and friends."

Lucy turned to stare at him, apparently much struck by the notion. "If that were true," she said slowly, "he would seem to be of a most generous disposition."

"I believe he is not an unfeeling man," replied Carmichael in what might be construed as judicious tones.

Lucy nodded absently and took two steps forward and back. "On the other hand, it could be interpreted as a desire to keep his future bride confined to the country," she speculated direly. "After all, he cannot truly be interested in someone he has never met before, and once he sees her he is very likely to wish to keep her hidden away while he pursues his pleasures elsewhere."

Carmichael's eyebrows snapped together over the bridge of his aristocratic nose. "You astonish me, Miss— er— Miss . . ."

"Powell," Lucy supplied absently, her mind still on the duke and his possibly nefarious plans for the future. "Miss Lucille Emily Powell."

The gentleman ironically inclined his head. "A pleasure, Miss Powell."

Lucy gave an impatient wave of the hand. "Likewise, Mr. Carmichael."

"As I was saying— " Carmichael coughed to clear his throat. "I had not thought you to be a woman of the world, Miss Powell. But then, appearances can be deceiving."

Lucy's head came up, sending a small cloud of dust into the air. "They can, indeed, Mr. Carmichael. Just because I have never been to London does not mean I am unaware of how the world goes on. I have read extensively all my life, and I

myself have aspirations of a literary nature. You
must not think me some naive creature."

Carmichael's smile was suitably grave. "You are
quite right to correct any misconceptions I might
have entertained, Miss Powell. You may be sure
that I begin to see you in a truer light."

"I am glad, Mr. Carmichael. You cannot know
how tiresome it is to be treated as a child constantly in need of being wrapped in white wool
when one has left the schoolroom quite some time
ago. I daresay you would not care for it at all."

"I should quite likely find it intolerable," agreed
the gentleman. Leisurely extracting an exquisite
Sevres snuffbox from his coat with the air of a
man gathering his thoughts, he inhaled a pinch of
what was undoubtedly his favorite mixture. "You
have my sympathy, Miss Powell," he said, returning
the box to his pocket. "But as to the subject of His
Grace, you would seem to know a great deal about
the duke and this potential bride of his. Would
you be surprised to discover that I find it difficult
to believe Lathrop would consent to marry a complete and utter antidote such as you would seem
to have described?"

Lucy flushed. "I never said she was an antidote,"
she declared heatedly, her eyes flashing with resentment. "She is simply not in the usual style— if,
that is, she is who I think she is. And, as for His
Grace, I have never laid eyes on the man and know
him only by his reputation as a Nonesuch and an
arbiter of fashion."

"Ah, no doubt that would explain your aversion
to him then," murmured Carmichael with only the
faintest hint of irony. "And who could blame you?
I myself find little to recommend in society frib-
bles."

Lucy had the grace to suffer a sudden twinge of conscience at that pronouncement. Faith, put in that light, she was made to appear rather too judgmental and shallow— she, who had always prided herself on viewing the world with an expanded sense of awareness. "I beg your pardon. I never meant to imply that His Grace was a fribble. Nor do I hold him in aversion. The truth is I know nothing about him and consequently cannot entertain any feelings toward him one way or another."

"I stand corrected, Miss Powell. You will admit, however, that a man who would abandon his wife in the country in order to pursue a life of dubious pleasure in the City would seem to have little to recommend him. And no doubt you are in the right of it. Certainly I should never dream of disputing a lady's opinion."

"Then I am afraid I shall be forced to think less of you, Mr. Carmichael," Lucy declared tartly. "Obviously you cannot think very much of me or my opinions. Not if you haven't the courage to take exception to those with which you cannot agree simply because I am a lady and you are a gentleman."

"Perhaps, Miss Powell, I am not the gentleman you think I am. Does it not occur to you that you know even less about me than you do my employer, the duke?"

"But you are wrong, surely," Lucy countered, stung that he apparently expected she must think less of him simply because he was forced to work for his living. "I have been talking to you for all of fifteen minutes, which is a deal more than I can claim for the duke. Why, we are well on the

way to becoming good friends, are we not, Mr.
Carmichael?"

"I should like to think so, Miss Powell," replied
the gentleman with a humble air, "though you
might very well wish me to the devil when you
come to know me better."

"I wish you will not be absurd, sir. You will find
that I am by nature intensely loyal. I am not easily
persuaded to turn on a friend." She paused, her
gaze reflective. "Speaking of friends, Mr. Carmichael," she said, glancing pensively back at him
over her shoulder. "Are you well acquainted with
Lathrop?"

Carmichael studied her from beneath drooping
eyelids. "Tolerably well, Miss Powell. I believe I can
say with complete honesty that, having been acquainted with him all my life, I quite possibly
know him as well as I know myself. Why do you
ask? Have you a personal interest in His Grace?"

"Indeed, Mr. Carmichael, I believe you might
say that I do." Feeling herself blush, Lucy turned
away to stare out over the purplish moors. "You
see, my father, the Earl of Bancroft, only just recently received a missive from Lady Barrington,
who, as you may or may not know, is the duke's
aunt and my godmother. The letter informed Papa
that the Duke of Lathrop, having decided it is time
he set up his nursery, would be calling to pay his
addresses to the eldest daughter of the house. I
am the eldest daughter, Mr. Carmichael."

"I see." Carmichael hesitated, his gaze specula-
tive on Lucy's averted face. "Am I correct in as-
suming you do not welcome the duke's
attentions?"

"Yes, Mr. Carmichael, you are." Lucy made an
impatient gesture. "Naturally, he is doing it solely

as a favor to Lady Barrington, and because he requires an heir. In which case, any female who is of good health and reasonably well to look upon will do. I, however, require more of a husband."

"More than a title second only to royalty and a fortune that would inspire most people to avarice?" drawled Carmichael. "You astonish me, Miss Powell."

A reluctant grin tugged at Lucy's lips. "Yes, I suppose I must seem rather hard to please. But thanks to Lady Barrington I shall be well-provided for, so I do not require the duke's fortune. And as for his title, I have never looked for the distinction that being the Duchess of Lathrop would bring. Happiness does not depend on such material things."

Carmichael raised a sardonic eyebrow. "Does it not, Miss Powell?"

"No, of course it does not. Happiness in marriage requires mutual affection and understanding. And a great deal of patience. The ability to forgive counts far more than rubies or diamonds. And perhaps even more important than forgiveness is the willingness to forget petty grievances. Believe, me, as the eldest of seven children, I have seen that principle amply demonstrated. But, most important of all, I should never marry for anything less than an all-consuming love."

Carmichael, crossing his arms over his chest, regarded her with a curious expression in his glittery eyes. "And you are quite certain, without ever having had the pleasure of being introduced to him, that Lathrop cannot meet these requirements? Is it not possible that you are being a trifle precipitate in your judgment?"

"I do not think so," Lucy answered without the

least hesitation. "I have given this subject lengthy consideration. A great love, Mr. Carmichael, is based on mutual need and an uplifting passion, and only a man who has experienced an exquisite anguish in his life could possibly have acquired the depth of feeling from which such a passion must spring. I cannot think that the duke, who lacks for nothing but a brood mare to provide him with the requisite heir, would be at all destined for such a love."

"You are a romantic, Miss Powell," Carmichael observed cynically.

"Yes, Mr. Carmichael, I am," responded Lucy.

Carmichael bent a curiously compassionate gaze upon the girl's dirt-besmudged face. "It has been my experience, Miss Powell," he said quietly, "that romantic love is extremely rare in marriages among our kind. I fear you are doomed to disappointment."

"Not at all, Mr. Carmichael," Lucy countered, her chin tilted in an attitude of firm resolution. "I do not expect that I am destined for a great love, any more than is the duke. Which is why I have determined to remain unmarried. I shall content myself with writing tales of Gothic horror, mystery, and love triumphant."

"No doubt His Grace will be delighted to hear that, Miss Powell," Carmichael dryly predicted. "It is not every duke who finds himself less appealing to a beautiful young woman than a life of spinsterhood."

"And *I* feel quite certain His Grace will be relieved, sir, at finding himself so easily quit of a marriage he cannot possibly want," declared Lucy with unshakable conviction.

"Perhaps," Carmichael murmured. He gazed at

her thoughtfully as he appeared to digest that information. "You seem unusually adamant in the belief that the duke will find you unattractive," he ventured after a moment. "Would you think me forward if I asked why you are so certain that will be the outcome?"

Lucy favored him with a pitying glance. "I should have thought it would be obvious to you, sir," she said lightly. "Though it is kind in you to say so, I am well aware that, even when I am not covered with dust, I am far from being beautiful, and, worse, I am not, I fear, of a conformable disposition. As the oldest of seven children, I have become hopelessly managing, intractable, and independent in my thinking. Not exactly qualities highly prized in a wife, you will admit."

"Perhaps not in the norm, Miss Powell," Carmichael said with a strange sort of gravity that Lucy found vaguely disquieting. "There are some men, however, who would value such a woman—one, who, far from being insipid and malleable, was possessed of those very traits you have described. A man would never be bored with such a wife."

Lucy stared at him, feeling herself drawn into the pale gleam of his eyes. "Would he not?" she asked, her voice ridiculously husky.

"No, Miss Powell, he would not."

Lucy swallowed, her mouth suddenly dry as Carmichael leaned over her so that all in a moment his strong, handsome features were revealed to her in a splash of sunlight from the window. His eyes, she discovered for the first time, were the clear, brilliant blue of the North Sea on one of those rare, unclouded days, and with the same hint of danger, lurking just beneath the surface. With a single look they pierced her through and held her, unable to move. Indeed, her heart was pounding and her mind was stunned by what she conceived to be a blinding flash of sublime illumination, not unlike what Roanna had experienced upon exchanging first glances with the mysterious raven-haired Florian. Suddenly all thoughts of the absent duke fled before the impelling awareness of Phillip Carmichael's all too disturbing presence.

"You are wrong, you know," he said, gently brushing a smudge of dirt from the tip of her nose with a careless forefinger. "Even dust-powdered, you are really quite extraordinarily lovely. I cannot think His Grace will be in the least put off by your appearance."

"Can you not?" Lucy watched, fascinated, as the smile faded from the remarkable eyes to be replaced by a long, probing look, which, besides being markedly sober, glinted with a piercing intensity that rendered her peculiarly spellbound. The finely chiseled lips parted, but before he could answer, Lucy jerked sharply upright. "No, of course you cannot," she blurted and backed up a step, breaking the spell under which he had held her. "You are the duke's agent. Naturally you are bound to say or do what is necessary to further his suit."

Carmichael's eyes hardened perceptibly. "I am not in the habit of lying, Miss Powell, not even for the sake of the duke," he asserted with a singular lack of mirth.

"Then you are being kind." Lucy pressed a hand over her wildly palpitating heart. "But I assure you it is not at all necessary. I grew accustomed a long time ago to the fact that I am a throwback to Papa's Irish grandmama."

"No, did you?" Carmichael expelled a heavy sigh. "No doubt your stubborn streak can be traced to your Irish forbear as well," he speculated dryly, straightening to his considerable height.

Lucy, staring up at him, felt suddenly and absurdly short of breath. In the spill of sunlight he appeared a deal larger and more formidable than when first she had turned to see him looming out of the shadows. Faith, tall, broad-shouldered, his masculine frame enveloped in the many-caped greatcoat, he fairly exuded strength and power—and an aura of untamed recklessness that made her feel ridiculously weak in the knees. It occurred to her that had she been the stranger to Lathrop and not he, she might have supposed he had been born and bred to the wild moorland, a fitting inhabitant of the great brooding castle falling slowly into disrepair.

Indeed, had she been looking for someone after which to pattern one of her heroes of Gothic romance, she need not have looked any farther than Phillip Carmichael. Who was he, really? she wondered, noting, upon closer scrutiny of the hard countenance, the fine lines of fatigue about the eyes and mouth and, more intriguing yet, his unnaturally pallid complexion. He had the look of a man who had recently suffered greatly from illness or injury and was not yet wholly recovered.

"Have you been in the duke's employ for long, Mr. Carmichael?" she asked, her curiosity fully aroused.

The gentleman's black eyebrows snapped together at the sudden change in subject. "No, Miss Powell. As a matter of fact, I came into the position an exceedingly short time ago. Why do you ask?"

Lucy shrugged. "Somehow you do not have the

look of an agent. My father's man of affairs is of
a very different sort. He is rather quiet and unas-
suming, and though he is a good man and kind,
his interests appear to revolve around such matters
as ledgers and property improvements, rents, and
all that sort of thing. One could not in one's wildest imagination think of him as being arrogant or
commanding in either manner or appearance."

"From which I must assume that I do present
such an image, is that it, Miss Powell?" drawled
the gentleman, with an uplifted eyebrow.

"You must know very well that you do, Mr. Carmichael," replied Lucy, apparently not in the least
discomfited by a pair of gimlet eyes boring holes
into hers. "Had you not told me your occupation,
I should never in a hundred years have guessed
you were employed by the duke in such a capacity.
And I am generally considered a keen observer
and a good judge of character."

"Valuable assets, no doubt, for an aspiring
author," Carmichael observed dryly. "And in what
capacity do you see me employed, Miss Powell?"

Never one to back away from a challenge, Lucy
studied him thoughtfully. "From your air of command I should rather have expected you to be a
man more used to giving orders than receiving
them— and having them obeyed without question.
And I can more easily visualize you on a horse
than seated at a desk. I wonder, would you be so
kind as to remove your gloves, sir?" she added,
unabashed by his imperious lift of an eyebrow.
"Ah, just as I thought," she exclaimed, taking his
hands when he had complied with her request and
turning them up to reveal calluses on the palms.
"You are given to athletic pursuits. Indeed, sir, I

would venture to say that you are more used to wielding a sword or a pistol than you are a pen."

"Congratulations, Miss Powell." The gentleman inclined his head ironically. "As it happens, I was, until quite recently, pursuing a career in the military. I resigned my commission little more than two months ago."

"Why, sir?" Lucy asked, quick to respond to the steely edge in his voice. "Because you were wounded?"

Carmichael uttered a short, hard laugh. "No, Miss Powell. Because I had no choice in the matter."

Lucy, vibrating to the undercurrent of bitterness she sensed in that final utterance, hastily lowered her eyes. "Did you not?" she murmured. She glanced steadfastly up again. "How very disagreeable that must have been for you. There is nothing so detestable as feeling the right to determine one's own life has suddenly been snatched from one."

"You sound as if you are speaking from experience, Miss Powell," Carmichael observed, his face losing some of its hardness.

"Indeed, sir, I felt much the same way when I was told about my godmother's letter concerning the duke. You can imagine how it must have been. My parents are constantly assuring me I should be flattered by the honor the duke wishes to bestow upon me, and my sister Florence insists I should be selfish in the extreme to refuse an offer that could only benefit her and the others when it comes their time to enter the Marriage Mart. Will, the oldest of my brothers, has even felt it necessary to point out that I shall very likely never receive another offer."

"No, has he?" Carmichael murmured dryly. "But how very disobliging of him."

"Yes, even if he is in the right of it," Lucy rue-fully agreed. "I began to think it was my duty to marry the duke, regardless of how I might feel about it. It seemed I had lost control over my own destiny. It did, that is, until I analyzed the situation and realized things were not so desperate as I had begun to imagine them to be."

"Ah, hence the decision to become the free-spirited novelist. I believe I begin to see."

"But of course you do. One may not always have what one wants, Mr. Carmichael, but one always has a choice, even if it is between two evils, so to speak. It must have been a great disappointment to you to have to give up your career. I expect you must have been very good at what you did— and that you can have little love for your new occupa-tion. It must seem very tame, after all, to find yourself overseeing the duke's estates when only a short time ago you were risking your life for king and country. The important thing is to remember that nothing has really changed. You are the same man you have always been, a man who is still mas-ter of his own fate."

"I begin to wonder, Miss Powell," drawled Car-michael, eyeing her strangely. "I am afraid I am not at all the man I was just a very short time ago, and my fate, as you call it, would seem to have taken a sudden turn. A turn that I suspect is going to prove as irreversible as it was unexpected."

Lucy blushed, uncertain how to interpret that cryptic utterance, or the exceedingly dry tones in which it had been couched. "Yes, well, we cannot always see what our fate will be," she answered, wondering why this man would seem to be having such an odd effect on her sensibilities. "But I have found that, whenever something happens that may at first seem unlucky, with a little concerted effort on my part, it nearly always turns out to be for the better. Perhaps it will be that way for you, Mr. Carmichael."

"You cannot know how fervently I hope you are right, Miss Powell," replied the gentleman, his expression enigmatic.

Lucy felt a shiver go most unaccountably up her spine at his words, rather in the way Roanna had experienced a shudder of portent at her first meeting with Florian. Indeed, if she did not know better, she would almost have believed that what she was experiencing with Phillip Carmichael was a momentously prodigious discovery, one of those rare instances when two people of destiny meet and are suddenly awakened to a mutually sympathetic awareness of one another. But that was absurd, she told herself firmly. Such moments were reserved for those fortunate few who were destined for a great, all-consuming love, and it was inconceivable that she could be counted among their number. Florence might be suited for such a role, or perhaps one day even the sweet, gentle Josephine, but not the eminently sensible Lucille Emily Powell, who aside from the indisputable fact that she lacked the essential ethereal beauty of a true romantic heroine, was far too hopelessly practical. If one of love's arrows were ever launched in her direction, she wryly speculated, it would more than likely simply glance off, repelled by her stubborn refusal to succumb to anything so irrational as fits of the doldrums, crying spells, or melancholia— mental states to which lovers were well known to be subjected but to which she was not in the least prone. She considered this an unfortunate flaw in her character; one more thing, like her red hair and freckles, that she owed to her father's Irish grandmama.

Still, she was not without certain positive attributes, she consoled herself. She had been blessed with a keen eye and a discerning heart, which told her that there was a deal more to Phillip Carmichael than he appeared willing to divulge.

"Forgive me, Mr. Carmichael, for forgetting my manners," she said, noting for the first time that his greatcoat and curly brimmed beaver showed distinct signs of travel. Obviously he had only just arrived. "You must be tired after your journey, and certainly the last thing you could have been expecting was to have to entertain a guest so soon upon your arrival. Especially one who was not invited."

"On the contrary, Miss Powell," Carmichael replied, "I am the one who has been vastly entertained. It is, in fact, my sincere hope that you will continue to feel free to visit Lathrop Castle whenever you wish." I expect to be in residence for some few weeks and would be grateful, not only for the company, but to have someone who is intimately acquainted with the area to serve as my guide."

"I should be only too happy to introduce you to your neighbors and the surrounding countryside," Lucy answered, smiling. "Though I daresay you may find you will have any number of Powells eager and willing to inflict themselves on you. Good God," she gasped, staring with sudden fixity out the window, "if I am not mistaken, you are about to make the acquaintance of a substantial portion of them in a very few moments."

"I beg your pardon?" queried her companion, his eyes narrowing on her at that startling announcement, couched in tones very nearly resembling horror.

Lucy did not hear him. "Oh, dear," she exclaimed, at the sight of the small procession setting out along the lane from Greensward to the castle, "I had quite forgot about Francine and the others. I daresay they have been worried sick about me. And now look. I promised I should be only a few minutes behind them, and now they are coming in full force, no doubt thinking to wrest me from the clutches of a ghost. Botheration, if I am not mistaken, they have not only seen fit to inform Papa of my supposed peril, but they have brought Mama with them as well."

"A hideous prospect," observed Carmichael, with a gleam of amusement. "I daresay the Ghost of Lathrop Tower must be all atremble."

Lucy awarded him a moue of disgust. "You may well laugh, Mr. Carmichael. It is not you who must face my parents' displeasure. Indeed, I am afraid you will have to look elsewhere for your guide, sir. I shall no doubt be confined indefinitely to my room on a diet of bread and water when they behold my disreputable appearance."

"Then we must make sure they do not see you like this," pronounced Carmichael. Taking her arm, he drew her toward the secret passage. "I should say we have time enough for you to wash your face and brush your hair if we hurry." Carmichael's eyes met hers as he felt her hesitate. "Come, my dear, it would not be at all like a budding writer of Gothic romance to balk at the prospect of exploring a secret staircase. And you, after all, are a free and independent spirit. If it is the

ghost of Lathrop Tower you fear, I promise to protect you."

Lucy choked on a giggle. "I wish you will not
be absurd. You know very well I am dying to see
where your secret passage leads. It is only that I
am suddenly reminded that I am quite alone with
a gentleman in circumstances of which my parents
could hardly approve." How much greater, then,
would be their disapprobation at discovering their
eldest daughter *inside* that gentleman's domicile!
Lucy thought with a sinking feeling in the pit of
her stomach. It really did not bear thinking on.

Mr. Carmichael, however, appeared remarkably
undaunted at the prospect. "If it is the proprieties
that concern you, rest assured: You are in no danger of being compromised. I give you my word."

Lucy hesitated only an instant longer. He looked
so large and commanding, so very sure of himself!
"Well, then," she said at last, dimpling up at him,
"what are we waiting for?"

Before he could answer she grasped his hand
and took the first step into the stairwell, spiraling
downward into darkness.

"Oh, I cannot see a thing," she gasped as the
circular stone slid back into place. "How did you
do that?"

"Here." Strong fingers grasped her hand and
guided it to a brass wall sconce, which presumably
had been meant at one time to house a torch. "You
have only to turn it counterclockwise."

"How did you know?" queried Lucy, thinking
she would not soon forgive the twins for having
kept the secret of the passageway to themselves.

"The Dukes of Lathrop are noteworthy for their
extensive libraries and records. Nothing is too insignificant to preserve, it would seem," drawled

Carmichael, holding Lucy's hand as he groped his way down the steps, guided by the wall. "I was fortunate to discover the original diagrams for the castle in the duke's library at Hollingsworth before I left. They proved to be most instructive."

"Instructive! Faith, what an understatement!" exclaimed Lucy thrillingly. "What I shouldn't give to see them. And then to explore every dungeon, hall, and parapet. Just the thought of it gives me gooseflesh."

Strangely, the sound of a deep, masculine chuckle had a similar effect on her, she was instantly to discover.

"Such an excursion would give most females of my acquaintance gooseflesh, but for entirely different reasons, I suspect," came Carmichael's amused observation. "As it happens, I shall be doing extensive prowling through the duke's ancestral hall. Should you care to join me on occasion, I should not object to the company."

"Oh, I should like it above all things," Lucy averred, "though I cannot be certain my parents will see it in a favorable light. Perhaps they could be persuaded to allow it were I to bring Francie with me however," she added a trifle doubtfully.

"Francie, being, I must presume," replied Carmichael, "one of the six siblings with which you have been endowed. Does, she, like you, aspire to write romance?"

"Heavens, no," laughed Lucy, amused at the very thought of her tomboy sister sitting still long enough to write a paragraph, let alone a story in its entirety. "She is, however, as lacking in delicate sensibilities as am I, and would be just as keen to explore even the gloomiest castle simply for the adventure of it."

"Then naturally the invitation is extended to young Francie as well, and any other of your siblings you would like to have with you. On the condition, of course, that I am always present to ensure their safety."

"You are very kind, sir," Lucy said, thrilling to the stale scent of the long-unused passageway and the hollow echo of their footsteps in the impenetrable gloom. "I should limit the invitation to two Powells at a time were I you, however. More than that would likely discourage you from the notion of ever setting up your own nursery."

"Do you think so?" drifted enigmatically back to her. "I am not, I warn you, easily discouraged."

She did not answer. Not only had the stairway come to an intriguing end, giving way to a level floor, but they had taken a sudden turn, immediately after which she had heard the distinct sound of a door sliding shut behind her. The cold clamminess of the stone wall, smooth beneath her palm, sent a delicious chill down her spine, even as the clinging caress of a cobweb across her face startled a low gasp from her lips. Grimacing in disgust, she brushed the loathsome thing away. Immediately thereafter, however, she was smiling delightedly to herself in the darkness. Oh, but it was simply lovely. Indeed, she had never had so marvelous an adventure. And best of all, it was just as she had imagined it would be when she described it in *The Lord of Lathrop*.

No sooner had that thought crossed her mind than she came up unexpectedly against a very large unmovable object— Carmichael, who had come to a halt.

"Softly," he murmured, reaching back to steady her. "We are at the end of the passage." She sensed him, even in the dark, grope for something. "It's here somewhere," he muttered, more to himself, she suspected, than to her. "Ah, yes."

A hollow rasp, like stone grating against stone, sounded loud in the silent gloom. A sliver of light sprang out of nowhere, widening into a golden shaft that spilled through an open doorway, and beyond, Lucy, squinting and blinking against the sudden brightness, beheld a room, which, if a trifle shabby, was yet spacious and pleasantly warm with tapestry wall hangings, bright Oriental floor coverings, ceiling-high shelves of books, and, most welcome of all, a blazing fire in a great open fireplace.

"Oh," she breathed in apparent alt, "this is everything that is magnificent!"

"Welcome, Miss Powell," drawled Carmichael, watching her, "to the Lord of Lathrop's study."

Three

Lucy completed the final stitch on Timothy's torn cuffs and, tying off the knot, broke the thread between her teeth.

"There," she said with a comical grimace. "The final reparation for my misdeeds."

Folding her brother's shirt and dropping it on the pile of mending she had completed that morning, she let her gaze stray, not for the first time, to the scene outside her window.

From the attic room beneath the eaves, which she had long ago adopted as her private haven away from the usual turmoil created by the profusion of Powells at Greensward, she espied the figures of her twin brothers casting lines into the fishing holes along Bancroft Beck. A flash of color in the paddock beyond the stables briefly engaged her attention— Francie putting Jester, the green colt her Papa had given her to train, through his paces on a lunge rein. Absently, Lucy's mind registered the fact that Florence was practicing her Mozart on the pianoforte, and no doubt Josephine was in the garden with Mama cutting fresh flowers for the house. That left only Will, who presumably had ridden out earlier with Papa, she thought, gratified to escape for a time the bantering and teasing of her younger siblings.

They had whisked her off to the schoolroom the evening before and bombarded her with an unending stream of questions about Carmichael, the Ghost of Lathrop Tower, and, most uncomfortable of all, what she had been doing all that time alone with a gentleman she had never met before.

"Nothing," she had repeated for at least the fourth time to Florence's persistent interrogation on the subject. "We only talked, mostly about the duke."

"What about the duke?" demanded Florence. "He is still coming, is he not?"

"Of course he is coming," interjected Francie in disgust. "Don't be an idiot. Why else would he send Mr. Carmichael to Lathrop?"

"You ought not to be so hard on old Flo," commented Tom, amusing himself by bouncing a rubber ball against the wall. "She cannot help being an idiot. On the other hand," he added, neatly ducking an eraser Flo hurtled at his head, "I don't see what one has to do with the other."

Francie plopped down on the windowseat and gave a careless shrug. "But it's obvious, isn't it? The duke will need someplace to stay while he pays court to Lucy."

"I don't see why," Tom retorted.

"He is not *going* to pay court to me," Lucy averred.

"He could stay with us," Timothy supplied, taking up where his brother had left off as if Lucy had never spoken.

"But why should he, when he owns a castle less than ten minutes' ride from Greensward?" Josephine gently pointed out. "And of course he is going to pay court to you, Lucy. It's why he is coming, after all."

"Exactly so," Francie applauded. "I know how hard it is for the rest of you, but just try and think for a moment. Mr. Carmichael is the duke's agent. Why should Lathrop send him here if not to spruce up the place for the duke, hire some staff, and make Lathrop ready for His Grace to take up residence?"

"As a matter of fact, that is exactly why he is here," Lucy submitted, giving in to the inevitable. "But you are wrong about Lathrop. He will not be courting me because I intend to inform him without roundaboutation that I must refuse his kind offer."

"Unfortunately *he* does not know that," Francie said, going instantly to the heart of the matter. "It only takes a modicum of reason to explain Mr. Carmichael's presence. It's the ghost that we really want to know about, Lucy. Did you see it? Was it deliciously terrible?"

"Oh, it must have been dreadful," Josephine said with a shudder. "Though they pretend nothing happened, I saw Tom and Timothy when they came out of the tower. They were white as sheets, and they ran right past us without saying a word."

"No, did they?" murmured Lucy, suppressing a grin at the sight of Timothy, who had assumed a preoccupied air, and Tom, who appeared suddenly absorbed in contemplation of the toe of one disreputably scuffed boot. "Then no doubt you should ask *them* about the ghost, because I never saw it."

"Who said anything about a ghost?" shrugged Timothy, red-faced beneath an unruly thatch of fair hair. "We were just having a race to see who could reach home first."

"Gammon. You were scared half out of your wits

and you know it," Flo said with her customary air of superiority.

Naturally incensed at this disparagement of their courage, Tom bridled. "You're one to talk, Florence Faint-of-Heart. If there had been a ghost, do you think we should ever have run? I daresay there isn't a ghost alive who could scare Tim and me."

"But ghosts aren't alive, stoopid," Francie observed, pouncing with relish on the glaring flaw in his argument. "They are disembodied souls condemned to torment, and they like nothing better than to frighten little boys with ghastly moans and blood-curdling wails. Are you quite certain that is not what sent you fleeing *ventre à terre* from the castle tower?"

"Who are you calling 'little'?" demanded Tom. Thrusting his face within inches of his tomboyish sister's, he neatly sidestepped the significant question.

"You," Francie retorted. "And your dwarf-sized twin, of course."

Upon which Timothy felt compelled to enter the fray. "Dash it all, Francie, you're only a year older than us."

"A year and two months," she corrected. "And I'm a head taller than either of you."

"You are not," declared Tom, standing as tall as he might, which was indeed a good six inches shorter than Francie's lanky height.

"Am too," retorted Francie, making a face at him, "and I'm not afraid of any old ghost."

It was at this juncture that Lucy, in no mood to endure one of the "am-too, are-not" debates that the three combatants were quite capable of indulging themselves in to a point ad infinitum, had settled the matter unequivocally by promising in dire tones that they were all likely to suffer stunted growths if they did not immediately take themselves off to their rooms.

And that had been that, reflected Lucy, propping her chin on her elbow on the arm of her chair. She felt her gaze drawn, as if of its own accord, to the purple haze of moorland rising above the verdant downs. There, crouched on the heather-covered hill, Lathrop Castle brooded, a stark reminder of the curious events of the previous day.

She still had difficulty believing she had managed to escape with only a minor scold from her mama when she had been certain she would receive nothing less than a year's worth of mending in return for the stunt she had pulled. No doubt it had helped somewhat that she had managed to make herself rather less disreputable in appearance by washing her face and hands and brushing out her hair before presenting herself in the duke's surprisingly well-appointed, if somewhat dusty and antiquated, parlor.

Even so, she had approached the heavy carved oak door acutely aware that her gown was soiled and that she would have a deal of explaining to do. After all, she had not only caused her parents extreme anxiety on her behalf, but she had allowed herself to remain unchaperoned for longer than twenty minutes in the company of a gentleman to whom she had not even been properly introduced. In light of the fact that the Duke of Lathrop had all but made it plain he meant to offer for her hand, the possibility that she might very well have jeopardized her good name and compromised herself with a stranger should have, at the very least, put even her normally most understanding of par-

ents into a taking, she had reasoned, and had
steeled herself for what promised to be an extremely unpleasant confrontation.

Instead, she had been greeted by the sound of
her mama's laughter and the surprising aspect of
her papa lounging at ease in a great overstuffed
chair before a blazing fireplace over which Phillip
Carmichael towered, one elbow propped casually
on the mantelpiece. Perhaps even more startling,
however, was the complete absence of the younger
Powells, who, it soon turned out, had been sent
home immediately after it was ascertained that
their sister had not been abducted by the Ghost
of Lathrop Tower or anyone else, for that matter.

"Ah, Miss Powell," Carmichael drawled,
straightening to his full, impressive height.

Lucy's heart inexplicably gave a leap as he came
toward her, striding with an easy, supple grace that
sent a soft thrill coursing through her. Then, what
the devil? she wondered as, bending his head to
salute her knuckles, he deliberately winked an eye
at her. "Mr. Carmichael," she had said on a swal-
low and hastily dipped him a curtsey.

Carmichael smiled with what could only be construed as a conspiratorial air; then, tucking her
hand in the crook of his arm, he turned to face
the earl and his countess. "I was just telling Bancroft and Lady Emmaline about our chance encounter in the tower room and how, in the
excitement of discovering we share a mutual interest in old houses and hidden passageways, I failed
to consider the deplorable condition of most of
the castle. I deeply regret that, because of my
thoughtlessness, Miss Powell ruined her gown during our exploration of the secret staircase."

"Nonsense," spoke up the countess, a twinkle in

her lovely eyes. "The gown can be cleaned. And I'm sure Lucy enjoyed her little adventure immensely, didn't you, dear?"

"Indeed, Mama," Lucy replied, all but heaving a sigh of relief. How very clever of Carmichael to come up with something so very simple as the truth to tell her parents. Lies tended to prove so very cumbersome. And if it was not exactly all the truth, at least what her parents did not know could not, in this case, possibly hurt them. "The secret staircase was everything I could have hoped it to be, and Mr. Carmichael everything that is kind. He has generously invited Francie and me to join him when he explores the rest of the castle. Oh, please do say that we may! I have always wished to see a dungeon. I should like above all things to discover it is still furnished with wall chains and any number of engines of torture."

"Lucy, for heaven's sake," gently reproved her mama. "I pray you will not be absurd. Those are hardly interests suitable to a young woman of refinement."

"On the contrary, Mama, judging by the continuing popularity of the Gothic romance in ladies' reading circles, females of refinement are obviously fascinated by such things."

"That is hardly a recommendation, my dear," observed the earl in tolerant amusement. "In any case, you are bound to be disappointed. All that sort of thing went out of fashion centuries ago. A pity, really. I have often thought wall chains and engines of torture just the thing for bringing up children."

"You never thought any such thing," objected the countess, awarding her spouse a scandalized look of reproach. "Do not believe him, Mr. Carmichael. He has been the best of fathers. I daresay he has never lifted a hand to any one of his children."

"Indeed, no," chuckled his lordship. "I leave all that sort of thing to you, my love. Which reminds me: We really should be getting home. The thought of our numerous progeny left untended for any length of time is hardly conducive to comfort. Mr. Carmichael." Having earlier risen from his chair at his daughter's entrance, the earl extended a hand to his host. "It has been a pleasure, sir. May I be the first to welcome you to our neighborhood? I hope you will make it a habit of calling on us at Greensward. I should be pleased to show you my collection of rare and antique books."

"Now, William," admonished his wife, coming to her feet and fondly taking his arm, "you must not frighten Mr. Carmichael away with your promised treats. Not everyone has as keen an appreciation for moldering old books as do you."

"But, Mama, Mr. Carmichael is something of a student of antique manuscripts," Lucy interjected, an imp of laughter in the look she lifted to Carmichael. "The dukes of Lathrop, it seems, never discard anything and consequently have an extensive collection of rare old things. You must ask Mr. Carmichael to tell you about the original drawings of the castle he located among them."

This had the effect of galvanizing the earl, who positively beamed on the newest inhabitant of Lathrop Castle.

"By Jove, what luck. I should dearly like to see those diagrams, sir."

"Then, naturally, nothing would give me greater pleasure than to show them to you, my lord," replied Carmichael. "In fact, I suspect you could be of no little help to me in deciphering some of the notations. My Latin is somewhat better than adequate, but the quality of the manuscript has suffered the inevitable effects of age, rendering parts of it nearly illegible."

"Did you hear that, Emmaline? A puzzle to be solved. When would you like to start, sir? I myself am available immediately."

"Mr. Carmichael, however, has just sustained a long journey and consequently must soon be wishing us at Jericho," admonished the countess, exchanging an understanding glance with their host. "You must come for dinner one evening soon, Mr. Carmichael. Shall we say day after tomorrow? I cannot promise you a French cuisine, but you may be sure of good English cooking."

"I should be honored, Lady Emmaline," said Carmichael, inclining his head, "and more than gratified. I'm afraid the entire staff at Lathrop at present consists solely of the caretaker, my coachman and groom, and my own personal servant. Until I can engage a cook and kitchen help, as well as household servants, I shall be dependent on what my valet can prepare."

"Oh, but that will never do," blurted Lucy, appalled somehow to think of his existing on what must amount to little better than camp fare. "You must come and take your meals with us." A blush invaded her cheeks at the sight of her papa's bemused lift of an eyebrow. "Must he not, Mama?" she ended, raising her head and plunging recklessly on.

"But of course he must," had been Lady Emmaline's inevitable conclusion. "We should be pleased, Mr. Carmichael, were you to think of our home as your own while you are here. You need only drop in, and you will find there is always a place for you at our table."

"Excellent," pronounced the earl. "Then it's settled. We shall expect you for dinner at five, sir."

Mr. Carmichael, however, while exceedingly grateful for their kindness and though certain he would be pleased in the coming weeks to take frequent advantage of their generous offer of hospitality, graciously asked to be excused from dinner that evening. He had dined earlier at the village inn and, foreseeing something of the difficulties involved in setting up housekeeping at the castle, had taken the precaution of providing himself with foodstuffs enough to last him for the next few meals.

Lucy, staring at the castle from her attic window, did not know whether she felt relief or disappointment that the mysterious Mr. Carmichael had not been persuaded to come to Greensward sooner than the earlier invitation for the morrow. Inviting an almost complete stranger to practically run tame in her parents' house without having first taken the precaution of asking their permission was hardly her usual custom. She had been every whit as surprised as they must have been when she acted on impulse, and one, which had been prompted, she little doubted, by her awareness of the evidence writ on the unnaturally pallid features of what must certainly have been his recent suffering of an acute anguish of some sort.

Even now a blush came to her cheeks at the memory of her precipitate outburst. Faith, no wonder he had cried off. Indeed, she little doubted that he must consider her, at the very least, childishly impetuous and, at the very worst, unfemininely coming. The possibility that, indeed, he might very well believe she had deliberately set her cap for him was mortifying in the extreme.

"Oh, hell and damnation!" she uttered to the edification of the empty room. "What can it possibly matter *what* he thinks! I know, if no one else does, that mine was purely a compassionate gesture. I haven't the least interest in Mr. Phillip Carmichael, or anyone else, for that matter."

That much settled at least, she should have felt immediately better. Unfortunately, however, she could not shake the notion that the real reason for the gentleman's reticence was something else altogether.

It had come to her as she lay in her bed the previous night and it had gradually grown to what amounted to a conviction that Carmichael was far from well. Obviously he was a proud man, and everyone knew proud men did not readily admit to any sort of weakness. Having most probably only recently risen from a sickbed, he had come all the way from Hollingsworth in Hampshire to the North York Moors. How greatly must his strength have been taxed by a journey covering almost the entire length of England.

Naturally he would have no desire to socialize and make small talk. Very probably he had wished only to escape to the privacy of his room, and there, shut away from prying eyes, to give in at last to his fatigue. Very likely he had contracted a fever from overtaxing his strength and even now lay alone and suffering in his bed with only a gentleman's gentleman and the old caretaker to know and look after him.

How like a man, she thought, to choose to endure his illness alone when he might have had her to soothe his hot brow with lavender water and to doctor his fever with chicken broth and willow bark tea. Heaven knew she had helped to nurse her younger brothers and sisters often enough.

A sigh escaped through her lips as she allowed fancy to conjure up the image of herself administering to Carmichael as he lay delirious and wracked with fever. She was just at the point at which he opened his eyes to behold her bending over him and had just visualized the leap of recognition in the fever-lit orbs, followed swiftly by a blaze of tender passion, when she was jolted back to reality by the realization of just exactly where her unruly imagination was taking her.

"Good God," she gasped and bolted to her feet, bosom heaving, her hands clapped to heated cheeks. "Lucille Emily Powell, what in heaven's name are you about? Obviously you have been tucked away in the country far too long!"

Twenty minutes later, having changed from her morning gown into her riding habit, she was mounted on Wind Star, her dappled grey mare. Lifting the reins, she set the grey into a trot along her favorite trail, which, climbing out of the valley onto the craggy moors, skirted the rocky headland overlooking the sea.

She had always loved the mist-laden coast with its many small, rough bays and high, rugged cliffs. Perched on a rock with the sea swells beneath her and the castle, stolid and seemingly impregnable, on the headland across from her, she could daydream and concoct, seemingly out of the mists, any number of romantic tales of love and heroism. Here, she had composed *The Lord of Lathrop* nearly in its entirety, the words and images flowing effortlessly onto the pages of her journal. It was like nothing she had ever experienced before, that fe-

verish outpouring of ideas. Indeed, she had felt
intoxicated with her sense of creative power.

Whatever it was she had felt then, however, had
apparently deserted her, she reflected, glancing
ruefully down at the empty page of her journal.
She had been staring mindlessly into space for at
least forty-five minutes, she judged. No, she corrected, not mindlessly, exactly. She did not suppose
one's mind could ever be totally blank. There were
always thoughts of some sort, and hers, to her disgust, had been usurped by Phillip Carmichael.

It was bad enough that she was plagued by unwitting images of him, which seemed to pop into
her mind at the most inconvenient times. Like that
morning, for example, at breakfast. One moment
she had been telling Timothy not to gobble down
his grilled kidneys and the next Mama was chiding
her to stop toying with her food and eat. With a
start, she had come to amid the smirks of the
younger Powells to discover that she had been sitting for quite some five minutes contemplating the
peculiar effects on one's sensibilities of eyes the
clear blue of the North Sea on an unclouded day.

Oh, yes, that was bad enough. But even more
disturbing to her equanimity was the sense of mystery that seemed to emanate from his very being.

Who was he, really? she wondered, not for the
first time since she had been startled half out of
her wits by his unexpected materialization in the
tower room. While he had seemed perfectly willing
to discuss his employer, the duke, he had proven
maddeningly elusive when it came to revealing the
least little information about himself.

Mentally, she tallied the meager tidbits she had
managed to glean: He had been in the military;
he had left the military suddenly and apparently

against his will under circumstances that had allowed him no choice but to have done; he had a better than adequate mastery of Latin; and he had known the duke intimately all of his life. All in all, it was not very elucidating.

It was, in fact, only enough to pique her curiosity and drive her half mad with imagining all sorts of intriguing scenarios, when what she really wished to do was banish him from her thoughts altogether. How else was she to get any writing done?

"Blast the man!" she exclaimed, knowing she was being unreasonable to blame him for her inability to do what she had come to do but not caring. "It is all his fault for turning up out of the blue to complicate my life, when I was perfectly happy never knowing he existed."

Determined not to waste the time remaining before she must ride back to Greensward, she deliberately turned her back on the tantalizing aspect of the castle.

"Now, let me see," she murmured, chewing on the tip of her quill pen; "where was I?"

She was exactly nowhere, not even having come up with that most important of all lines in any story—the very first—before she had lost herself in speculation of what events could possibly have resulted in Carmichael's being forced to resign his commission.

Deciding that a description of the setting might be the very place to begin, she dipped the pen in ink and wrote, "The night was dark with portent, too horrible to contemplate, as . . ."

"H-m-m-m," murmured Lucy, brushing the quill feather against her cheek. "Who shall it be sallying forth in the face of the storm? Letitia, perhaps?

Marguerite, Pamela, Isabel, Charis?" She giggled
at the thought of Prudie or Hortense. "No, Leon-
ora. Or, better— Evalina. Oh, yes, most certainly
Evalina. Evalina what?" She toyed with various sur-
names, none of which pleased her, until, experi-
menting with merely putting syllables together,
she came up with Drackman. "Drackman. Drackman. Evalina Drackman. Oh, but I like it. It has
just the right exotic flavor."

Dipping the pen once more in the ink, Lucy
wrote, "Evalina Drackman stepped down from the
carriage before the deserted . . ." A sudden gust
of wind caught the page and fluttered it at the
very instant that a large drop of rain splattered
itself against the neatly inscribed "Evalina," smear-
ing it.

"Hellfire and damnation." Lucy slammed the
journal shut.

In her preoccupation, first with Phillip Carmichael and then with the exotic Evalina Drackman, she had failed to note the sudden swift
gathering of rainclouds overhead. She knew at
once that she was in for a wetting long before she
could reach Greensward. But not, perhaps, she reflected, her eyes going to the castle, before she
could reach Lathrop.

Fleetingly it occurred to her that the proprieties
might be considerably bruised were she to burst
in on Mr. Carmichael uninvited and without so
much as a groom to accompany her. Still, she could
hardly be blamed for seeking shelter from a storm,
she reasoned, and it was not as if she would stay
overlong. Summer showers came and went with
equal suddenness. Firmly refusing to allow that
she might be motivated more by a desire simply
to see Mr. Carmichael again than to escape a wet-

ting, and reassuring herself with the certainty that
Mama would never forgive her if her eldest daughter were to contract a fatal inflammation of the
lungs, she quickly tucked her writing box in the
pouch slung from her saddle for that purpose;
then, mounting, she sent the mare at a gallop for
the protection of the castle.

Nearly blinded by the howling wind and her
hair, whipping madly about her face, Lucy gloried
in her wild dash along the cliff tops. Perhaps
rather than anything so staid as a carriage, Evalina
Drackman should make her entrance in just such
a fashion: a reckless flight on horseback into the
very teeth of a storm, with masked riders in hot
pursuit! What a glorious beginning to a tale of
adventure and romance that must be, she thought,
as her mount thundered through the castle gates
and plunged to a halt—just in the nick of time.

Lightning slithered across the sky, giving forth
with a resounding clap of thunder, and the heavens opened up.

Lucy clung to the saddle as Wind Star sidled in
fright and reared. "Easy!" Lucy called to the mare.

From out of nowhere a figure appeared. From
the back of the plunging mare Lucy caught sight
of powerful shoulders and raven hair. It was Phillip Carmichael, looking surprisingly healthy for a
man who was supposed to have been wracked with
fever only the night before. A lean, strong hand
caught the mare's bridle.

"Hang on!" Pulling the mare's head down, Carmichael led the horse across the bailey into a covered passageway. Shut out by thick stone walls, the
sound and fury of the storm instantly receded to
a distant rumble.

Lucy laughed, her blood still surging from the

thrill of the ride and the sudden eruption of the elements. "I beg your pardon for this unexpected intrusion, sir. The storm caught me quite unawares. Oh, but is it not glorious, Mr. Carmichael!" she breathed. "It is what I especially love about the moors— the suddenness and unpredictability of the weather."

Coming to a halt, Carmichael turned to look at her.

Lucy's breath caught at the sight of him. Clad only in a white shirt, open at the throat, and breeches tucked into the tops of Military Long Boots, he exuded masculinity and lean, powerful strength, all of which created an odd, queasy sensation in the pit of her stomach. But it was the burning intensity of his eyes that quite took her breath away.

"Little fool," he growled. "Have you any notion of the danger you risked in riding neck or nothing over the cliff trail? One stumble and you and your horse would have plunged to your deaths in the bay. By God, if I were your father, I should turn you over my knee and beat some sense into you."

Lucy's exuberance quite effectively squelched, she went rigid with resentment. "Then thank heavens you are not my father, sir," she retorted, her eyes flashing green sparks out of stormy grey depths. "I have ridden that trail since I was a child and have never once come remotely close to plunging over the cliffs to my death. No doubt I am grateful for your concern, Mr. Carmichael, but I assure you it is entirely misplaced."

"Oh, brava, Miss Powell," Carmichael murmured dangerously. "You have given me back some of my own, have you not? I am well aware I haven't the right to read the Earl of Bancroft's daughter a curtain lecture, but you will heed me nevertheless."

Reaching up without warning, he encircled her waist with his hands and, lifting her from the saddle as easily as if she weighed no more than a child, set her firmly on her feet.

"If you have any wish to explore the castle with me, my girl," he said, holding her with steely eyes, "you will promise me never again to risk your life in heedless abandon."

Lucy stared at him, her lips slightly parted as she considered not so much the content as the implications of his words.

"What a very odd man you are," she declared testily. "I cannot think why it should matter to you what I do. You hardly know me, after all."

A short bark of laughter seemed forced from him. "I am well aware you haven't the least inkling why I should bother myself with your welfare. But you are begging the question. Have I your word, Miss Powell?"

Lucy hedged, feeling herself trapped. "Surely you must see how pointless it would be. How should I possibly know what you would consider risking my life heedlessly? I daresay I could be injured simply climbing out of bed. And I certainly have no intention of riding at a sedate walk. I have been used to horses all my life."

"I have no doubt you are a bruising rider," conceded Carmichael, who, only moments earlier, had been made a grim spectator to her skill on horseback. "I shall nevertheless have your word."

"Will you give me yours that you will take me to the dungeon?" Lucy countered, her eyes changing all in a second from stormy grey to impish green. "What could be more marvelous than to prowl a dungeon on a day like today?"

"Prowling the picture gallery, Miss Powell," Carmichael stated unequivocally. "At least it had better be, since that is all I am prepared to show you until I have had the opportunity to study the diagrams more thoroughly."

Lucy made a wry grimace of disappointment. Still, the picture gallery was better than nothing, she told herself and she, after all, was not one to hold a grudge. "Oh, very well. If that is the best you can do. I give you my word, Mr. Carmichael, that I shall not be heedless of my safety."

Carmichael, no fool, was well aware that that was not precisely the promise he had demanded of her. Still, the last thing he wished was to deny her access to the castle, and he had every intention, after all, of being in a position to quell whatever propensity she might have for recklessly endangering herself. Deciding that he would do well to be satisfied with at least the token of victory, he wisely forbore from pressing her further. Still, he was far from being pleased either with her or himself as, taking up the mare's reins once more, he said, "I shall hold you to it, Miss Powell."

Lucy smiled ruefully as she turned to follow him along the arched passageway. Instantly her nostrils were assailed by the aroma of horses and freshly thrown hay, and she realized he had brought her to the stables.

"The groom and coachman are away to one of the farms to procure hay and feed for the horses," Carmichael remarked, leading the mare into a large stall, which had been newly cleaned. "And hopefully, a stable lad or two." Lucy watched as he removed Wind Star's saddle with swift, sure hands and, after rubbing the mare down, pitched her some hay from the loft above. "Fortunately I have been used to looking after my own cattle on more than a few occasions."

"Where? On the battlefield?" Lucy asked, giving Wind Star a pat before following her host from the stall.

Carmichael laughed. "On the battlefield there are subordinates for that sort of thing. As it happens, my orders kept me away from the troops more often than not. My fighting was, for the most part, confined to skirmishes followed by hasty retreats."

"You were a guerrilla," Lucy exclaimed, her eyes fixing on him with eager curiosity. "Where? On the Spanish Peninsula?"

A single arrogant eyebrow arched toward his hairline. "You astonish me, Miss Powell. What the devil can you know about *guerrillas* in the Peninsular Campaign?"

"I know there were British officers who joined the Spanish guerrilla bands in order to further the resistance movement begun by Don Julian Sanchez. My Uncle Ned, who is Papa's youngest brother, is in the Forty-third Light Infantry under Crauford. He has mentioned Don Julian's guerrillas in his letters."

"Has he? And what makes you think I was one of them?"

"Perhaps because you used the Spanish pronunciation of *guerrillas*. And because I know Don Julian's guerrillas fight in the only way they can—ambushing the enemy from cover and then vanishing into the land they know better than any Frenchman possibly could, because it is their homeland. Did you know Don Julian? To think that one man from humble beginnings could rally twenty thousand men to his cause. Is he commanding of appearance and heroic in bearing? Is that why so many have joined his band?"

"They joined him because he was ruthless," Carmichael answered with a chilling deliberateness. "And because he hated the French enough for some cruelty they perpetrated against his family to butcher three soldiers as they lay sleeping in the woods. That was the beginning of Don Julian's resistance movement, Miss Powell. Do you really wish to know more?"

Sickened, Lucy gripped her hands behind her until the pain forced the faintness away. If he had deliberately meant to shock her, he had succeeded admirably, but she would rather die than let him know that. "Such things as you describe may indeed be beyond my experience, sir," she managed to retort with convincing firmness. "However, I have two younger brothers who have already expressed a desire to pursue careers in the military. I should be a poor creature indeed if I could not bear to hear what they might one day be forced to witness for themselves."

"Should you?" murmured Carmichael, silently cursing himself for a bloody fool. He had recognized from the very first moment he laid eyes on her that Lucille Emily Powell could never be anything but pluck to the backbone. The last thing he had meant to do was quash her impetuous youth and innocence, which, after Spain and his final role in the Peninsular Campaign, he had found singularly refreshing. Hellfire, even he was not so lost to all sense of decency as to wish to sully her ears with things no woman should ever have to know. War was not for women; especially not the sort of war that he had fought in the company of Don Julian and his *guerrillas*.

He had, however, still been laboring under a host of unfamiliar sensations that being forced to watch her wild flight across the headland had aroused. Bloody hell! He would wring the girl's neck if she ever again put him through such a moment as that had been. And then to see her, flushed and beautiful, glorying with her whole being in the excitement of the storm and her ride. Suddenly he had wanted nothing more than to shake her until she swore she would never again risk her life in such a manner. Instead he had lashed out at her and, with a ruthlessness that was well known to his intimates, had thoroughly squelched her high spirits.

By all rights she should have been crushed by his deliberate attempt to dispel any illusions she might have entertained concerning glory in war, especially Don Julian's sort of warfare. Instead she had demonstrated an unshakable fortitude and a penetrating insight that would have done credit to a veteran soldier. Suddenly he had been made to feel ashamed of his boorish behavior, a sensation that was not only unfamiliar to him but that he had found distasteful in the extreme. And now she was calling his bluff, even going so far as to dare him with those cursed lovely eyes to further add to his ignominy by telling her more about Don Julian Sanchez.

"Indeed, sir, I would know more," she was saying, her delightfully stubborn chin tilted in an attitude of firm resolve. "And you may rest assured I shall endeavor not to disgrace myself by falling into a swoon."

He had been staring with fixed rigidity at the

mare, feeding quietly in the stall, but now he lifted
his eyes deliberately to the girl's. Her gaze remained steady and unflinching. "What exactly
would you like to hear, Miss Powell? That Don
Julian went out again, night after night, stalking
the enemy? Murdering them where he found
them. That he was so successful in his own personal vendetta that others began to join him? Only
two or three at first. Then a small band and finally
an army. Perhaps he is heroic, even commanding.
In the end, one might even say he is a patriot. He
showed the others how it could be done, and his
guerrillas have done more to aid the British Campaign than any ten Spanish regiments."

Lucy shuddered, seeing Don Julian Sanchez
through Carmichael's cold, passionless eyes, but,
more than that, seeing Carmichael, embittered and
hard behind his arrogant facade.

Why? she wondered. What had happened to
make him what he was? Something inside her
made her want to reach out to him, to ease, somehow, the harshness from his face. Instead she stood
like a mindless idiot, unable to find the words to
break the silence.

She was grateful when the mare gave a low
whinny, which was answered by a tall, rangy fellow
in the opposite stall. Lucy uttered a low exclamation
of delight at the sight of the tapered head that
thrust itself over the gate to peer at them.

"Oh, you are a beauty, are you not?" she crooned,
reaching out with the instinct of a born horseman
to touch the white blaze on the animal's forehead.

Carmichael moved with her to the stallion. "His
name is El Guerrero," he said. "The Warrior."
Stroking with long familiarity the powerful, arched

neck, he watched the girl's unbridled pleasure in the black's clean lines and magnificent proportions.

"He has the build of an athlete. I daresay he could carry even your weight all day with perfect ease."

"He has done so," agreed Carmichael, "on numerous occasions."

Lucy nodded, never doubting that the magnificent creature had probably saved his master's life more than a few times on the field of battle. "And he is fast, too, I should wager. He has the mark of it on his off-hind leg," she said, indicating the right hind foot, which, bearing a white stocking, was considered a sign of speed. Save for the blaze on the forehead, it was the only mark on him. "He is a perfect gentleman, is he not? Oh, but he is grand," she breathed, laying her cheek against that of the stallion. "I have never before seen anything more beautiful."

An odd sort of smile twisted at Carmichael's lips at that. Obviously she had not the least notion of the striking image she presented at that moment. The slender girl and the warrior stallion— it was a picture that would haunt his sleepless nights. She was all sweet beauty and youthful innocence. Still, he did not make the mistake of thinking her either a child or a fool. He knew she was neither.

Bloody hell, what a coil he had made for himself! He must have been mad to let himself imagine that, given time, he might win her for himself. He could not put the duke off indefinitely. One day before the summer was through, Lathrop must inevitably make his appearance. And then she would learn the truth about Phillip Carmichael. He did not fool himself into believing that at that moment he would not lose her. It was as inevitable

as was the duke himself. She would turn from him
in anger and disgust.

His bitter certainty must have shown in his face.
The girl, glancing up at him, stilled, her eyes huge
and questioning on his.

Carmichael laughed, a harsh sound in the silence.
"You must forgive me," he said, cynical at last. "I
have not truly forgotten what it is to be a gentleman,
though after this afternoon's demonstration you
must find that difficult to believe. Would you care
for some tea, Miss Powell? I can even offer you a
tolerable biscuit. It seems my manservant once
served in the capacity of cook before he attached
himself to me as my batman."

"I believe I should like that, Mr. Carmichael.
And, Mr. Carmichael, as far as this afternoon
goes—" Lucy smiled gravely, revealing twin dimples
in either cheek. "I believe you need not fear for my
delicate sensibilities, sir. It is true that as a female
of gentle birth I have been protected all my life
from knowledge considered unsuitable for my sex.
Faith, is it any wonder women of my class so often
present the appearance of fatuous, shallow creatures? I believe women are better than that, Mr.
Carmichael. We are stronger, more intelligent, and
far more capable than our society would have us."

Carmichael bowed. A gleam of humor in his eyes
relieved the hardness of his face. "I shall endeavor
to remember that, Miss Powell. And now, tea and
biscuits, if you will."

"And a grand tour, Mr. Carmichael." Lucy
smiled gaily. "The picture gallery. You promised,
sir."

Four

Some fifteen minutes later in the parlor, under the watchful eye of Mr. Jessop Oakes, Lucy gingerly balanced a cup and saucer on her knee with one hand while she accepted with the other something that might loosely have been termed a biscuit.

"Thank you, Mr. Oakes. They look delicious," she offered, thinking it was fortunate that she was not prone to fits of hysterics. She had little doubt that had she been Florence, she very likely would have swooned at her first sight of Mr. Carmichael's manservant.

A great hulk of a man of indeterminate years, bowed and bent, his huge hands gnarled by exposure to the elements, Mr. Oakes had the appearance of one who had been subjected to the worst sort of tortures.

Not the least of his deformities was the absence of one eye, redress for which had been attempted by substituting a facsimile made of glass. Lucy could not but think the result was less than fortuitous, since the facsimile had the tendency to stare disconcertingly to the off-side, while the genuine article was trained straight ahead. It little helped, moreover, that the ill-favored defect had the added misfortune of being located midpoint along the jagged line of a hideous scar that extended from above the left eyebrow to below the corresponding cheekbone. No matter how hard Lucy tried not to have done, whenever she had cause to look into the disfigured face she invariably erred, to her discomfort, in addressing the sightless orb. She had just been forced for the third time to correct her error when she glimpsed a wry gleam of sympathy in that single living eye. Maddeningly, she felt herself blush.

"I beg your pardon, Mr. Oakes," she blurted, thoroughly ashamed of herself. "I truly do not mean to stare. It is only that I have seldom the privilege of meeting someone who has so obviously braved the perils of battle. I hope you can find it in yourself to forgive my unseemly curiosity."

The effect of that ingenuous speech was to produce a great, gape-toothed grin that utterly transformed the poor ravaged face.

"Forgive you, miss? Why, there's nothing to forgive. Jessop Oakes is a frightful sight for the likes of a lady like yourself. Most folks can't bear to look on him. They treat him like he wasn't even there. So don't you fret yourself none, miss. Not for doin' what others haven't the stomach for."

It was, Lucy surmised, a lengthy speech for the former batman, and one that demonstrated a rough but elemental kindliness. In spite of his unprepossessing appearance, he was undoubtedly a man capable of the finer sensibilities. And, indeed, when she had been left alone in his care while Carmichael went to make himself more presentable, Oakes had been most solicitous of her comfort, insisting on dragging the cumbersome Charles II carved oak armchair closer to the fire and dusting it off with his neckerchief before allowing her to be seated; and occasionally she was sure she had glimpsed a gleam of humor in the hazel depths of his one remaining eye, which led her to believe that beneath his rough exterior there lurked a bluff, good-natured soul. Most of all, however, he demonstrated toward Mr. Carmichael an unmistakable, almost dogged devotion, which she was quite sure owed its source to a fiercely stubborn sense of loyalty to his master.

Lucy would not, for the world, have wished to hurt the man's feelings.

She hardly knew what to expect as she bit into the crumbly, misshapen mass cooked to a golden brown and smelling of cinnamon and ginger. Certainly she had not thought to experience a delectable burst of almond flavor or the exquisite sensation of sugar and saffron melting in her mouth. Her eyes widened in pleasured surprise as she emitted an eloquent "M-m-m" of delight.

"Oh, but, Mr. Oakes," she exclaimed when she had swallowed, "these are marvelous. I believe I have never before tasted anything quite like them."

The wooden expression Oakes had carefully maintained as he waited at attention for her reaction gave way to a hardly disguised glow of pride. "I'd be tolerable surprised if you had, miss," he said, nevertheless, with an admirable aplomb. "It's my own concoction what I invented for the cap'n when he was laid up in his bed this last time. Even the doctors thought he'd not pull through, but we fooled 'em, eh, Cap'n?"

"Yes, Mr. Oakes, we fooled them," Carmichael answered quietly from where he stood beside the fireplace. "Thanks in large part to your stubborn refusal to accept the doctors' learned prognoses.

And now I believe you were to be occupied for a time elsewhere, were you not?"

To Lucy's amazement the burly giant, shifting his weight self-consciously from one foot to the other, blushed as rosily as a girl at that gentle reminder, a reaction that was just as swiftly supplanted by an obstinate hardening of the jaw. "Beggin' your pardon, Cap'n, but my place is here with you. I'd just as lief stay and serve you and the young lady."

"Your place, Mr. Oakes," Carmichael replied evenly, "is where I say it is. Now kindly do as you are told. Miss Powell and I do not require your services."

A look, which seemed fraught with meaning, passed between the two men, the one resembling a great, bristling mastiff that had been unjustly rebuffed and the other the master, unmoved and unyielding in his manner. Oakes gave in first. "Next you'll be tellin' me I'm of no use to anyone, and likely you'd be right," grumbled the former batman. "Then so be it. No need to say more. I'm goin', Cap'n, though I'll not say I like it. By your leave, miss," he added stiffly to Lucy and, making an about-face, shuffled, muttering to himself, from the room.

Hardly knowing what to think of the scene that had just been enacted before her, Lucy carefully set her cup on the cherrywood sofa table. "You have hurt his feelings," she said, keeping her eyes on the cup.

"Not his feelings, Miss Powell. His pride," answered Carmichael, who was still staring thoughtfully at the door through which Oakes had departed. "Which means a deal more to him."

Leaning his hand against the fireplace mantel, he lowered his eyes to the fire.

In the silence that settled uneasily over the parlor, Lucy was left to stare at him, wondering if he even remembered she was there. She nearly jumped when Carmichael broke the silence.

"Mr. Oakes is not so young as he was used to be," he said quietly, as though that explained everything— his arbitrary behavior toward a loyal servant and his reticence toward a guest. "And, though he would never admit it, he feels the discomfort of old wounds. He has already done the work of two men this morning and would continue doing that of two more if I did nothing to prevent him." At last he looked at her, a wry glint in his eye. "I am not quite the ogre you think me, Miss Powell. I have merely sent him to his quarters for a much-needed rest."

With an effort, Lucy subdued the sense of confusion that swept over her with the realization that she had, indeed, grossly misjudged him.

"You are right, of course," she said ruefully. "I'm afraid I did misunderstand. You are fond of him, are you not?"

Carmichael appeared amused at the notion. "I should never have thought of it in such terms, but perhaps I am fond of Oakes. I daresay we have grown comfortable with one another. He has been with me since I was a raw leftenant."

"He appears not to have done so unscathed," she remarked, sensing the bond between two men of such disparate stations in life could only have been forged by a great many harrowing adventures. "He lost an eye and must have come very near to losing his life. How did it happen?"

She had spoken gently, moved by sympathy and

a wish to understand what lay behind Carmichael's strange moods.

Suddenly it was as if a shutter had dropped over Carmichael's features, leaving them utterly devoid of emotion. Unwittingly Lucy shivered.

"He had the poor judgment to put himself in the way of a French cavalry officer who was intent on driving his sword through my chest. And you are right: It very nearly did cost him his life. Tell me, are you always so inquisitive about matters that should not concern you? I can think of more pleasant topics to discuss with a female companion over tea."

"No, can you?" Stung by his harshness, Lucy clenched her hands in her lap to stop their trembling. "Something along the lines of ladies' fashions, perhaps? Or did you have in mind the latest *on-dits* from London? I daresay if neither of those appeals to you, you can always resort to metaphors describing my maidenly beauty."

"A January sea chased by rainclouds."

"I-I beg your pardon?" Lucy faltered.

"Your eyes, Miss Powell. A moment ago they were the green of the sea in winter, and now they are the ocean-grey of an overcast day."

Lucy stared at him, thunderstruck. "You are roasting me, Mr. Carmichael."

"Not at all, Miss Powell. I was paying you a compliment."

Lucy's hand fluttered in a dismissive gesture. "Then your currency was Spanish coin, sir."

Carmichael's smile was singularly mirthless. "And you, I must suppose, prefer plain pounds. Very well. The truth is, Miss Powell, that you are worse off than Oakes. He at least can see, while you, with two perfectly good eyes, apparently are blind."

Lucy drew in a sharp breath. Really, nothing was going at all as she had imagined it would. She had not the least idea why they should have come so suddenly to loggerheads, when she had expected something quite different after their momentous meeting the day before. Indeed, for a single, nerve-tingling moment as he had winked at her and enjoined her to conspiratorial silence, it had occurred to her that here was a spirit kindred to her own. She did not fool herself into thinking there could ever be anything of a romantic nature between them, but she had thought that at least he might be her friend. Then what had she done but spoil everything by poking her nose into matters which he was quite right in pointing out were none of her affair, and he had punished her by paying her pretty compliments that, being obviously empty, had put her smartly in her place. Faith, if only she could learn to keep her curiosity bridled and her unruly tongue between her teeth!

Lucy came to her feet, her bosom heaving and her cheeks flushed with embarrassment.

"I beg your pardon, Mr. Carmichael," she said stiffly. "You are quite right to bring me to task for prying into something that is clearly none of my affair. However, I assure you it is not at all necessary to pay me compliments in order to stop me from speaking out of turn. I really should not have come. If you will excuse me, I am sure I can find my own way back to the stables."

She was rewarded with the sound of a heavy sigh from Carmichael, which only served to add to her confusion. Indeed, it was all she could do to stand her ground as he deliberately crossed to her.

"I'm afraid, Miss Powell, that it is I who must beg your pardon. I did warn you of my deplorable manners."

"D-did you?" replied Lucy, who was wishing him, without remorse, to the devil, or at least to a safe distance from her. How patently unfair that he should appear insufferably cool, when she was experiencing a peculiarly queasy sensation in the pit of her stomach. It had just occurred to her that she must be suffering from a hitherto unsuspected allergic condition, triggered, no doubt, by the subtle scents of shaving soap and clean linen at exceedingly close range, when she nearly flinched at the touch of his hand beneath her chin. Gently, he forced her to look at him.

"You are stubborn, impetuous, and a hopeless romantic, but you stand excused of prying." A wry smile touched his lips. "I have a particular aversion to discussing my experiences on the Peninsula, especially with an engaging young woman. Not only have I had my bellyful of war, Miss Powell, but I find that I am becoming more reconciled by the moment to my sudden change in career. I have, for example, been looking forward to showing you the duke's picture gallery— if you can overlook my earlier boorishness. Say you will stay to accompany me on the grand tour."

"Really, I shouldn't. The rain has stopped, Mr. Carmichael," Lucy pointed out. "Indeed I . . ."

"It will take only a few moments," Carmichael interjected, tucking her hand in the crook of his arm and taking up a lighted candelabra. "I shall tell you the tale of why the Twelfth Duke of Lathrop abandoned his castle."

"But I have already heard the tale, Mr. Carmichael," Lucy protested, allowing herself nonetheless to be led from the parlor into the Great Hall, which boasted, placed strategically about the room, sentinels of armored suits draped in cobwebs, and a marble stair ascending from a parquetry tiled floor to an open gallery above. Lucy could not but thrill to the soft scuff of their shoes echoing eerily through the huge empty room or to the writhing of shadows cast by the candlelight. How Francie would have loved the nerve-tingling whisper of draughts playing among the hanging tapestries. Lathrop Castle seemed a deliciously brooding, haunted place.

Nervously, she cleared her throat and recited, "Patrick Windholm, the Twelfth Duke of Lathrop, fell in love with the rector's daughter, who was not only ethereally beautiful, but pure of heart. It is said that she returned his love, but could not bring herself to forsake her lifelong desire to serve as a missionary any more than he could renounce his title or his worldly possessions. She married a man of the cloth and died, ministering to the sick and the poor in India, and the duke, his heart broken, refused ever again to set foot in the castle. He vanished after getting himself a wife and heir and was never heard from again."

They had climbed to the head of the stairs as Lucy related the tale of the lost lord of Lathrop, and now Carmichael stopped before a gilt-framed portrait. "The lady's name was Patience Merriweather, Miss Powell. Some might think her beautiful. I consider her somewhat insipid for my tastes."

Lucy felt a tingling along her spine as, startled, she glanced from Carmichael to the portrait. Huge

eyes framed in a heart-shaped face of delicate
beauty stared hauntingly back at her.

"This is *her* likeness!" Lucy exclaimed softly in
tones touched with something of the awe she felt.
How often had she imagined the star-crossed lovers,
here in this very castle! Patrick Windholm's love for
Patience Merriweather had been all-consuming;
losing her, the exquisite anguish that awakens the
soul to the highest form of passion. He was the
apotheosis of the romantic lover and the model
upon which Lucy had patterned her own Lord of
Lathrop, who had been doomed to a slow, agonizing
death at the loss of his Lucinda.

Lucy's hand went out reverently to touch the
faded portrait. "He must have kept it here like a
shrine, until he could not bear to look upon it any
longer. He left it just as it was. Do you feel it, Mr.
Carmichael?" Lucy said thrillingly. "It is almost as
if her spirit still lingers, forever captive in Lathrop
Castle."

"Then no doubt she will be the first His Grace
will consign to obscurity in the attic," Carmichael
predicted with a sardonic lift of an eyebrow.
"Along with Patrick Windholm, who allowed his
ancestral pile to fall into disrepair. From what little
I have seen, it is my considered opinion that the
cost to the duke for his grandfather's negligence
will not be insignificant."

"Oh, but he mustn't!" cried Lucy, grasping Carmichael's sleeve in horror. "Patience Merriweather
and Patrick Windholm are legendary in this part
of North Yorkshire. One does not consign legends
to the attic."

"One does when the portrait is badly done,"
Carmichael replied, passing on to the next portrait
in line. Settling back on his heels, the side of an

index knuckle to his chin, he appraised the likeness of a bewigged nobleman attired in brocade
of crimson and canary yellow. "The artist has, perhaps, captured the eyes," he commented critically.
"But the nose is not quite right, is it? And he has
failed abominably with the Windholm chin. I have
it on good authority that all the Windholm men
bear a strong family resemblance."

"No, do they?" murmured Lucy, staring at the
portrait with a peculiarly arrested expression.

"Indubitably. I myself can attest to the fact that
the present duke is the spitting image of his father
and his great-grandfather before him. Unfortunately, we have only this likeness of Patrick in the
flower of manhood. I should say he was about my
age— nine and twenty— when he had the thing
done."

Lucy appeared not to have been listening. "Did
you say *all* the Windholm men bear a strong resemblance?" she asked without taking her eyes off
the portrait that seemed wholly to have absorbed
her attention.

"It is, I believe, a family trait," replied Carmichael, his gaze enigmatic on her face.

"How very odd."

"Odd, Miss Powell?"

"Yes, odd." Lucy lifted her eyes to his. "Patrick
Windholm would seem to bear a strong resemblance to *you,* Mr. Carmichael."

If she had hoped to elicit some sort of response
from him, she was to be sadly disappointed. Carmichael's features remained maddeningly unreadable. "Do you think so, Miss Powell?" he
murmured.

"Yes, Mr. Carmichael, I do. I should even go so

far as to say you bear a striking similarity. And please do not deny it."

"Indeed, why should I, when I quite agree, Miss Powell? The resemblance is uncanny, is it not?"

"Oh, positively." Lucy stared at him expectantly. "Well, is that *all* you have to say to it? You are a Windholm, are you not?"

Carmichael's lips curled in sardonic amusement. "One could say, I suppose, that the duke and I enjoy a certain kinship," he reflected. "You might even say we are closer than brothers. I did tell you I had known him all my life."

"But your name— Carmichael . . . ?" Lucy frowned, trying to put all the pieces together.

"Is my mother's," Carmichael finished for her in such a manner as left little doubt he meant that as an end to the matter. "And this, of course, is Lathrop's great-grandfather," he continued with hardly a pause. "He was, I am told, a favorite of the French actress Madame Lecouvreur, to whom he lost his heart upon the event of her first appearance at *le Comedie francaise.*"

Lucy, who could not, at the moment, have cared less about Madame Lecouvreur or her affection for the eleventh duke of Lathrop, nevertheless pretended to smile and nod with interest as Carmichael related the Windholm family history.

She was still reeling from the discovery that Carmichael was a deal more to the duke than he had previously allowed. Indeed, a great deal about Carmichael would seem to have been made suddenly and quite patently clear. She no longer need wonder either at his bitterness or his reticence about himself. He had all but admitted, after all, that he was a close relative of the duke's, one, moreover, who went by his mother's surname, and for that there could be only one interpretation.

What bitter gall for a man of pride, she thought, lowering her eyes to hide the pity she felt, to be forced to live his life as a Windholm by-blow!

Very likely his mama had been an actress or—no, a beautiful young widow of slender means, who had had no choice but to give the child of an illicit love over to his father to rear. Or perhaps she had died, no doubt in childbirth, leaving the father little alternative but to take in the poor motherless infant. As an acknowledged but illegitimate son, he could not have had a happy childhood. It did not seem likely, after all, that the duchess would have been pleased to be presented with a daily reminder of her husband's transgression. Liaisons might indeed be countenanced among those of their class, but only so long as they were conducted with discretion. And what if he were the elder of the duke's two sons? How dreadful to be denied the birthright that legitimacy would have bestowed upon him! Faith, it did not bear thinking on, and yet it seemed she could think of nothing else.

Lucy, lost in contemplation of what it must have meant to Carmichael, growing up in the duke's household, unloved and unwanted, was brought to awareness by the sound of her own name.

"I-I beg your pardon," she stammered, blinking foolishly up at Carmichael. "What did you say?"

"Nothing, apparently, of any significance," replied Carmichael, his tone faintly amused. "It had only just occurred to me that, little as I might like it, it is perhaps time that I took you home— before your parents start to scour the countryside looking for you."

Lucy fairly snapped to attention.

"Oh, good heavens!" she exclaimed. "I forgot all about the time. I should have been home long before now. They will very likely be imagining I have been carried off by Gypsies or some such thing."

"Then I suggest we repair to the stables without further delay," drawled Carmichael, turning to escort her back the way they had come. "As delightful as I find Lady Emmaline and the earl, I do not relish the thought of having them storm the castle so soon again in search of their errant daughter."

Lucy, casting a last lingering glance at Patience Merriweather's portrait, could only agree with him on that cogent point. She had escaped yesterday's fiasco with impunity. She could hardly hope to do so a second time.

Wind Star was contentedly munching the hay Carmichael had provided when Lucy and her host came to the stable by way of the postern. She would have saddled the mare herself had not Carmichael insisted on doing it for her. When he led El Guerrero from his stall, however, with the intention of saddling the black and accompanying her, she protested that there really was no need for him to do so.

"On the contrary, there is every need," Carmichael returned, lightly flinging the saddle over the stallion's long, rangy back. "How else am I to explain to your parents that, having run into you during the rainstorm, I invited you to accompany me in its wake on a tour of the countryside?"

Irrepressibly, Lucy grinned. "I fear, Mr. Carmichael, there is a streak of the rogue in you."

"I begin to believe you are right, Miss Powell," Carmichael replied resignedly, as, with swift, capable hands he finished the task of saddling the black. "Certainly I am discovering a facility for artifice that I previously never suspected in myself."

"Then obviously you were not reared in a houseful of siblings," Lucy commented guilelessly. "Greensward is a bed of artifice and intrigue. It is not exactly lying, after all, when one simply does not tell all the truth. It is more like preserving one's parents' peace of mind. Why should they be burdened with the knowledge that Timothy and Tom were swinging from the hay mow when they ripped their trousers, or that Francie was attempting to teach herself to swim when she fell into a fishing hole on Bancroft Beck one summer? My parents would only have been unduly upset over milk that was already spilt."

Carmichael, handing her up into the saddle, leaned for a moment with his hand on the cantle. "Let me see if I understand you, Miss Powell," he said, gazing up at her in such a manner as brought a faint tinge of color to her cheek. "It is your considered opinion that subterfuge, if it is in a good cause, ought to be excused, is that it?"

Lucy frowned as she considered her answer. "I should think that, in general, one should be truthful, but, yes, Mr. Carmichael. If the cause warrants it, I believe subterfuge might, on occasion, be forgiven, don't you?"

"Oh, by all means, Miss Powell," replied Carmichael, mounting the black in a single effortless motion. "One might even say I am counting on it."

It was on Lucy's tongue to ask what he meant
by his final, cryptic utterance, but Carmichael,
gathering up the reins, had already set the stallion
in motion. She was given no choice but to follow
at a clatter behind him; and, when they emerged
moments later from the castle walls, Lucy all but
forgot Carmichael's comment as she inhaled the
sweet scent of rain-freshened heather.

The sudden shower had left the moors sparkling
in sunshine, and the road lay before them, a
muddy ribbon, weaving back and forth on itself as
it descended the hill to the meadows and downs.
With Bancroft Beck trailing a silvery path through
the greensward before her and the gloomy envi-
rons of the castle thankfully behind her, she suffered a sudden surge of affection for the
Elizabethan manor house that had been her refuge
through all of her nineteen years. It came to her
suddenly that no matter how she might long for
adventure or how greatly she might yearn to travel
to far and distant places, she would always wish to
return again to Greensward.

She was still thinking of her home and how
deeply were her roots sunk into the valley that had
belonged to her ancestors for seven generations as
she set her mount off at a walk. "Where do you
call home, Mr. Carmichael?" she asked, glancing
sideways at her companion.

"I was born in Surrey, Miss Powell, and spent
my boyhood at Hollingsworth in Hampshire," replied Carmichael. "Why do you ask?"

Lucy shrugged. "I was just thinking that a soldier must have need of a place to call home when
he is very far from all that is familiar. I know I
should long terribly for Greensward in similar circumstances. Only just look around you: I daresay

there is nothing more beautiful than the North Yorks in summer."

"There is London at the height of the Season, Miss Powell," observed Carmichael, studying the effects of the sunlight in her rebellious red hair. "Have you no desire to forsake your beloved Yorkshire hill country for the allure of the City?"

"I wish you will not be absurd," Lucy countered, laughing. "It is hardly the same thing. Naturally I look forward to a Season in London. Indeed, what girl would not? London, however, could never be home, could it? It would only be a place to visit."

"Oh, most assuredly," agreed Carmichael without the flicker of an eyelash. Obviously Miss Powell had not the least inkling how novel would be such a notion to the vast majority of those with whom he was acquainted. Rustication in the country, after all, was something that must be endured when the summer heat made the City intolerable, and even then it was far preferable to pass the time of exile at one of the more fashionable seaside resorts or watering holes. But then, Miss Powell, he was discovering more and more, was something of an original, as was demonstrated by her next inquiry.

"Does Lathrop fish, Mr. Carmichael?" she asked, staring at a point between Wind Star's ears.

"Upon rare occasions. Having only come recently into the title, he has been a great deal abroad. I believe he was not left with much time for such leisurely pursuits." He paused as though to reflect on the matter. "No doubt you will pardon my curiosity, Miss Powell, but can it be that fishing is another of your prerequisites for marriage?"

"As a matter of fact, I have a passion for fishing. I believe I am not bragging when I say I tie the best flies in the valley. Furthermore, I have the distinction of being the only one ever to snag 'Old Slippery.' "

" 'Old Slippery,' I must presume, is something of a local legend," speculated Carmichael, faintly smiling.

"He is only the grandest trout to be found anywhere in Bancroft Beck. I should say he easily spans the length of your arm and weighs upwards of fifteen pounds. It was the most glorious day of my life when I hooked him with one of my very own flies. I should have landed him, too, had Francie not chosen that particular moment to try her hand at swimming."

"Ah, yes. The ill-fated experiment in aquatics you mentioned earlier. You, naturally, were compelled to fish your enterprising sibling from the water at the supreme sacrifice of your fish."

"She was only ten at the time," Lucy corroborated in explanatory tones. "I really had little choice in the matter."

"No, I daresay you had not," mused Carmichael, guiding his mount around a puddle in the road. "Are you called upon often to rescue your younger siblings from their youthful peccadilloes, Miss Powell?"

Having reached the bottom of the hill during this exchange, Lucy laughed and lifted Wind Star into a canter. "Practically on a daily basis, Mr. Carmichael," she called gaily over her shoulder. "It is the price one pays for being the eldest."

A peculiar glint in his eye, Carmichael watched as the trim figure atop the long-legged mare drew away. The girl's hair shone, a glorious halo of fire in the sunlight, just as he had predicted it would, and she sat her horse with the graceful ease of one born to the saddle. Unspoiled, spirited, intelligent, and caring, she was a magnificent creature— perhaps all the more so because she had not the slightest notion just how singularly lovely she was. She was, in fact, everything he had been led to believe her to be, and much, much more, he reflected grimly, as he let the black out. Whether she wished it or not, Lucille Emily Powell would make a duchess of whom any duke would be justly proud, and he was all too aware that Lathrop would be a damned fool to let her slip through his fingers.

The rest of the ride to Greensward was accomplished in short order; and, as they arrived coincidentally with William, who was strolling to the house after having delivered his and the earl's mounts to the stables, and since the twins had just returned from fishing and the girls had just been released from their lessons, it was not long before Carmichael and Lucy were surrounded by eager young Powells.

"I say, sir," said William, when the introductions and vociferous greetings were over, "that is a prime bit o' blood, if ever I saw one. I'll wager he's a sweet-goer."

"He has shown his heels to some of the best on the Peninsula," replied Carmichael, running his hand down the stallion's neck. "Otherwise, I should not, in all likelihood, be here today."

"The Peninsula?" exclaimed Timothy and Tom in rapt unison. "Have you come from the Spanish Campaign, Mr. Carmichael?" added Tom with the first definite signs of what Lucy doubted not would fast develop into hero worship.

"Pray don't be an idiot," interjected Francie, inserting herself between Wind Star and El Guerrero, the better to examine the black. "He would hardly have gone to the Peninsula for a holiday. And besides, his horse is obviously no stranger to battle. See here: He has been marked by a bullet. And if I am not mistaken, he owes this scar on his flanks to a glancing blow from a lance."

The immediate result of this pronouncement was to bring the boys crowding around Francine. "Egad, Tom, look at that," breathed Timothy in accents of awe. "Singed him with a musket ball."

"And here," whispered Tom. "Lucky he wasn't gutted."

"Really, Tom, that is quite enough," pronounced Florence from the porch in withering accents. "I cannot imagine what Mr. Carmichael must think of us. I should think, Will, as our father's heir, you could assert some positive influence over the boys. Such language is better suited to the stables."

Lucy, who had gone from hot to cold with dread at what she sensed must be coming next and Carmichael's probable reaction to it, was for once exceedingly grateful for her sister's almost prudish adherence to the proprieties. Clearly, the twins had been on the point of demanding the complete and no doubt gory details of El Guerrero's close encounters with death, something that she had already learned was likely to earn Carmichael's displeasure. Still, Lucy, noting her eldest brother's ominous rise in color, could not but reflect that it was unfortunate that Florence had chosen to make Will the unwelcome focus of attention.

"I should like to see you exert any influence over them," he responded in stiff resentment. "Or over Francie, for that matter. I daresay I could box their ears for them, for all the good it would do."

"Oh, but I shouldn't think it would do any good

at all," spoke up Josephine with childish seriousness. "Except, perhaps, to put Papa out of frame.
You know he believes reason preferable to violence
in all things. And, besides," she added, favoring
their tall visitor with a shy glance, "I suspect Mr.
Carmichael is not so awfully offended. I daresay
he himself was a boy once."

"I believe I was— once." Carmichael laughed. "A
very long time ago." Then, to William, he added,
"I understand, Viscount Lethridge, that you have
undertaken to learn the business of running your
father's estates. As I find myself in somewhat similar circumstances, I should be interested in hear-
ing your views on farming techniques. Perhaps you
would care to ride out with me one afternoon to
show me the improvements you and your father
have instituted."

William fairly bridled with pleasure at this mark
of distinction, coming as it did from one who so
obviously commanded both the respect and admiration of his younger siblings. "I should be both
pleased and honored, sir," he replied, refraining,
no doubt with a deal of effort on his part, from
casting a look of triumph at his sister Florence.

Lucy, looking on, was both moved to admiration
by the ease with which the captain had salvaged
William's wounded pride and touched at the
thoughtfulness that must have motivated it. What
a strange man he was, to be sure. Though he obviously took great pains to hide it, she could not
be fooled. Captain Phillip Carmichael was a discerning man with a not insignificant capacity for
kindness.

Carmichael, glancing up at her at that instant,
was met with a look that quite took his breath away.
Indeed, he was not certain whether to be relieved

or vexed that the earl chose just then to step out
on the porch, his face lit with pleasure at the sight
of his unexpected guest.

"Mr. Carmichael," he boomed, striding forward,
hand extended. "Welcome, sir, to Greensward."

Five

The old manor house seemed to swell with the bubbling vitality of the Powells who swept in through the front door and then, as if the great hall, with its high-paneled ceiling and mural-painted walls, could not contain them, spilled over into the countess's favorite withdrawing room. Because of its solid front of windows overlooking the evergreen labyrinth and the rose garden, she was want to refer to this as the "Summer Room."

Here, as might be expected on any midafternoon of June through September, they found Lady Emmaline, looking, in a high-waisted round gown of pale rose sarcenet, her short curls parted in the middle *a la Madonna*, nearly as young and quite easily as lovely as her two oldest daughters. With an embroidery frame before her upon which she had been making delicate stitches, she presented an altogether charming picture, Carmichael decided, as he was ushered unceremoniously into her presence.

"Emmaline, dear," exclaimed Bancroft, "I told you there was no cause to worry about Lucy. Here she is, quite safe and sound. And just look whom she has brought with her."

"It is Mr. Carmichael, Mama," said Florence, settling prettily on the sofa beside the countess as the other Powell progeny flocked around their mama. "They have been riding together."

"You should see his horse, Mama," exclaimed Timothy. "His name is El Guerrero, which means 'The Warrior' in Spanish."

"Does it indeed, dear? But how very interesting," responded his mama, setting aside her embroidery in order to give him her full attention.

"He has been in any number of perilous battles," Tom instantly appended. "He bears the most marvelous scars."

Will next proclaimed him to outshine all the stud horses in the North Yorks, a position to which Francie took instant exception, declaring that when her own Jester reached his full growth he would give Mr. Carmichael's El Guerrero a run for his money. The very suggestion made Florence blush in embarrassment for her hoydenish younger sister and their papa to proclaim in regret what a race that must have been if it could only have been held before Mr. Carmichael got away. Yes, but it could not be helped, Lucy was moved to point out. Jester, after all, was little more than a green colt. It would be at least another year or more before he was up to El Guerrero's weight, and even then it was doubtful he would be in the same class as Carmichael's black.

This, quite naturally, set off a whole new discussion concerning Jester's potential, based on character, build, and a bloodline that could be traced all the way back to the Godolphin Arabian.

In the general enthusiasm over Mr. Carmichael's horse, Mr. Carmichael seemed quite forgotten, the novelty of which at any other time or place he might very well have found, if not galling, then most certainly a prelude to boredom. Strangely

enough, however, with the Powells he felt neither.
On the contrary, he was, to his surprise, vastly entertained. Had anyone told him as little as three
days ago that he would discover anything remotely
charming in being in the company of a boisterous
lot of schoolchildren, untried fledglings, and in-
genues, he would have considered his informer
either mad or a fool. But then, that was before he
had met Lucille Emily Powell and been given to
see her singular family through her remarkable
eyes.

Startled from his silent musings by a tentative
tug on his coat sleeve, he glanced down into the
delicately lovely features of the youngest of the
Powell hopefuls.

"You mustn't mind them, Mr. Carmichael,"
Josephine advised kindly. "When you get to know
us better you will discover that the Powells, for the
most part, are simply mad about horses. Mama
says it cannot be helped. It is in our blood, you
know."

"No, is it?" answered Carmichael, properly
grave. "But not in yours, I take it."

Josephine's enchanting young face lit up. "Oh,"
she exclaimed, "but I love horses. Indeed, I think
they are the most beautiful creatures on earth."
Just as suddenly her face fell, and she glanced self-
consciously away. "It is only that I have never
learned to ride. I am not exactly robust, you see.
At least not like Lucy and Francine." With a sigh
she looked back at Carmichael. "Lucy says it is
because I was sent to be a comfort to Mama in the
midst of chaos."

"Your sister Lucy is obviously a female of great
insight," observed Carmichael, who was witness to

just such chaos as must surround Lady Emmaline daily. "And what do *you* think?"

Josephine shrugged. "I think she only says that to make me feel better about not being able to do all the things the others take for granted," she answered candidly. "I do try, for Lucy's sake, not to show it, but it is so very tiresome sometimes, being confined to quiet pursuits when everyone else is outside, having the most marvelous adventures. Until yesterday in the castle tower, I had never had an adventure. And I daresay I shall never have another."

"Shall you not?" murmured Carmichael, smiling faintly. "You are mistaken, surely?" Puzzled, Josephine tilted her head back the better to look at him. "I have had a great many. More than I care to remember," he said. "Consequently, you may believe me when I tell you, you are fated to experience the grandest sort of adventure."

"Do you really think so?" queried Josephine doubtfully.

"Oh, you may rely on it. A woman, such as you give promise of being, could not escape it even if she wished to have done."

The topic of Jester versus the black having reached an impasse that required a judgment from El Guerrero's master, Carmichael was drawn away from the child, who stared after him with a wondering light in her eyes.

"Ah, Mr. Carmichael," Bancroft said when his guest was pressed into the circle of Powells. "We were wondering, sir, about El Guerrero's bloodlines. Will and I have been speculating that, his color notwithstanding, he has the look of Herod by way of the Byerley Turk. Lucy is most obstinate, however, that he is of Spanish stock."

"And how not," broke in Lucy, "when he has the athletic build of the Hispano and the wavy mane and tail of the Lusitano? And you cannot dispute the scooped forehead of the Arabian, surely." Her eyes flashed to Carmichael. "Tell them, Captain. El Guerrero is Spanish, is he not?"

Carmichael, met with the passionate blaze of those glorious grey-green orbs, reflected that a man would be moved to swear to anything for just such a look. Fortunately, in this case, he would not be required to perjure himself.

"As it happens, the black was presented to me by Don Julian Sanchez, in return for a service I performed for him."

"It must have been a very great service," Timothy speculated suggestively.

"Don Julian so considered it at the time," agreed Carmichael, smiling, but refusing to take the bait. "El Guerrero was the don's own personal mount, bred by the Carthusian monks of Jerez from pure Andalucian stock. Unfortunately, his coloring is a throwback to the earlier Barb, which, because the white, grey, or bay is generally predominant and naturally preferred, made him unsuitable for breeding purposes. He has the fire and agility one sees in the Lipizzaner, which owes its origins to the Andalucian; but the scooped profile of the head must surely be due to an Arabian influence somewhere in the bloodlines, possibly a Spanish Arabian mare."

"Then I was at least partially right," Lucy exclaimed, her face aglow with triumph. "The Lusitano is very like the Andalucian in appearance."

"Except for the size," mused Bancroft, reluctant to admit he could have been mistaken. "He is taller than most of the Spanish breeds."

"A trait that the monks found undesirable," Carmichael admitted. "Which is another reason he was deemed unsuitable for their breeding purposes."

"I should breed him, if he were mine," Francie breathed. "I should cross him with a good English Thoroughbred."

"And end up with a colt that could outperform Jester; admit it," teased Will.

"I admit nothing," Francie retorted with a toss of her obstinately straight blond hair. "Jester has the heart and blood of a champion. I shouldn't sell him short if I were you."

"Nor shall we," interjected Lady Emmaline, who had not missed the slight tremor in her daughter's voice. "I believe we have exhausted the subject of Mr. Carmichael's remarkable horse for one afternoon. Indeed, in our enthusiasm for this El Guerrero, we have failed deplorably in our hospitality." Smiling gently in amusement, she extended her hand to their guest. "Mr. Carmichael, how nice to see you. I do hope you have come with the intention of joining us for tea."

"Indeed, ma'am." Carmichael, taking her hand, lightly saluted her knuckles before lifting twinkling blue eyes to hers. "I find that all this talk about horseflesh has given me a thirst."

"Then it is not tea but a glass of Madeira that is called for," Bancroft announced. "I've an excellent malmsey I have been saving for just such an occasion."

It was at that point that the countess took note of the disreputable condition of the twins, whose nankeens were mud-soiled and smelled distinctly of fish, and of Francie, whose hair was something less than immaculate and about whom there issued an unmistakable aroma of the stables. Amidst a chorus of groans and protests, the younger children were ordered upstairs where, they were informed, they could enjoy their tea and biscuits within the confines of the schoolroom.

"Lucy, dear, you may ring for the tea tray," said Lady Emmaline a few moments later, when peace and quiet had descended once more over the Summer Room.

"Well, Carmichael, how do you find things at the castle?" Bancroft inquired conversationally, as Lucy crossed to the bellpull. "The old pile appears solid enough from the outside, but fifty years of neglect cannot but have taken its toll."

"It has not benefitted from it," agreed Carmichael, taking the chair across from the countess. "Lathrop may be grateful that the caretaker saw fit to employ the services of rat-catchers on a regular basis. And, naturally, it was advantageous that Lathrop's father maintained a skeleton staff until recent years. Still, the roofs on several of the outbuildings are in need of extensive repairs, and the kitchens are deplorably outmoded. Many of the rooms will require considerable renovation to render them merely habitable, let alone comfortable and aesthetically pleasing. As for the grounds, I believe they speak for themselves. It will necessitate a small army of groundskeepers to return the gardens and orchards to their former state, and an equally large force merely to rid the interior of the castle of all its vermin and dirt."

"My, what a formidable project for the duke so soon after acquiring the title," reflected Lady Emmaline. "I wonder that he would wish to undertake it when he must have inherited a great many other responsibilities."

"Still, it is Lathrop's family seat," Lucy pointed
out as she rejoined the others and seated herself.
"And there is no denying that the land provides
him with a tidy income. Surely it is time the dukes
of Lathrop put something of themselves back into
it. Why, just think what it would mean. Not only
would it provide gainful employment for all manner of people, but it would bring prosperity to the
village as well."

"You are right, of course," Carmichael admitted
with a wry gleam of a smile. "There is no denying
that the castle would contribute substantially to the
local economy. The truth is, however, that Lathrop
is only one of His Grace's lesser holdings. Hollingsworth alone brings in nearly twice the income.
And the duke's shipping interests are even more
lucrative."

"Are they, by Jove?" rumbled the earl. "Was
tempted myself to invest in British shipping, but
decided instead on the Funds. The security, you
know."

"I say," interjected Will, "no wonder the dukes
have preferred Hollingsworth to Lathrop, even if
it is the family seat. I mean, it stands to reason,
doesn't it? Why live in a drafty old castle when
Lathrop must have any number of more congenial
houses for that sort of thing?"

"Perhaps the new duke is motivated by something more important than comfort or convenience," Lucy said, more sharply than she had
intended. Faith, surely they must realize Lathrop
Castle was not just any place. Within its vast old
halls the Lost Lord of Lathrop had mourned the
loss of his beloved Miss Merriweather. The castle
was the epitome of everything that was marvelous
and romantic. "There is the matter of roots, for

example, and—and pride in one's ancestral home," she added passionately by way of explanation. "His Grace may very well have come to realize that Lathrop Castle is a deal more to him than just an old pile of stones."

"I daresay he will have a sudden change of mind once he sees it," dryly predicted Florence, whose most recent visit to Lathrop Castle had left her anything but enchanted.

"Actually, I am afraid that if Lathrop is to be persuaded not only to make the sizable investment required to renovate the castle, but to remove from Hollingsworth to the North Yorks as well, he will need some added inducement," Carmichael told them, his eyes carefully avoiding Lucy's.

"Indeed, Mr. Carmichael, and what inducement is that?" queried Lady Emmaline, signaling the servant who had just entered with the tea tray to set it on the sofa table before her.

Lucy's gaze lifted to Carmichael and held with a dread sense of foreboding.

"But it is obvious, isn't it?" said Florence, glancing from Carmichael to Lucy and then back again. "His Grace would require a wife."

Will's face brightened with sudden intelligence. "But of course," he exclaimed. "But not just any wife. It would have to be—"

"A Yorkshire wife," Lucy finished for him, and nearly groaned as she felt all eyes fasten on her, one pair of compelling blue orbs in particular. The devil, she thought. How dare Carmichael deliberately seek to promote the duke's suit when she had made her own feelings on the matter quite plain? And then to go so far as to maneuver her into a coil of her own making! She was quite sure she had never met anyone more conniving or underhanded. Instantly, her head came up, her chin jutting in unconscious defiance. "I'm sure I wish him luck in that regard. As for myself, I shall be far too busy pursuing a career in writing."

Lucy steeled herself for the proverbial roof to fall in in the wake of that pronouncement. To her surprise, the earl appeared to take in stride what clearly amounted to mutiny in the ranks, while the countess hardly batted an eyelash.

"But of course you will, Lucy dear," said Lady Emmaline, calmly pouring tea. "One lump or two, Florence?"

The rest of the conversation over tea consisted of mundane topics concerning nothing more disturbing than the bouquet and texture of the earl's prize Madeira, various farming innovations that Will was attempting to persuade his father to initiate, and the debate among the gentry as to whether the waltz should be accepted at the local assemblies. Lucy, still fuming over Carmichael's defection from her cause, when she had been sure they were on the way to becoming fast friends, was noticeably quiet, leaving the field to Florence, who clearly basked in Carmichael's odiously charming presence.

It had been, she decided some forty-five minutes later, when Carmichael, firmly but graciously declining to remain for dinner, thanked his hosts for a delightful visit and departed, the most disagreeable afternoon of her young life. And, worst of all, it was not over yet, she realized, as Florence followed her up the stairs, clearly with the intent of rhapsodizing over the first grown man ever to pay her more than a passing attention.

By the time they had reached the second story, Lucy had been made to endure with what she was sure was the patience of Job, Carmichael's com-

plete and detailed canonization. Obviously he was
a gentleman of no little distinction, but with such
a pleasing air of condescension as rendered him
quite the most charming and delightful of com-
panions. Furthermore, his conversation demonstrated a refinement of wit that could not but
please, an informed intelligence that must be considered gratifying in the extreme, and an enlight-
ened outlook that could never be anything less
than uplifting. While Job's patience may have been
boundless, Lucy's was sorely tried long before
Florence had exhausted her supply of superlatives.
Asked for the fifth time if Mr. Carmichael was not
the most praiseworthy of gentlemen, Lucy at last
turned on her sister.

"Oh, indeed. He is, I have no doubt, the most
admirable, most exemplary, most estimable gentleman ever to walk the face of the earth. Mr. Carmichael is a paragon among men, a model of
everything that is pleasing. I am sure there has
never been nor ever will be his equal again."

Instantly she regretted her outburst at the sight
of Florence's expression of hurt disbelief.

"Oh, Florence, I am sorry. I am afraid I am
simply not myself. The truth is, I could not be
more pleased that you enjoyed Mr. Carmichael's
company. It is only that I have contracted a split-
ting headache." Smiling wanly, she reached for
Florence's hands. "Do forgive my unruly tongue."

Taken by surprise, Florence visibly wavered. This
was Lucy, who was never ill. Indeed, Lucy, the
peacemaker, the problem-solver, the oldest sister,
who was always in perfect control, the one to whom
the others always listened and looked for sympathy
and advice.

"I did notice you were uncommonly quiet at tea," she ventured, albeit grudgingly.

Lucy grimaced wryly. "I am afraid I was not very good company. Believe me, I was glad you were there to help Mama entertain our guest. Indeed, I am sure I do not know what we should have done without you."

"Really?" Florence said. "You are not just saying that?"

"But of course, really," Lucy answered. "Why should you doubt it? You are nearly eighteen, are you not? And about to make your come-out? Why, by this time next year you might very well be a bride."

Florence blushed becomingly at the thought, and yet it was true. In April she would make her come-out, and it was, of course, her hope, as it was every gently born woman's, to find herself betrothed at the end of her first Season in London. It was simply that with Lucy yet to enter Society, she, Florence, was still used to thinking of herself as the younger sister, always waiting for her turn to arrive. Perhaps, however, her time *had* finally come. Mr. Carmichael, after all, had not treated her like a schoolroom miss. Indeed, he had been most charmingly attentive.

But then, that must be it, she thought: the reason for Lucy's unheralded headache. Thinking back, it seemed that he had quite forgotten Lucy in favor of herself, and it had been obvious from the very first that Lucy was more than a little attracted to him. Oh, how could she have been so blind as not to see it before she had been idiotic enough to wax eloquent about Mr. Carmichael— and to Lucy, of all people! She might have caused her older sister to miss her come-out by being so foolish as to contract the mumps, but she would not be responsible for breaking that same sister's heart. She would just have to give Mr. Carmichael up— if, that was, it was not already too late. Perhaps Mr. Carmichael had already been pierced by Cupid's dart, in which case there would be nothing she could do to alter the course of true love. Oh, poor dear Lucy. She would never forgive her, and all because she, Florence, was cursed to be the Beauty of the family. At that moment she would have given anything to be able to trade places with Lucy, red hair, freckles, and all.

Stricken with conscience at the tragedy she envisioned before her, Florence smiled convulsively and squeezed her sister's hands. "But of course I forgive you. You must go and lie down at once, Lucy. We can save any further discussion of Mr. Carmichael for when you are feeling better."

Stifling a tremulous gasp, Florence turned then and, without waiting for an answer, fled down the hall to her room.

"Now what the devil," muttered Lucy, staring after the other girl in perplexity. She did not pause overlong to ponder her sister's odd behavior, however. She was much too preoccupied with her own.

She could not imagine what in the devil had possessed her to rip up at Florence in such a manner. It was not as if she had not in the past seventeen years had plenty of practice learning to hold in her temper where Flo was concerned. Of vastly different temperaments, they had been at loggerheads for practically as long as Lucy could remember. As the eldest, however, it had been impressed on Lucy from earliest childhood that it was incumbent on her to set a good example for the others. And, indeed, she had learned early on that her own life was a deal more pleasant if she maintained at least a modicum of peace among her younger siblings. It was inconceivable that she should now suddenly find herself flying up in the boughs over what amounted to little more than her sister's girlish infatuation for Phillip Carmichael.

A plague on the man, she thought, flinging herself irritably across her bed. In just two days' time he had managed to unsettle the even tenor of her life, disturb her tranquility of mind, and transform her into some shrewish creature she hardly recognized as herself. And the unkindest cut of all was that, in spite of everything, she could not stop herself from liking him.

Indeed, it seemed that he had cast some sort of a spell over every member of her family. It was one thing to win over the twins, who were like rollicking puppies ready to tumble over anyone, and her papa, who always looked for the best in everyone. And Carmichael was, after all, the sort of man who would naturally command the respect of other males. Added to his manly bearing was an ease of manner that must inevitably earn their liking as well. No doubt he had been the sort of officer whom men would follow into the very teeth of death, if need be. It was, when one came right down to it, inconceivable that her papa would not like him. And Will, too, for that matter, and for the very same reasons. But he had charmed her mama, as well, and that was a different matter altogether.

Lady Emmaline might appear the very picture of gentleness and delicate femininity, but beneath that deceptively fragile exterior there lurked an iron will and an acutely perceptive mind. No matter how manly his bearing or charming his conversation, no man who was not worthy of her regard would have been given what amounted to an invitation to run tame in her home, certainly not with her children always about. She would sooner have invited a serpent into her house. And yet, that was exactly what she had done with Carmichael at his departure, telling him to come often and to feel free simply to drop in whenever he liked. Faith, one might have thought, from the ease with which they laughed and conversed in one another's company, that they had been acquainted for years instead of an hour or two.

It was as if they were all in a conspiracy against her, Lucy, she thought, flinging herself over on her back. A conspiracy to woo her into accepting Lathrop's imminent proposal of marriage. Certainly Carmichael had done his best to give that impression. Indeed, he might as well have broadcast his intent to the world, she fumed, still stinging at what, she realized even in her agitated state, she perhaps unreasonably considered his betrayal.

Face it, Lucille Emily Powell, she told herself sternly: Phillip Carmichael might be perfectly willing to treat her with the consideration and kindness due a neighbor, but he had absolutely no other interest in her. He was merely being a thoughtful host in escorting her through the picture gallery and entertaining her with what he obviously considered a lot of romantic nonsense about Patience Merriweather and the Twelfth Duke of Lathrop. In the circumstances, he was perfectly within his bounds to do his utmost to promote his employer's suit. It was, in fact, practically his duty to do so.

"Oh, drat the man!" Lucy uttered out loud. In

a sudden excess of nervous energy she bounded off the bed and began to pace fitfully about the room. Nothing seemed to make any sense. She simply could *not* be mistaken in thinking Carmichael had been more than a host performing the duties of entertaining an unexpected guest. Such a view did nothing to explain his behavior toward her in the stables. She blushed hotly at the memory of his strong hands about her waist, the steely flash of his eyes. He had been furious with her, and all because he had witnessed her wild flight along the cliff trail. This was not the behavior of a man who was totally indifferent to her. And neither had it been, later, in the duke's study, when he had stood so close to her that she had been acutely aware of the pulse throbbing in the strong column of his neck. He had liked her then; she was sure of it. And she was equally sure there had been no misunderstanding between them concerning her feelings about marrying the duke.

Carmichael *had* deliberately betrayed her trust and the friendship she had so freely offered. But why? How could he be so insensitive to her feelings? Surely he was not afraid of the duke? Carmichael did not seem the sort to be afraid of anyone or anything. And yet, what if Lathrop held something over him, just as Lord Faxon had done over Florian— something that demanded Carmichael's loyalty? Would that not go far in explaining Carmichael's odd behavior? But what could it be? Lucy pondered, sinking down once more on the bed.

In search of a possible clue to the duke's power over Carmichael, she once again went over the bits and pieces of Carmichael's background that she had managed to glean. Immediately it came to her that what had struck her most forcibly was his bitterness at being forced to resign his commission. Indeed, he had declared he was given no choice in the matter. She had assumed at the time and later, from the things Oakes had let drop, that the seriousness of his wound had necessitated his retirement from active duty, but what if it had been something else entirely?

Obviously an act of cowardice was out of the question; Carmichael was incapable of such a thing. Nor could she imagine that he could ever for any reason be guilty of failure to perform his duty. It simply was not in his character. Then what? A scandal of some sort? Something quite serious, like striking a superior officer, perhaps. Or refusal to obey an order that would have led to a senseless and costly loss of life. It could hardly be anything less than that, after all, for Carmichael to commit an act of insubordination. Or perhaps he had fought a duel.

A duel! she thought, sitting bolt upright. But of course. It was not in the least difficult to imagine Carmichael facing an opponent at twenty paces over drawn guns. Or perhaps it had been swords at dawn. In either case, it would make perfect sense. Carmichael, wounded nearly to death on the field of honor but killing his man, would clearly have been given no choice but to sell out. The question was, how could Lathrop use such a thing against him?

Unable, even with her fertile imagination, to come up with an answer to that particular aspect of the puzzle, Lucy reluctantly shelved it for later consideration. After all, the two might be totally unrelated, she reasoned, sinking her chin on an elbow propped on one knee. Indeed, it might

make more sense to approach the problem from
the angle of Carmichael's relationship to the duke.

Instantly she was aware of a sudden prickle of
gooseflesh along her arms. Good God, she could
not truly be thinking what she was thinking! And
yet the idea was already taking firm root in her
mind. What if Carmichael's mother had not borne
an illegitimate son at all? What if there had been
an elopement and a marriage, which, perhaps because of the bride's unsuitability or the fear of
scandal, was kept secret? Had she been breeding
at the time, indeed, even close to her time of con-
finement?

Lucy had little difficulty envisioning a hideaway
somewhere in the country and a young woman
waiting in pain and fear for the arrival of her lover
with a magistrate to perform the marriage cere-
mony. She could almost hear the anguished mur-
mur of the spoken vows as the child threatened at
any moment to arrive. And then he had been delivered, but his mama, weakened by months of
anxiety and fear, had perished giving him life.
What had happened then? Had the duke acknowledged his son but not the marriage? Had another
already waited, ignorant of the events that would
have displaced her future son from the direct line
of inheritance? And the duke— what of him? Had
some small vestige of conscience prevented him
from destroying the marriage certificate? Had he
caused it to be hidden in the one place where it
might always be safe— the castle in which the lords
of Lathrop had sworn never to set foot again? And
on his deathbed, had he confessed all to the true
heir of Lathrop, leaving that son with the desperate hope of one day uncovering a metal box that
held the proof of his stolen inheritance? Was that

why Carmichael had come to Lathrop and why, playing for time to find the box, he pretended to further the interests of his brother, the usurper?

The very thought of such a possibility made Lucy's head spin. It was, after all, exactly what she had recorded one day as she perched on a boulder on the clifftops, Lathrop Castle brooding on the headland across from her and the words flowing from her pen onto the pages of her journal.

It was *The Lord of Lathrop, or the Watcher in the Tower,* just as she had written it.

Six

One might have thought the Prince Regent himself was coming to dinner, Lucy reflected wryly, as she viewed the preparations that were going forth in the manor.

Mama had ordered the table laid with the second-best plate, reasoning, no doubt, that the best plate would have been too obvious a condescension for what was supposed to be an informal dinner party. The fact that the meal was set for five o'clock, in keeping with the earl's preference for adhering to country hours, had not prevented Lady Emmaline from insisting on employing their finest damask tablecloth or from planning a nine-course menu topped with consomme and thick soup and forging through successive dishes of oysters, stuffed quail, roasted pigeon, a saddle of lamb— for digestive purposes a peach sorbet flavored with brandy— Italian truffles, green salad, asparagus in white sauce, and finishing with a lemon ice. Nor had the countess scrupled to furnish every vase in the principal rooms with freshly cut roses from the garden.

Mr. Carmichael, it seemed, had made a good impression indeed.

Though Lucy might marvel that Mama would go to such lengths, however, for someone who was expected simply to run tame about the place, Lady

Emmaline was not the only one in a stir over the much anticipated event of Carmichael's first dinner at Greensward. In the past two hours alone Lucy had been summoned on four separate occasions to render judgment on Florence's appearance, and each time her sister had been resplendent in a wholly different gown, new accessories, and altered hairstyle. And each time, though she had been a picture of loveliness and, indeed, would have been, dressed only in sackcloth and ashes, Flo could not be persuaded to believe she did not look the veriest dowd. Lucy smiled in sardonic amusement, certain that she would be called upon yet again before the magical hour of five to give her opinion that Flo had never looked better in still another of her many dresses, all of which were in the first stare of fashion and seemingly designed solely for the purpose of setting off Flo's indisputable beauty to perfection.

Lucy had, in addition to catering to her younger sister's attack of the nerves, been required to swear a sacred oath to the four youngest Powells that she would entice Carmichael up to the schoolroom before dinner; been prevailed upon by Papa for Carmichael's sake to find among the litter of papers and books in his study the 1740 first edition of Richardson's *Pamela, or Virtue Rewarded,* which Richardson had allegedly printed himself on his own printing press; and been cajoled into stitching a new pair of lace cuffs to the sleeves of Will's white linen dress shirt.

All of which had left her precious little time to attend to her own preparations.

She had hardly left her bath when the hall clock struck the half hour before five and, discovering Nanny Yates was occupied with dressing Florence's

hair over again for the fifth time, had no recourse
but to hastily tug a comb through her own thick
curls, which, made frizzy from her bath, was no
simple matter. Hurriedly she slipped into her silk
underthings and, reaching in her wardrobe for
practically the first thing that came to her hand,
donned it.

Moments later, giving her reflection in the looking glass only the most cursory of inspections,
Lucy gathered up her ivory-handled folding fan
and stole from her room in the hopes of intercept-
ing Carmichael upon his arrival.

The doorknocker sounded coincidentally with
her own flurried descent down the final set of
stairs into the great hall, so that she fairly landed
at the foot of the stairs, cheeks flushed and bosom
heaving, her skirts hiked midway to her calves, at
the very moment that Carmichael was being admitted by Timmons, the butler.

An involuntary "Oh!" escaped her lips at the
sight of Carmichael, who, having divested himself
of his greatcoat, curly brimmed beaver, and York
tan kid gloves, stood revealed before her in evening attire. Obviously a follower of Beau Brum-
mel's tenant that clothes should never draw
attention to themselves, he was undeniably elegant
in a double-breasted cutaway coat of dark blue superfine, white marcella waistcoat, and grey
kerseymere pantaloons. His neckcloth, tied in the
Oriental, boasted a single diamond pin, his only
ornament save for a gold fob across the front of
his waistcoat and a signet ring on the little finger
of his left hand. His black patent shoes gleamed
with an unearthly sheen, and his hair, brushed in
the Windswept, shone blue-black in the light of
the chandelier.

Lucy had never seen a finer-looking specimen of the male gender.

Indeed, she was made suddenly not only aware that she wore a gown that was neither new nor more than marginally fashionable and that her hair, which she had tried haphazardly to subdue in a loose knot on top of her head, had escaped its fetters to fall in a rebellious mass of curls about her face and shoulders, but that she still stood with her skirts hitched well above her ankles.

With a furious blush she hastily dropped them.

"Mr. Carmichael. Welcome to Greensward."

Carmichael, who had been given to view as shapely a pair of ankles and calves as had ever been his privilege to see, graciously saluted her hand. "Miss Powell." Straightening, he looked directly into her eyes. "May I say you are looking particularly fetching this evening."

Lucy choked on an unwitting burble of laughter. One would have had to be blind or an idiot not to apprehend the gleam of amusement in the look he bent upon her.

"I am sure I have no control over whatever despicable thing you might say," she retorted in repressive tones. "I am well aware that my appearance is only just short of being reprehensible. You may, no doubt, attribute it to the eccentricities of an artist. And please do not argue. There isn't time." Taking his hand, she pulled him toward the stairs. "We have an assignation to keep."

"You intrigue me, Miss Powell," murmured the captain, allowing himself to be led up the staircase. "It was my impression yesterday at tea that you had taken me in aversion."

"And so I did, Mr. Carmichael," Lucy replied. "As well I might after the way you tricked me. You know perfectly well that I have no intention of marrying the duke, or anyone else for that matter.''

''I believe,'' drawled Carmichael, insufferably cool, ''that I made known to you my own views on the matter that first day in the tower. You have all the qualities that would make you an admirable duchess, Miss Powell. I should not be doing my duty if I did not try to persuade you that it is in your best interests to accept the duke.''

''Your duty . . . !'' Lucy came to a sudden halt on the first-floor landing and turned to face him. ''Your duty to the duke notwithstanding, Mr. Carmichael, it was still a despicable thing to have done. There is, after all, a matter of trust between friends. I trusted you to honor my feelings, just as I should honor yours were our situations reversed. But then, I would seem to have been stupidly naive. I thought you liked me at least a little, but obviously I was mistaken.''

Had she meant to break through his formidable defenses, she was to be amply rewarded for her efforts.

Carmichael's hand came up flat against the wall, scant inches from the side of her face. ''You, Miss Powell, are exceedingly naive,'' he said, his eyes glittery in the lamplight. ''It is one of the things I find most endearing about you. But you are far from being stupid. It must be obvious to you that I am not some callow youth to be lightly played with and then as casually dismissed. If it is a friend you wish, you have it, gladly. But I should consider carefully, were I you. You know nothing about me. It might very well be that I am not the man you think I am.''

''Then I should take you on trust, Mr. Carmichael," Lucy said, returning his look steadily. "As you would have to take me on trust. That is the nature of true friendship, is it not?"

"Aye, trust," murmured Carmichael, eyeing her strangely. "And if I should, in the end, prove false to your trust, Miss Powell, what then? Would you cast me from your circle of friendship?"

Lucy frowned, considering the possibility. "How can I answer that, Mr. Carmichael?" she ventured at last. "If I cannot know in what manner false? Were you false in all else, but in your heart true to your friend, then how could that friend cast you off? I can tell you this: that I am not one to take friendship lightly, nor do I offer it so."

"Then so be it, Miss Powell," Carmichael said with an odd sort of finality. "Such a friendship as you envision may, in the end, prove costly— to both of us. Nevertheless, here is my hand on it. Be very sure before you take it that you are prepared to accept the risks that come with it."

Lucy stared at him. She had the oddest feeling that her life was about to be changed forever. But how absurd; she was accepting an offer of friendship, not making a pact with the devil. If there was risk involved, then it must reside in whatever secret lay between Carmichael and the duke, and in that case Carmichael might very well have need of her as a friend.

Deliberately Lucy placed her palm in his. Given a choice, she could not but choose to stand by Carmichael and take her chances than play it safe and turn her back on him. "I am sure, Mr. Carmichael," she answered. It was, after all, hardly in her nature to do otherwise.

"Friends, then, Miss Powell?" His strong fingers closed over hers.

"Friends, Mr. Carmichael," Lucy said, reflecting that Florence had been quite right when she had claimed that one could lose one's self in Carmichael's eyes. Then, suddenly and acutely aware of her hand clasped in his, she started away from the wall. "And now if you please, sir. I did give my word. I should never hear the end of it if you failed to put in an appearance."

At the quizzical lift of a single arrogant eyebrow, Lucy grinned irrepressibly. "Come now, Mr. Carmichael. You did not think your assignation was with me? I should never be so forward. In addition to Florence, who believes she has never met a finer, more distinguished gentleman, and my mother, who has never been in the habit of inviting the neighbors to run tame about the place, it seems you have made a conquest among the younger set." Coming to a halt before a closed door, she reached for the doorhandle. "How, by the way, do you feel about children?" she asked suddenly and seemingly inconsequentially.

A wry smile twitched at the corners of Carmichael's lips. "Children, Miss Powell?" he queried politely.

"Yes, children, Mr. Carmichael. You know—smaller versions of ourselves."

"It is true my experience with the offspring of our species has been limited in the extreme, but I do know what they are, Miss Powell. As it happens, I have not given the matter a great deal of consideration. Why do you ask?"

"Because your assignation, Mr. Carmichael," Lucy announced, turning the handle and opening the door, "is with my younger brothers and sisters."

* * *

For a man who, by his own admission, had had little experience with children, Carmichael was proving amazingly adept with them, Lucy reflected some ten minutes later. Indeed, it was apparent from the looks on their rapt young faces that he had a natural talent for engaging and holding their interest. And for spinning tall tales, she decided, hiding a smile of amusement at the very notion of Carmichael engaged with a company of French soldiers in a game of "Catch Me As Catch Can."

The sly little devils, she thought. Had she guessed her siblings' purpose was to cajole their unsuspecting guest into telling the story of how he had won Don Julian's gratitude and the gift of El Guerrero, she never would have agreed to bring him there. Indeed, she had been as close as she had ever been in her life to losing her temper with them the moment their object became mortifyingly clear. Fortunately, Carmichael had immediately diffused the situation. Assuring Lucy that he did not consider the request either an imposition or an impertinence, he had ordered them all to be seated.

Lucy had hardly known what to expect as she reluctantly allowed herself to be led to a chair. At first she had been uneasy as Carmichael began to tell the story of how one of Don Julian's most trusted lieutenants, through trickery and betrayal, had been taken captive by the French. After all, he was speaking to the tender young ears of children, Josephine included among them. Almost immediately, however, she was made to relax as she realized she should have trusted Carmichael to know what was suitable for his audience to hear.

The tale that unfolded quickly assumed the humor and charm of a children's story.

It was not until later, when he had come to a hilarious account of how, after tagging a number of the French soldiers in the dark, putting them out of the game, he had at last been taken captive and removed to a castle where he was made to participate in a duel of Twenty Questions with the commandant, that she realized the story, in essence, must be true.

After that she went by turns hot, then cold, as she translated the children's fantasy into what must have been the reality of Carmichael's desperate mission to rescue Don Julian's confederate from the French. How well he must have mastered the Spanish guerrilla tactics to be able to stalk and disable the enemy, one after another, in the dark, until the odds had finally turned against him. Taken captive, he had been cruelly interrogated, starved and beaten, no doubt, for, as one of Don Julian's guerrillas, he could hardly have been expected to be granted the status either of a British officer or a prisoner of war.

Seen in such a light, Lucy had little difficulty in identifying the giant, who, in the company of a "hardy band of thieves," had breached the castle's defenses and rescued the captain. It could have been no one other than the ever loyal Jessop Oakes, along with a handful of Don Julian's guerrillas. With the captain to lead them, they had found and freed their lieutenant, with whom they had escaped in time to join the British forces who were even then gathering for the battle of Rolica.

"That was a ripping good tale, I must say," exclaimed Tom, grinning hugely, when the captain had come to the end. "But you can't gammon me. It wasn't the real story, was it?"

"You didn't really play tag with the French. Or duel at Twenty Questions with the French colonel," Timothy scoffed, emboldened by his twin's declaration of disbelief, though it was plain he was not quite so sure of himself as he would have the others believe.

It was at that point that Josephine stood up, her delicate features set with uncharacteristic determination. "Pray don't listen to them, Mr. Carmichael," she said, moved to champion her newfound friend. "I think it was a marvelous story. Oh, how I should like to be friends with a giant like yours. You don't think he would eat me alive, do you?"

"Oh, very likely," Francie felt obliged to speculate. "*If*, that is, there were any such thing. Who's ever seen a real giant, after all, especially one who could make himself invisible by donning a magic cloak?"

"*I* have," declared Lucy, getting firmly to her feet. "And so will you one day soon, since Mr. Carmichael's giant is presently in residence at Lathrop Castle."

"No, is he?" exclaimed Josephine, torn between fear and alt. "Then it was indeed a true story!"

"Every word of it. Now thank our guest for being so kind as to humor you." Lucy frowned with mock severity. "If ever again you try to use me for such an ulterior purpose, you may be sure I shan't be nearly so understanding as he has been."

Josephine was the only one among the young rapscallions who had the grace to look chagrined for her part in misleading her beloved eldest sister. "You will forgive us, won't you, Lucy?" she pleaded, her face troubled. "Please do say you are not angry."

"But of course she is not angry," said Francie with utmost confidence. "Could you not see she enjoyed Mr. Carmichael's story every bit as much as did we? For which we do thank you, sir, even if it was stretching the truth just a bit. And you will let us come meet your giant very soon, won't you?"

"You may be sure Mr. Oakes and I shall look forward to it," replied Carmichael, who had maintained an aspect of tolerant amusement throughout. "I believe you will find that he has a great many stories to tell."

"Which, if you are on your very best behavior, he will no doubt relate over tea and the most delicious cinnamon biscuits," Lucy said, adding that it was time she delivered Mr. Carmichael to Lady Emmaline and the earl.

"Tell me the truth," demanded Lucy of Carmichael moments later on the stair. "Was there really a castle, or was that only an embellishment on the story for the benefit of the others?"

Carmichael's dark head went back in a chuckle. "It was, in fact, a country house on the outskirts of Vimeiro. One roughly along the same lines as Greensward, though in the Spanish style. Fortunately, it lacked fortifications, or it is highly unlikely I should be here in your charming company this evening."

Lucy, who had experienced a soft thrill at the sound of his laughter, subsequently suffered a chill at the thought of what a very near thing it must have been for him. "I'm glad, then," she said simply. "I haven't so many friends that I should wish to be deprived of even one." She paused before the withdrawing room door to give him a long, searching look. "Thank you for your kindness to my brothers and sisters, though I fear you may live to regret it. I suspect you are going to find yourself besieged by young Powells from this time forward, all of them suffering from acute cases of hero worship. Shall you mind very much, do you think?"

Carmichael, bemused by the soft grey warmth of her eyes, gave a twisted smile. "I shall undoubtedly fob them off on Oakes," he answered, "who will take great delight in adding to my heroic image. Will you be among them?"

Lucy shook her head. "By no means, Mr. Carmichael." Then, as she saw him accept her pronouncement in silence, she dimpled naughtily. "How can I be with them," she said laughingly, as she tucked her hand in the crook of his arm, "when I shall be with you, sir, exploring the dungeons?"

"Wretch," he murmured with obvious feeling. "Be careful you do not end up a permanent fixture in Lathrop Castle."

"I shall be very careful, you may be sure of it." Lucy laughed and turned gaily to enter the withdrawing room, where the rest of the dinner party were already gathered.

Dinner, in spite of the accusing glare with which Florence greeted her sister's entrance on the arm of the guest of honor and the stiff self-awareness of Will, dressed in the sartorial splendor of a Jean de Bry coat with outrageously high padded shoulders, voluminous Petersham Cossacks with a flounce around the ankle, and pointed toed shoes, laced across the front and having three-inch heels in the manner of an aspiring Town Tulip, was a merry affair.

Lady Emmaline, after two highly successful seasons in London, during which she had been well on her way to establishing her reputation as a hostess, might indeed have chosen retirement in the country in order to rear a sizable brood of young hopefuls, but she had not forgotten how to perform with consummate skill those duties that made for a perfect meal. Under her tutelage the conversation flowed with as great an ease and regularity as did the various courses, which were excellent.

But then, Lucy reflected, her mama was amply aided in the success of her endeavors by having as guest a man who was as adept at drawing others into talking about themselves as he was at parrying any questions about himself.

Carmichael could have charmed the purse off a miser had he wanted to, she realized, watching him coax Florence, without seeming to have done, so completely out of her petulance at Lucy's earlier usurpation of what she must clearly have considered her own just due as to join wholeheartedly in the general merriment. Only those intimately acquainted with Florence could appreciate the Herculean accomplishment that was, Lucy reflected dourly. And as for Will, that young would-be sprig of fashion appeared to blossom under Carmichael's cultivation, so far forgetting himself that he positively radiated self-confidence and a newfound sense of importance. Nor was Lucy herself immune to Carmichael's compelling presence, she discovered, upon finding herself relating any number of amusing anecdotes about her childhood.

Carmichael listened and smiled. And though he was perfectly willing to entertain them with humorous *on-dits* about various members of the *Ton*, or to impart the latest news from London, and though he could discuss any number of topics, ranging from ladies' fashions to Napoleon's proposed Russian campaign, he revealed very little of a personal nature, except what might be gained by deduction.

Obviously he moved in the best circles and had a large acquaintanceship among the Beau Monde. He was well-read, keenly observant, and possessed of a quick wit and a wide-ranging intellect. He must have been, Lucy realized, invaluable to Wellington, who would know how best to use the tools at his command. What had happened, then, to terminate what must have been a singularly promising career? she wondered, absently jabbing at her lemon ice with a spoon.

For a time the room receded, along with the laughter and merriment, as an image rose up before her of Carmichael, bitter, yet proud in the face of ignominy, while all around him, his men fought and died without him to lead them. Had there been no one besides Oakes to know or care what he must have been suffering?

Irresistibly, she drifted off in a daydream in which Carmichael was cast as a tragic hero with herself in the role of his sole supporter and champion. A sigh breathed through her lips, while, forgotten before her, her lemon ice melted.

It was not until Lady Emmaline rose, suggesting that they retire to the withdrawing room, that Lucy was jarred from her thoughts to sudden and instant awareness. She glanced up and, for the barest instant, found herself staring directly across the table into Carmichael's eyes. Inexplicably her breath caught.

A faint, sardonic smile touched his lips and, furiously, she felt herself blush. The devil, she thought, hastily averting her gaze. He must have been watching her for some time. Indeed, unless she was very much mistaken, he well knew she had been thinking about him. The realization was mortifying in the extreme. Still, she would rather have died than let him know that.

Rising from the table, she awarded him a look that was meant to be cool and composed.

"Tell me, Captain," she murmured, smiling ingenuously at him over the top of her fan as he came around the table to join her, "do you always cast a spell over everyone who comes into your presence?"

"Everyone, Miss Powell?" queried the captain, odiously sure of himself. "Surely you exaggerate."

"On the contrary, I am not exaggerating in the least. If you must know, I have never seen my mother so positively enchanted with anyone. And in case you have failed to notice, my sister cannot take her eyes off you. I should be careful if I were you. She is inexperienced in the art of light flirtation and shall very likely fall head over ears in love with you."

"Unlike you, Miss Powell, is that it?" he had the gall to answer her.

Lucy narrowed her eyes at him, certain that he was laughing at her. "You, sir, may be certain of it," she retorted. "It is true that I have never been farther from Greensward than Scarsborough, but I am neither green nor gullible. I am a good deal older than my sister. Furthermore, you are not the only gentleman of my acquaintance. I have attended the local assemblies on a regular basis since I was turned sixteen."

"An unconscionably long time," agreed the captain. "I wonder that you are not jaded by all the gaiety *that* must have afforded. I shall no doubt come to look forward to your assemblies with an eagerness to match your own."

The very thought of Carmichael at the local assemblies was too much to contemplate with a straight face. Lucy choked on a helpless burble of laughter. "I wish you will not be absurd, Captain. You will do no such thing. You must know very well they are perfectly insipid."

"Quite so, Miss Powell." Carmichael smiled, apparently having accomplished his purpose; then, bowing, he left her for the earl, who was beckoning his guest to join him at the grog tray.

The earl, ever a congenial host, had forborne out of deference to his wife and children to bring up until after dinner his fondest topic of conversation, which was his passion for antiquated manuscripts and books. Now, however, he did not hesitate to mention, albeit with an assumption of casualness, that he maintained a correspondence with the proprietor of a certain rare old books shop in Cheapside who had been instrumental in supplying him with any number of treasures, his most recent acquisition being an exiguous first edition of Richardson's *Pamela*.

"A rare treasure, indeed, if it is the 1740 edition," Carmichael observed. "It occurs to me that

I have had dealings myself with this proprietor. A Mr. Aloysius Trent, am I not mistaken?"

"Indeed, sir, you are not," exclaimed Bancroft, delighted at Carmichael's familiarity with the little-known dealer in antiquities. "It is the very same man. Are you a connoisseur of rare books, Mr. Carmichael?"

"Merely a dilettante, I'm afraid," replied Carmichael. "I recently consulted with Trent concerning the authenticity of various works contained in the duke's library at Hollingsworth. I found him to be remarkably knowledgeable in the subject."

"He is indeed, Mr. Carmichael," the earl readily agreed. "I wonder, sir, would you care to see my collection. I have promised my wife not to detain you overlong."

Graciously, Carmichael bowed. "I should naturally be delighted, my lord."

Fairly beaming with pleasure, the earl reiterated his promise to Lady Emmaline not to tarry overlong and led his guest from the room. They were followed soon after by Will, who, claiming he had an early day before him on the morrow, kissed his mama good night with the intention of retiring.

"Oh, how *could* Papa be so selfish as to take Mr. Carmichael away?" said Florence, plopping disconsolately down on the sofa beside her mama. "I should have thought you could persuade him to put off his precious books for another day."

"Then you were very much mistaken, my dear," replied the countess, calmly taking up her embroidery frame. "I should never dream of depriving your father of his enjoyment."

"And nor should you, Flo," Lucy said, seating herself at the pianoforte and running her fingers

Allow us to proposition you in a most provocative way.

GET 4 REGENCY ROMANCE NOVELS *FREE*

An $18.49 Value

NO OBLIGATION TO BUY ANYTHING, EVER.

An $18.49
value.
FREE!
No obligation
to buy
anything, ever.

absently over the keys. "It is not often Papa meets someone who can appreciate his collection."

"Oh, certainly. *You* can say that." Florence's lovely eyes flashed with resentment. "You thought nothing of stealing off with Mr. Carmichael in order to have him to yourself."

Lucy's fingers stilled on the keys. "I am sorry if that is what you think. The truth is, I took him to see Francie and the others. Josephine particularly requested it of me."

"Josephine requested it? For heaven's sake," said Lady Emmaline, amused. "Whatever in the world for?"

Lucy smiled reminiscently. "She and the others wanted Mr. Carmichael to tell them a story, which he did in great style. They enjoyed it immensely, Mama."

"As we all should have done, no doubt," Florence declared, awarding her sister a meaningful look.

"I believe there is no sense in belaboring the subject, dear," said the countess, never pausing in her embroidery work. "I'm sure Lucy did not mean to exclude you from what was clearly meant as a treat for the younger children."

Lucy drew a long, steadying breath. "No, Mama, Florence is right. She would have enjoyed it, and I should have thought to include her. The truth is, however, that I didn't think of it. I'm sorry, Flo. Please believe that I never dreamed what the little schemers intended. If I had, you may be sure I should never have promised to take Carmichael to them."

"Yes, well, it's your own fault, Lucy," Florence declared, getting up from the sofa. "The truth is, you never think to include me." She wandered to the piano and stood for a moment before sitting down on the bench beside Lucy. "However, in this instance," she said, starting to play, "I do believe you."

When Carmichael and the earl rejoined the ladies some twenty minutes later it was to the merry sounds of song and laughter.

Carmichael, met with the sight of Florence at the piano and Lucy performing an earthy country song in her rich contralto, paused, bemused, just inside the door.

The Misses Powell, it seemed, were full of surprises. Obviously the younger sister was a more than accomplished pianist, and with her fair good looks she would upon her come-out soon find herself much sought after by any number of hostesses. It was the older one, however, he reflected, smiling a little, who, given the chance, would take London by storm.

Lucy Powell had that rare quality that others would always draw upon— an exuberance for living that the world-weary members of their set could not possibly resist.

It shone now in the merry sparkle of her eyes and in her animated features. She was no simpering miss, but a vibrant woman, infinitely charming and wholly desirable. Indeed, she fairly exuded vivacity and an originality that quite set her apart from the other young beauties of his acquaintance. Most intriguing of all, however, was the fact that she was totally unaware of it.

And there was the rub. He had never been in the position of having to convince a beautiful young woman that, far from being a dowd, she was

a diamond of the first water. And yet if the duke
was to have his duchess, that, apparently, was precisely his task.

A sardonic smile touched his lips. How infinitely
ironic that, where Miss Powell's heart was concerned, Captain Phillip Carmichael appeared to
have better than even odds in his favor, while the
titled and enormously wealthy Lathrop would
seem to have little or no chance at all. If nothing
else, it put him in a most damned untenable position, and all the more so because he was discovering the more he was around her just how little
he liked the thought of losing her.

Seven

June had given way to July and Carmichael had been at Lathrop for five weeks when Lucy exited the manor early one afternoon and stalked across the back lawn to the stables. She could not have been more relieved to be able at last to escape the house and, most especially, Florence, who seemed determined to drive her older sister to distraction.

Moments earlier, Lucy had been as close as she had ever been to utterly losing her self-control with Florence.

With an effort she reminded herself that her sister was in the throes of her first infatuation with an older man and would very likely become a deal more trying before the painful experience was behind her. Had not she herself once entertained the belief that she was destined to love Mr. Thaddeus Wilkerson, Will's former tutor? Of course she had only been thirteen at the time, and she had never let anyone know she was stricken with her first and only case of misplaced infatuation. She had been unbearably hurt and embarrassed when Mr. Wilkerson, upon receiving a much awaited government appointment, announced his betrothal to a Miss Mary Ellen Sanderson. What Lucy had supposed to be a deep and abiding affection for herself she had been suddenly made to realize was nothing more than a grown man's kindness to a gawky adolescent.

While she had survived the experience without any lasting scars to her emotional well-being, she had never forgotten the terrible pangs of her disillusionment in love. She supposed, on retrospect, that it had not quite been of the magnitude of an exquisite anguish, but it was as close to it as she had suffered before or since. The symptoms of her case, moreover, bore a striking similarity to those Florence was manifesting.

That morning alone, Florence had gone from humming mysteriously to herself over a bouquet of wildflowers she had picked to falling into a distempered freak over something so innocuous as Lucy's comment that Carmichael had at last pronounced the dungeons safe for exploring.

"And now I suppose you will prevail on Mr. Carmichael to show them to you," Florence declared peevishly. "Just as you have imposed yourself on him nearly every afternoon since he arrived. I wonder that you are not the talk of the countryside, the way you fling yourself constantly in his way."

"I beg your pardon," Lucy said in awful tones. Gripping her hands tightly before her, she strove for her normal composure. "I do *not* fling myself at him. You know very well that I do not," she tried in a reasonable vein. "Mr. Carmichael has been kind enough to ask for my suggestions in the renovations going forth at Lathrop. As I recall, he invited you to do the same."

Florence had the grace to blush at the veracity of that statement. It was obvious her temper had betrayed her into saying what she had never meant to have done, and now that she found herself

trapped in the toil of her own making she simply
could not bring herself to back down.

"You know very well that I cannot bear to be in
that dreadful old castle," she said, flinging away
from Lucy. "It is cold, miserably damp, and
gloomy. It gives me the shivers just to think of it.
And you have taken unfair advantage of my sensibilities. I daresay you spend more time at
Lathrop than you do at home, and do not think I
do not know it is because you want Carmichael for
yourself."

Lucy, who could not deny that she had been a
great deal at Lathrop of late, suffered an unexpected twinge of conscience at this possible interpretation of events. And yet how unfair; she had
behaved with perfect decorum, never going without one or more of her siblings in tow for propri-
ety's sake, and always with the full consent and
approval of her parents. The devil! she fumed,
striking her crop against her skirted leg. Her
friendship with Carmichael had afforded her great
pleasure, and she was dashed if she would give it
up just because Florence was jealous.

Surprisingly enough, Lady Emmaline, having
entered the room in time to hear Florence's final
accusation, had interceded on Lucy's behalf, reminding Florence that she was not yet out of the
schoolroom, while Lucy, had circumstances not
dictated otherwise, should already have had her
come-out.

"Perhaps your father and I were mistaken in allowing you to join in entertaining company," the
countess suggested gently to Florence. "If we were
premature, then I am sorry for it—and for you,
my dear. I cannot like to see any of my children

unhappy. I believe, however, you owe Lucy an apology."

Florence had not apologized. Her face had gone beet red, then pearly white. Then, raving something to the effect that it was not enough the duke was to be Lucy's for the taking, but she must be allowed to have Carmichael as well, Flo had burst into tears and dashed willy-nilly upstairs to her room.

Lucy sighed, feeling the anger drain out of her. It was highly unlikely that Carmichael would ever feel anything more than a brotherly affection for either one of them; and while Lucy had never allowed herself to look for more than that, Florence, unfortunately, had apparently entertained great expectations.

The thought was a sobering one for Lucy, who could see nothing in it but disillusionment for Florence. Very likely Flo would need her eldest sister before long; in which case Lucy was determined not to allow a rift to come between them. She might even, with patience and understanding, succeed, she reflected sardonically— if, that was, she was not driven first to throttle her younger sister.

Twenty minutes later, Lucy, mounted on Wind Star, cantered across the paddock to meet Francie, who, having finished putting Jester through his paces, was just turning the colt over to a stable lad.

"It's about time," called the younger girl, exchanging Jester for Piebald, the venerable black-and-white gelding upon whom all the Powell children had variously taken their first riding lessons. "I thought you would never come. Very likely the captain has gone exploring without us."

Lucy laughed. "He would not dare. Come on, I'll race you to the gate."

"On this sway-backed, knock-kneed bag of old bones?" Francie grimaced. "Not without a ten-minute head start."

"Gammon. I'll give you a twenty-count and not a second more."

Francie swatted the old gelding across the rump with her riding crop. "Then catch us if you can!" she cried as the big horse lurched into motion.

At least Francie had not been changed by Carmichael's intrusion into the peace and tranquillity of Greensward, reflected Lucy, smiling at the sight of her daredevil sister pounding across the down on Piebald. She was the same incorrigible young hoyden she had always been, and Lucy loved her for it.

In spite of Piebald's lead the race was every bit as one-sided as Francie had predicted it would be. Lucy's Wind Star thundered through the gate a full three lengths in front of the lumbering gelding.

Laughing out of pure enjoyment, Lucy pulled the mare in and waited for Francie to come up to her.

"It isn't fair," Francie protested, hauling against the gelding's iron mouth with all her might. "Piebald was well enough when I was seven, but I'm a good deal older now. I daresay I could ride anything in the stable, and Papa still insists this spavined old mule will do until Jester is ready. A whole year, Lucy! I shall have every bone in my body jarred loose long before then."

"Poor old Pie," Lucy crooned sympathetically as she reached out to rub the old horse between the ears. "It is only Papa's way of providing you with the proper incentive, Flo. Jester is like the carrot at the end of the stick, and Old Pie is the spur to urge you on. You will work harder to train Jester properly, if only because he is the means of ridding yourself one day of Pie."

"It is far more likely that Pie will be the end of me," Francie predicted with a comical frown as she struggled to pull Pie's head up away from a succulent tuft of grass by the side of the road. Laughing, Lucy set out once more for the castle with Francie, who was hard put to keep the old gelding from snatching a mouthful of grass at every other step.

In five short weeks Carmichael had accomplished a great deal more than Lucy would have thought possible had she not seen it for herself. With a veritable army of groundskeepers at his command, Oakes had overseen the refurbishing of the bailey, including the pruning and thinning of the apple orchard, which some later Duke of Lathrop had caused to be planted between the parallel moats that had formerly guarded the approach. The once-famous rose gardens had been re-planted and the topiary garden on the west side of the keep returned to a semblance of its former magnificence. As for the stables, the stalls had all been cleaned and furnished with feed and hay, and men were even then working to repair the roof under the auspices of Carmichael's groom.

The keep itself, isolated within the bailey, was comprised of a single great rectangular tower with an octagonal turret at each corner, in one of which Lucy, weeks before, had read her tale of *The Lord of Lathrop* to the girls. At one time or another the

keep had been added to and modernized in order
to afford the inhabitants greater comfort.

It was in the process, Lucy noted as she and
Francie were ushered into the Great Hall, of being
modernized yet again. Crews of laborers were
everywhere at work, and where they could not be
seen, the sounds of their progress could be clearly
heard.

"Faith," whispered Francie to Lucy, "Carmichael
must have half the able-bodied men in the county
employed here today. It would seem no cost is too
high for His Grace when he makes up his mind
to a thing."

Though half the number of able-bodied men in
the county was a gross exaggeration, Lucy could
not but be similarly impressed. Indeed, she could
only wonder with a sinking sensation in the pit of
her stomach if Lathrop actually had taken on the
project simply for her benefit. But that was absurd,
she told herself. The man would have to be either
exceedingly arrogant or a fool to spend a fortune
for the sake of a woman he had never met, one,
moreover, who had yet to receive a formal offer
of marriage let alone accept it. Clearly he had to
be motivated by something else.

Left, in all the chaos, to themselves, the two girls
wandered in search of Carmichael, who, it was
variously reported, could be found in the north
turret checking the newly repaired stairway, in the
study, revising the plans for the new servants' quarters, and in the kitchens, supervising the installa-
tion of the new cast-iron cookstoves.

"Obviously he cannot be everywhere at once,"
Lucy reasoned, smiling in bemusement at her sister. "Why don't you check the kitchens, and I shall
investigate the study."

Its having been agreed upon that they would meet once more in the Great Hall, Lucy made her way up the curving staircase to the picture gallery, which, stripped of its portraits, appeared forlorn somehow and quite barren. She suffered a small pang as it came to her to wonder if Miss Patience Merriweather and the Twelfth Duke of Lathrop would ever again hang side by side in Lathrop Castle.

At length, having ascended a circular staircase and traversed a dimly lit corridor, Lucy came at last to the study. When a rap on the heavy oak barrier failed to elicit a response, Lucy hesitated only briefly before pushing the door open. Curiosity and the memory of her one and only previous visit there, prompted her to enter.

The room was just as she remembered it on the auspicious occasion of her first encounter with Carmichael, save for the fact that it had taken on more of the personality of its temporary master. Maps of the county, the castle, and presumably the duke's estate littered the great oak desk along with a scattering of books that Carmichael had brought with him from Hollingsworth presumably to read during his leisure hours. Glancing curiously at the titles, she was given to surmise that the gentleman's tastes were varied, ranging from architecture and agricultural treatises to a slender volume of Thomas Campbell's latest verses. She was examining a field telescope and compass when a flat walnut box caught her attention.

She stood for a long moment, running her fingers over the smooth surface while she struggled against temptation. In the end, curiosity won out over conscience. After all, she was only going to take a peek, she told herself, and lifted the lid.

She experienced a cold prickling at the nape of her neck at sight of the brace of weapons laid out against a red velvet lining. She had never seen dueling pistols before, but only an idiot or a child could mistake what they were. In dread fascination she ran her fingertips over one of the octagonal gun barrels. How smooth and cold to the touch! Involuntarily she shivered. Perhaps ten inches long, the barrel shone a dull blue against the velvet, as did the gun mountings, made of polished steel. The stocks were plain, without carving or ornament, save for the checkering on the grips, intended, no doubt, to allow for a firm grasp.

The weapons were beautiful and quite deadly, she little doubted. Had Carmichael ever used them? she wondered, her fingers lingering on the stock's polished surface.

"Are you considering a meeting at twenty paces, Miss Powell?" queried an exceedingly dry voice behind her.

With a gasp she turned to find Carmichael watching her from the doorway. Her heart gave a lurch at sight of his tall masculine form, casually elegant in buff riding breeches and coat of bottle green superfine.

"I wish you will not be absurd," she retorted. "I was just looking for you. Someone said you might be in your study."

"And being of a curious nature, you naturally stayed to examine my dueling pistols." He smiled ironically as her cheeks took on a charming tinge of color.

"Oh, how odious you are." She gave a wry laugh. "I'm afraid you have caught me, fair and square. What, sir, do you intend to do with me?"

With a single appreciative glance, Carmichael

took in the slender figure clad in a velvet green riding habit, which, in spite of the fact that it had seen a great deal of service, seemed peculiarly suited to her somehow. Indeed, from the absurd black beaver hat perched at a precarious angle atop a riot of red curls to the toes of her well-worn riding boots, she presented a charming picture of alluring femininity.

He could conceive of any number of methods of punishment that would have afforded him no small measure of satisfaction, crushing her to his chest and sampling her enticingly sweet lips being only the least of them.

"I promise to give the matter my due consideration, Miss Powell," he promised ironically. Propping a broad shoulder against the door frame, he studied her from beneath drooping eyelids. "Pray don't mind me." He nodded significantly toward the gun case. "Take one out and examine it freely."

"Oh, but I could not possibly—" Lucy stammered, taken by surprise.

"Come now, Miss Powell. You know very well you not only can, but you want to. There's no need to play missish with me. Take it up. How else are you to know what it is to have the feel of it in your hand?"

The devil, thought Lucy, to tease her so. But then, he was perfectly in the right of it. She did want very much to know what it would be like to hold it in her hand, simply in order to be able one day to describe it with thrilling accuracy.

"Yes, that's right." Carmichael smiled as he read capitulation in the sudden determined tilt of her delightfully stubborn chin. "Hold the grip firmly, but not too tightly. In a duel you have only a split second to shoot. Stiff fingers or a cramp in the palm could prove damned inconvenient."

"Faith, how heavy it is," Lucy exclaimed, feeling the weight of the barrel drag at her arm.

"A dueling pistol is designed to give the duelist the greatest possible advantage. The excessive weight of the barrel provides a measure of compensation for the possibility of a nervous jerk of the trigger. The aim is less likely to be affected. Notice as well the dull sheen of the metal. It is deliberately blued in order to minimize the glare. Nothing, after all, must be allowed to divert the gentleman at the point of risking his life on the field of honor. For the same reason the stock is severely plain. Only a fool or an amateur would employ a pistol with pearl handles or silver or brass mountings. A split second of distraction can mean the difference between living and dying."

"Yes, I suppose it would," agreed Lucy, both fascinated and repelled. Lifting the pistol to eye level straight out before her, she sighted down the barrel.

"I fear, Miss Powell, if you take such a stance, you will have little chance of walking away from a meeting at dawn. You present an altogether too inviting target."

"No, do I?" Lucy lowered the weapon in order to look over her shoulder at Carmichael. "And how, pray tell, sir, should I stand?"

Inexplicably she felt her pulse quicken as Carmichael straightened and crossed leisurely to her. "I should suggest you present your right side to the opponent, your back straight and your stomach in, in order to present the smallest possible target. No, no, Miss Powell. Hold your shoulders back— like so." Lucy was hard put not to flinch at the unexpected weight of his hands on her shoulders, straightening them. "In addition, your right arm should be positioned to protect as much of the chest as possible." A faint, ironic smile touched his lips. "Naturally, a woman's physique presents a unique problem in that regard. Perhaps that is one reason why dueling has always been a man's pursuit."

"Do you think so?" Lucy replied sweetly. "I, on the other hand, suspect it is because women are far too intelligent to engage in anything so patently foolhardy. There. Have I got it right, Mr. Carmichael?"

"I should say you have it exactly right, Miss Powell," answered Carmichael; but whether he meant her stance or her pointed observation was not entirely clear to her.

"Thank you, Mr. Carmichael. And now, I suppose, I aim and fire?"

"You hold in your hand, Miss Powell, one of the finest dueling pistols ever made. It does not require that you aim it. You have only to point and fire. With such a pistol, no doubt even you could hit your target three times out of four at twenty paces."

"Not aim? I don't believe you, Mr. Carmichael. Indeed, you are roasting me, are you not?"

An arrogant black eyebrow arched toward Carmichael's hairline. "I should not dream of it. Allow me to demonstrate. Drop your arm straight down before you. On my count of three raise it and point at the target— shall we say the face of the mantel clock?"

Lucy, spotting the proposed target at the far end of the room, nodded her agreement. "Very well, Mr. Carmichael. I am ready whenever you are."

A smile twitched at the corners of Carmichael's lips at her fierce look of concentration. "One," he said, the thought crossing his mind that she might indeed be a throwback to her Irish great grandmama, but at the moment she presented more the aspect of an Amazon. "Two," he said. Then, "Three."

Lucy's arm swung up and held steady. "You are right, Mr. Carmichael," she exclaimed, squinting along the sights. The pistol's "point" was true. The sights were perfectly aligned with the target even though she had not made the least attempt to aim. "I should never have believed it had I not seen it for myself."

"You astonish me, Miss Powell," murmured Carmichael ironically. "One would almost believe you hold my word in doubt."

Lucy laughed and dropped the gun to her side. "But I should never do that. You might feel obligated to call me out. Please, sir, accept my apologies instead."

A wry smile twisted at Carmichael's lips. "I cannot accept what is unnecessary. On the other hand, since I fear I should prove a poor second to you in a duel, I suggest we settle on a truce."

"Now you *are* roasting me, Captain," Lucy said, eyeing him askance. "Mr. Oakes has assured me there is not your match with pistols or swords. I daresay you have yet to meet the man who could better you on the field of honor."

"Mr. Oakes is fond of puffing off my consequence," replied Carmichael dismissively. "At any rate, it hardly signifies. *You* are not a man."

"Indeed, sir," Lucy agreed. "But what has that to say to the matter?"

"Everything, I should think," Carmichael reflected, his expression maddeningly unreadable. "Thus far, you, my dear Miss Powell, have bettered me at every turn."

"I?" Lucy's startled laugh sounded unnatural in the quiet of the duke's study. "I am sure I do not have the least idea what you are talking about."

"I am aware of that," Carmichael responded in exceedingly dry tones. "I am, however, in hopes of rectifying the situation. No, pray do not trouble yourself," he added, lightly smoothing his thumb over the frown that had etched itself in her forehead. "It was not my intent to spoil your mood."

Lucy shook her head. "Nothing you have said could do that," she said, dropping her gaze. Aware suddenly that she was completely alone with Carmichael in what could only be construed as compromising circumstances, she carefully restored the pistol to its box. Only then did she lift her eyes once more to his. "You are my dearest friend, Captain," she said, surprised that her voice could sound steady when inside she felt ridiculously unsettled, "and I have enjoyed myself immensely. It occurs to me, however, that the purpose of my visit was to explore the dungeons. I really should be getting back to Francine. She probably thinks we have gone on without her."

"As a matter of fact," announced Francine in a peeved voice from the doorway, "that is exactly what she thought. Have you any notion how long I have been left to kick my heels down there? Long enough for Mr. Oakes to describe the entire siege of Rolica, and Captain Carmichael's part in it." Her eyes shifted appraisingly to Carmichael. "Did you really penetrate the city's defenses in the guise of a goatherd, Captain?" She gave a comical grimace. "I warn you, I find it inconceivable that any-

one would deliberately smear his person with goat
dung, even for the purpose of reconnoitering for
Wellington.''

Carmichael laughed. "You would be surprised
how the aroma of goat dung discourages even the
most hardened of soldiers from examining one too
closely. Filth and the appearance of poverty confer
a certain anonymity that I found advantageous on
more than a few occasions.''

"But of course. *Now* I understand." Lucy's face
brightened with sudden revelation. "The giant's
magic cloak. It was the one thing in your story for
which I could find no reasonable explanation. Mr.
Oakes dressed himself in rags and covered himself
with filth, which made him 'invisible' simply due
to the fact that no one wished to pay him any attention.''

"Brava, Miss Powell," applauded the captain.
"You have uncovered only one of the many lessons
we learned from Don Julian's guerrillas. And now,
if you still wish to uncover the secrets of the dungeons, I suggest that we should get started.''

"I was beginning to think you were never going
to get around to it," Francie declared, grinning in
complete agreement. "What are we waiting for?''

The dungeons, or, more accurately, prisons,
were located in the two lower stages of each of the
drum turrets. Two of them, Carmichael informed
the girls as he led them down the secret stair from
the duke's study, had been filled in with earth and
rock early in the previous century. The third had
been converted into a wine cellar by the Eleventh
Duke of Lathrop, which left only the fourth— be-

neath the tower room that had played a part in Lucy's *Lord of Lathrop, or Watcher in the Tower.*

Constructed without windows, the passageway brooded in darkness, cold and dank, beneath the tower's fastness. It seemed to Lucy that she could feel the weight of the castle bearing down on them, and she had a delicious sense that, here, time was somehow frozen. She squeezed Francie's hand to reassure herself that the gloom was not really haunted by the spirits of the dead, that the occasional rustle in the gloomy recesses was only the scamper of mice or rats, that the sudden cold breath against her cheek was nothing more than a draught from one of the hidden vents to the outside. Carmichael, holding the lantern aloft, loomed, nevertheless, all the more comfortingly large and formidable in the yellow glow of light.

Lucy suffered a shiver of anticipation as they came at last to a great iron door covered in rust and cobwebs. Handing the lantern to Lucy, Carmichael placed a shoulder against the barrier and leaned his powerful frame against it. The door gave a shudder and a groan that was, Lucy thought, feeling her flesh crawl, most certainly loud enough to awaken the dead.

Francie, as impatient as ever, lent her small weight to the effort as Carmichael braced himself for a second, more powerful shove. With a final shriek of indignation, the door gave way before their concerted onslaught.

"Just think," Francie breathed, clearly in alt, "this may be the first time anyone has set foot in here for centuries. With any luck we may find the skeletons of prisoners who were confined and then forgotten. It gives me gooseflesh just to think of it."

"I do hate to disappoint you, Francie," Lucy said, holding up the lantern to the door, "but, unless I miss my guess, someone has been here before us. Look at the hinges. There is not a speck of rust on them."

"Oh, you are right. Someone has replaced them," Francie concluded. Her glance went accusingly to Carmichael. "You have already made your exploration." Clearly he had slipped a peg in her estimation.

"No doubt I am sorry to disappoint you," drawled Carmichael, with only the faintest hint of irony. "I'm afraid I did ask Mr. Oakes to do what he could to ensure a safe passage. It seemed, in the circumstances, the wisest course of action. The dungeon is, for the most part, however, exactly as we found it a little over a fortnight ago."

Francie, who was not to be so easily placated, quickly pointed out that "for the most part" was not at all the same as "exactly." "Indeed," she demanded, "what is the use of exploring if there is nothing left to discover?"

"Well," ventured Lucy, "you must admit that whatever lies ahead will be no less new to us simply because Carmichael and Oakes have been there before us. Besides, I cannot think even Carmichael could have opened that door by himself if the hinges had been locked in rust, do you?"

"I suppose not," agreed Francie, who was by nature scrupulously just. Immediately she brightened, glancing up at Carmichael with twin imps in her eyes. "I suppose I shall have to forgive you, Captain— in spite of the shabby trick you played on us. The truth is I have never had a more marvelous time, and we haven't even seen the dungeons yet."

"You relieve my mind," drawled the captain in sardonic appreciation. "I am naturally pleased that the dungeons' appeal is sufficient to warrant your forbearance. I trust you will not be disappointed."

Lucy, who could already feel herself in the first throes of eager anticipation, considered such a possibility remote in the extreme. They were on the point of stepping into a remnant of the past, one, moreover, that could not but both horrify and thrill one's sensibilities. Even if the prison itself contained nothing overtly interesting, it must by its very nature excite the imagination.

Carmichael, once more in possession of the lantern, led the way past the iron door into the murky passageway beyond. Lucy and Francie, instinctively clasping hands, did not require the captain's stern reminder to stay close behind him. Indeed, Francie was moved to point out that so long as he had the lantern they were hardly likely to wander off on their own.

"We are coming to the upper chamber," remarked Carmichael, indicating in the distance an unexpected spill of sunlight beyond a second door, which, thankfully, already stood ajar. "The prisoner fortunate enough to be incarcerated in the top cell must surely have counted his blessings. At least he was granted the boon of a window, which, though it was too high to allow a view of the outside, yet afforded him the benefits of sunshine and fresh air. The wretch beneath him was not so fortunate. You will no doubt be fascinated to learn that the only access to the cell below is through a circular hole in the floor of the upper chamber, over which a stone slab was set, sealing the prisoner in utter darkness."

"Good God," murmured Lucy, appalled. "The

poor soul might as well have been buried alive in his tomb."

"As a matter of fact, the Eleventh Duke of Lathrop left a written account of the discovery of a skeleton in one of the lower cells. So far as I could find, none of the chambers had been breached for over a century previous to that. No doubt so gruesome a discovery was what motivated his grace to order the other cells to be filled in."

"But how simply marvelous," exclaimed Francie, clearly undaunted by the macabre aspect of Carmichael's account. "I wonder if the skeleton is still there. I have never seen a human skeleton before."

"And you will not see one now," Lucy informed her in dampening tones. Nevertheless, the image of that ill-fated prisoner, cut off from the world and condemned to die sealed in a tomb of complete and utter darkness, haunted her long after they had viewed the circular chamber with its single window and peered down through the entry hole into the lower vault. She was exceedingly quiet and preoccupied as Carmichael led them back through the secret passageway.

Once more in the duke's study, Lucy went directly to the window and flung back the drapes in order to drink in the blessed sunlight. How beautiful it was, and the green, rolling downs of Greensward! No doubt it had not been that much different over two hundred years ago. Certainly Bancroft Beck, the moors, the sea, the sky had all been there, little more than fifteen feet from that miserable wretch in the dungeon.

Who had the prisoner been— man, woman, or child? What crime had been terrible enough to warrant so inhuman a sentence of death?

She shuddered; then, feeling Carmichael suddenly behind her, instinctively turned into his arms.

How strange that it should feel perfectly natural to draw on the comfort of his strength at that moment. She was completely oblivious to Francie, who, mumbling something about going below to beg a cinnamon cookie from Oakes, precipitously fled. She knew only that her spirit was oppressed, and that Carmichael offered her a haven when she most particularly needed one.

She did not know how long she stood within the circle of his arms. It seemed an eternity but could not have been more than a few minutes before the impropriety of her position, clasped in the arms of a gentleman, interceded to bring her back to an awareness of herself.

Carmichael, feeling her stir, immediately loosened his hold.

Lucy stepped back. "I beg your pardon," she stammered, feeling her cheeks flooded with an unfamiliar warmth. "What a goose you must think me. I assure you, however, that I am not usually missish. I am afraid the dungeon and the tale of that poor unfortunate affected me strangely."

"It would be strange had it not affected you so," uttered the captain in chilling accents. Startled, Lucy glanced up.

"You must not blame yourself for my foolishness," she said swiftly, taken aback by the chiseled hardness of his face. "As horrifying as it was to realize men are capable of something so unthinkable, you must know that I still should have gone."

"You should be at home and, like your mama, at your embroidery. Or in your parlor surrounded by a bevy of moon-stricken young cubs. You should *not* be traipsing about filthy dark corridors and ghost-ridden dungeons. Perhaps it is time you got it through your head, Miss Powell, that you are not some eccentric spinster who must fill the dreariness of her days with imagined haunted castles and phantom lovers. You are a beautiful young woman in need of a man."

Lucy, stung by his unfair assessment of her and her ambitions, could only stare at him for the moment in stricken disbelief. She had been exceedingly foolish to imagine for one moment that he might be capable of understanding. She might indeed be a spinster and an eccentric, but her days were neither dreary nor empty. She was a writer of fiction. Her imagination conjured plots and characters out of everything around her, which was why she yearned for something more than to be mollycoddled and smothered with proprieties. All her life she had been the dutiful daughter, the dependable older sister, the long-suffering throwback to her father's Irish grandmama, while, inside, her spirit, longing to soar, had chafed at the smallness of her world.

The last thing she had expected was to hear Carmichael, of all people, try and put her in her place.

"Really, Mr. Carmichael," she said, managing at least the semblance of her usual composure. "I had thought better of you. I believed you understood. In spite of what you might think I am a writer. I cannot allow myself to be limited to what is femininely nice in my pursuits. I want to know everything, experience all that I can. Instead, I am bound by social conventions and the image of women as frail creatures in danger of shattering at the least unpleasant thing. Well, let me tell you, Mr. Carmichael, men are not really so different from women. We are all fragile in one way or an-

other. You have only to look at your Mr. Oakes to
see that. Or yourself, for that matter."

To her horror, her voice broke at the end, revealing an unmistakable tremor. Furious with herself, she turned hastily away. No doubt she would
have fled ignominiously, had not Carmichael
stopped her.

"Lucy— !" His tone was impatient, she noted dis-
tractedly, and with no little pique. Instinctively, she
stiffened.

"I beg your pardon," she said in accents meant
to freeze his very soul. "I believe I have not given
you leave to use my given name." Immediately, she
was ashamed of herself. "Oh, how very abomina-
ble you are," she exclaimed, coming back around
to face him. "Indeed, how dare you provoke me
into falling back on the very proprieties I have pro-
fessed to despise. I should naturally be pleased,
sir, to have you use my given name."

Had she meant to take him off his guard, she
succeeded admirably. But then, he had learned
some time ago that the unpredictable Miss Powell
was full of surprises. He laughed.

"Thank you for the honor you do me. But then,
we are friends, are we not? In which case you must
naturally call me Phillip."

Lucy blushed an even duskier red at the very
thought of doing any such thing. Indeed, she
could not imagine what Florence would think, let
alone her mama and papa. But then, no doubt
Carmichael was perfectly aware of the dilemma in
which she found herself. Certainly, she could not
mistake the ironic gleam of expectancy in his
hooded eyes. The devil, to maneuver her into this
coil of her own making! Obviously he was enjoying
himself immensely at her expense. Nevertheless,

she would be dashed if she would back down now before the odious Captain.

"Very well— Phillip," she said, pleased that she had managed the thing without stumbling over her own tongue, "I wish to thank you for a visit which has been as stimulating as it has been instructive. You have been everything that is kind to my sister and me."

"On the contrary," drawled Carmichael, his smile distinctly cynical, "I am never kind. And I never do anything that does not suit my purposes, which is why you will listen to me now. Lucy, you are greatly mistaken do you think for one moment that women have not always had their own battles to fight. A woman's lot may seem to you shallow and mundane, but I can conceive of nothing more heroic than daring to love a man and bear his children. I daresay there is no adventure more harrowing than living life from day to day, never knowing what new crisis may arise. Just look at your mother. Would she not agree that there is no challenge more daunting than striving to maintain one's sanity while preserving domestic peace and harmony week in and week out? That is the real stuff of life and a woman's strength. Because you want more than that does not mean you need settle for less. So please do not tell me I do not understand. I understand you better than you can possibly imagine. One day perhaps you will learn that, Lucy."

"Shall I?" murmured Lucy, gazing at him in perplexity. "I wonder. Or is it only that you persist in believing your duty lies in convincing me to marry your employer?"

She had never seen Carmichael quite so angry

before. She was totally unprepared for the sudden flash of steel in his eyes.

"You may be sure that it was not duty that motivated me to speak. But then, you must believe what you will. No doubt you are perfectly right to hold anything I might say in doubt. As a matter of fact, you would be wise to question everything about me."

"But I am not wise. Indeed, it would seem I have been exceedingly stupid," declared Lucy, ashamed that she could ever have suspected his motives. "I have failed in trust, when you have been nothing if not honest. Oh, blast it all! It seems I am forever finding myself in the position of having to apologize, and I am not at all good at it. Please say you will forgive me, and put an end to my misery. Truce?" she queried, extending her hand.

A soft thrill went through her as Carmichael took it. "To avoid any future misery," he said ironically, "I suggest we agree that there need never be apologies between friends."

Lucy's face lit up in a smile. "Agreed, sir. Henceforth, we shall lock horns with the clear understanding that, no matter how vexed we become with one another, there is always forgiveness in friendship."

"Yes, no doubt," murmured Carmichael, an odd sort of shadow flickering in the depths of his eyes.

That night, unable to sleep, Lucy sat propped against her pillows in bed, her journal open on her knees. Her quill pen moved feverishly over the page. On her face she wore a smile of concentration, and her eyes shone with a marvelous grey intensity. Coming to the end of the page, she started another and yet another as the climax of the tale rapidly unfolded. Late in the night, tears swimming in her eyes and a soggy handkerchief clutched in her hand, she smiled tremulously, paused to blow her nose in the lace handkerchief, and wrote "The End" at the bottom of the manuscript.

With a sigh she lay back against the pillows. It was finished, and it was undoubtedly the best thing she had ever written—thanks to Carmichael.

A soft dreamy light came to her eyes at the thought of the captain. She had never experienced anything quite like the feel of his arms around her. It was like suddenly discovering that one was no longer alone when one had never suspected oneself of being in the least lonely. But how perfectly ridiculous, she chided herself. How could she possibly be lonely in a house full of boisterous young Powells? If anything, she could do with a little more precious time to herself.

Abruptly she roused herself to set aside her journal and writing accouterments; then, impatiently plumping her pillows, she plopped down among them. No doubt what she had felt was only the result of an overstimulated imagination in the wake of her visit to the dungeon and Carmichael's blood-chilling tale, she told herself. Resolutely banishing any further thought of the troublesome captain from her mind, she closed her eyes.

Nevertheless, it was an image of Carmichael, darkly handsome and maddeningly mysterious, that accompanied her into her dreams.

Eight

In the days following the memorable visit to the dungeons at Lathrop it was remarked by the neighbors at large, and by Florence in particular, that Lucy and Carmichael were to be seen a great deal in one another's company. From the very first Lucy had sensed in Carmichael a spirit kindred to her own. Perhaps it was little wonder, then, that their relationship had evolved so quickly into an easy camaraderie. Well-read, quick-witted, intelligent, and possessed of an appreciation of the absurd every bit as keen as her own, he was everything she could have looked for in a companion.

More importantly, however, Lucy had at last found someone with whom she could communicate, knowing that she would never be met with a blank stare of incomprehension. When faced with an absurdity in a crowded room she had only to meet Carmichael's eye to know that he shared her amusement. Carmichael seemed always to know what she was thinking and to understand fully without the need for stultifying explanations.

It seemed only natural in the circumstances that Lucy should fall into the habit of confiding in him everything from her fondest hopes and ambitions to the latest of her many siblings' peccadilloes. It was a novel experience to meet a gentlemen who

was not immediately prey to boredom at the mere
mention of children or anything else that might,
no matter how loosely, fall under the category of
"domestic concerns." Carmichael seemed to enjoy
her company every bit as much as she did his.

As if by tacit agreement, neither the subject of
marriage nor the duke's pending visit was ever
mentioned between them.

One other thing Lucy kept to herself, a secret
so precious that she dared not share it with anyone
lest in the end it prove only a disappointment.
Flinging caution to the wind, she had sent her
newest literary endeavor to Mr. Tobias Pendergraft, Book Publisher, Number 10 Savile Place,
London. She hugged this secret to herself, conscious of a soft thrill of anticipation coupled with
trepidation whenever she allowed herself to call it
to mind.

In spite of her burgeoning happiness in Carmichael's company, Lucy could never quite forget
that one day it must all come to an end.

No later than the end of August, His Grace must
surely make his appearance at Lathrop, and with
the repairs to the castle nearing completion, the
duke's arrival would most certainly signal Carmichael's departure.

Carmichael had admitted as much to the earl
upon the occasion of their deciphering the final
inscriptions on the castle diagrams. Florence, who
had taken that opportunity to borrow a book from
her father's study, never mind that she seldom read
anything other than *La Belle Assemblee* or *The Ladies' Monthly Museum,* and quite probably had not
suddenly developed an interest in Lord Town-
send's advocacy of crop rotation, had overheard
the captain affirm that his role at Lathrop must

of necessity come to an end when the duke arrived to take his proper place. Nor had she been loath to impart that cogent information to Lucy.

"He will leave us, I tell you," she said tragically to Lucy upon finding her elder sister ensconced in her usual retreat in the attic room under the eaves. "Oh, how shall I bear it? Surely there is something we can do to persuade him to stay on at Lathrop. If only you were not set on the idea of turning down the duke. As his wife, you would have no little influence. You could convince His Grace to keep Carmichael here at least until the start of the London Season."

Lucy, who was still in the process of dealing with the suddenness of Florence's announcement, was rudely jarred out of her own preoccupation by her sister's final declaration. "I pray you will not be absurd," she uttered, perhaps more sharply than she had intended. "Surely you are not suggesting I accept the duke's offer solely for the purpose of keeping Carmichael here?"

Florence, who quite naturally could not like to hear what had seemed to her a perfectly reasonable solution to the problem reduced to such brazen terms, blushed a dusky hue. "Oh, how very like you to twist my meaning to make it something I never intended. Of course I should never suggest any such thing. There are innumerable reasons why you should marry the duke, all of which must be perfectly obvious to anyone but you, Lucy Powell."

Lucy, who had heard every one of them more times than she cared to count, was in no mood to have them enumerated for her yet again. Certainly not by Florence, who seemed never to tire of reminding Lucy of the advantages that marriage to the duke would confer on her younger sisters.

"You are quite right, Flo," she said in something less than her normally congenial tones. "They are not at all obvious to me. In fact, I cannot think of a single reason why I should marry the duke. Certainly not for the one you have suggested, since that would be to no purpose at all. Phillip will leave Lathrop, Florence, as soon as he has fulfilled his obligations. You must see there is nothing to hold him here."

"Oh, indeed. You have made certain of that," Florence declared in what Lucy could not but think was a rather excessively dramatic vein. "There might be something— SOMEONE— if you were not so selfish. If you do not intend to have him, you might at least have the decency to remove yourself from the competition."

Lucy stared at her sister, aghast at any such notion. "Good God, is that what you think?" she demanded in incredulous accents. "That we are in a contest, with Phillip as some sort of trophy? I cannot think he would appreciate the comparison, any more than do I. It is patently absurd, Florence. Phillip does not view either of us with anything more than a friendly affection, and it is highly unlikely that he ever will."

Florence turned on her sister with her glorious eyes flashing. "No doubt you would like to believe that, but you are wrong, Lucy. Phillip will see that *I* love him. I shall make him see it, and there is nothing you can do to stop me."

Lucy had beheld her sister in many guises, but never one to equal this. Her head regally high, her bosom magnificently heaving, her eyes ablaze in a face that had gone pearly white, she swept out of

Lucy's presence in what could only be described as a Grand Passion.

Instantly Lucy regretted her hasty tongue. She would have called Florence back had she not known how very pointless it would be. It hardly mattered now that she had been motivated by the wish to spare her younger sister. She had been plain spoken when she should have been sympathetic. Nothing could have been more calculated to render Florence impervious to anything further Lucy might wish to say.

In the succeeding days Florence, having adopted the mantle of the Ice Queen, maintained an impregnable barrier of frosty disdain whenever she happened to encounter Lucy, which, in the circumstances, was an all-too-frequent occurrence. At first Lucy treated her sister's faint sniffs, arched eyebrows, and cold shrugs with amused tolerance. Telling herself that eventually it would pall on Florence to be constantly at odds with the one person other than their mama to whom she might always go for sympathy and feminine confidences, she waited for the frost to melt. Eventually, however, tolerance changed to annoyance, and then finally to a sincere concern that Florence might entertain a more serious *tendre* for Carmichael than anyone had previously suspected.

There was no denying that Carmichael could be irresistibly charming when he chose to be. Indeed, had Lucy not considered herself a wholly unlikely candidate for his heart, she might herself have succumbed to his devastatingly masculine presence. As it was, she was insulated in the certainty that there could never be anything more than friendship between them.

Consequently, while she could not but view the

inevitability of his leaving with a sharp pang of regret, and though she thought perhaps her life would seem rather hollow without him, she told herself that she could sustain the loss. After all, she had never allowed herself to expect anything else.

Certainly that was her frame of mind when, one morning in early August, she came downstairs determined to let nothing spoil what gave every promise of being a gloriously beautiful day. Indeed, not even seeing that Florence was the only occupant of the breakfast room could dampen her spirits. Uttering a cheery "Good morning," which was pointedly ignored, Lucy breezed past Flo to the sideboard and, humming softly to herself, proceeded to fill her plate with scrambled eggs and dry toast and her cup with coffee before blithely taking a seat across from her sister.

Lucy picked up her fork and began to eat with a relish that apparently was not shared by her sole companion at the table. Wrapped in her cocoon of self-imposed silence, Flo poked desultorily at the food on her plate. And if, occasionally, she exhaled a languorous sigh or appeared to droop apathetically (while stealing a glance at Lucy from beneath the luxurious veil of her eyelashes), Lucy appeared not to notice.

That was too much for one who expected something quite different from the sister who had wronged her. "You seem in a cheerful mood," Flo ventured grudgingly, her curiosity piqued beyond endurance.

"I am," Lucy answered. Popping into her mouth her last bite of toast, covered thickly with jam, she chewed, then swallowed, and, dabbing at her lips

with a napkin, shoved back her chair preparatory
to leaving.

"Going somewhere?" Florence pursued with an
instinct born of suspicion.

Lucy stood up. "Uh-huh."

"Well?" Florence persisted, discarding all in an
instant any last, lingering pretense of indifference.

"Well, what?" Lucy countered with an ingenuous arch of an eyebrow.

"Well, where are you going?"

"Fishing," responded Lucy and, waving gaily,
breezed from the room before Florence, glaring
after her, could voice the next, obvious question,
the answer to which was that she was going fishing
with Carmichael, only he did not know it yet.

Thirty minutes later, mounted on Wind Star and
burdened with a picnic basket, she had left Greensward behind her.

It occurred to Carmichael, as he sat his horse
on the crest of a hill and watched the sun come
up over the sea, that he had been too long in the
military. Six months in England and he had yet to
know what it was to pass a night in uninterrupted
slumber. And how not, when in the past three
years he had slept more often than not on the
ground, most of the time without even the benefit
of a tent, until he had almost forgotten what it
was to lie in a bed with four walls around him and
a roof over his head. During the hellish weeks
when he had lain sweating in his bed, tormented
by fever and pain, he had found the stifling confines of the bed drapes intolerable, the four walls
of his room suffocating, the unfamiliarity of the
feather mattress unbearably soft. If one added to

those the fact that he had survived three years on the Peninsula primarily by means of keeping his wits about him and maintaining a never-ending vigilance, and it was hardly remarkable that the slightest noise jolted him awake, his mind instantly alert and his hand clawing for the pistol he still kept in readiness thrust beneath his pillow.

He had learned early on, after he was finally allowed to leave his sickbed, that, once awakened in the middle of the night, it was of little or no use to hope for renewed slumber. Since coming to Lathrop he had formed the habit of going late to bed and rising, when awakened, to ride until sunup over the mist-ridden moors. He was fortunate, at least, that he seemed able to thrive on the brief snatches of sleep such a schedule afforded him— the result, no doubt, of his training as a soldier and a guerrilla-fighter.

The sudden curl of his lip was distinctly cynical. Bloody hell! He was lucky indeed. He had survived, and with his body intact. But he would make a damned poor bed companion for a wife. The first time he had recourse to his pistol in the middle of the night would make for a charming episode, he did not doubt. He could think of few females who would not instantly fall into a fit of the vapors at such a moment, and none who were ladies of quality— save, that was, for one.

A wry gleam came to his eyes at the remembered image of the eldest Miss Powell with a gun in her hand. Woman or not, she would have presented a formidable presence on a field of honor. What a wife she would have made for a soldier!

She had both the courage and the heart for it, and a common sense oddly at variance with her propensity for indulging in romantic flights of fancy. No doubt that was the poet in her, a quality that he did not share with her. Whatever poetry he might have had in his soul had long since been eradicated on the Peninsula. Nevertheless, he recognized and prized it in Lucy. It was, in fact, the single ray of hope in all of this, he reflected somberly, the slender thread upon which depended the entirety of his strategy.

How ironic, really, that he had dared to gamble everything— honor, duty, the future, even, of a dukedom— on a lie and a girl's unshakable belief in romance. He was not proud of the deception he had taken on himself. The last thing he wanted was to hurt Lucy. And yet he could not see that he had any other recourse. Certainly, he had little choice now but to play out the hand he had dealt himself. He was committed, and with damned few aces left and little time in which to use them.

Damn Lucy's blind obstinacy! She would force him yet to play the single trump card in his hand— the lovesick younger sister.

The thought was not one conducive to comfort. Bloody hell! He had not set out to make Florence fall in love with him. Nor did he believe for one moment that it was anything more serious than a schoolgirl's infatuation. If he came to believe there was any danger of its becoming something else, he would not hesitate to disabuse her of the notion that he made a practice of robbing the cradle. In the meantime, however, she could be exceedingly useful.

His mouth thinned to a grim line at the prospect. Florence might be vain, spoiled, and selfish, as might be expected of the beauty of the family, but she was neither heartless nor vicious. One day, if fortune favored her, she would meet someone

with the strength and forbearance to put up with
her starts of temper, and then she might very well
turn out to be a woman not unlike her mama.
Certainly she did not deserve to be used in the
game he was playing. He would have to find a way
to avoid that, no matter what the cost. It would
save him at least the final shreds of honor that
were left him.

The sun stood well up in the sky when Carmichael rode through the castle gates and, dis-
mounting, turned the black over to a stable lad.
The crews were already at work, and Carmichael
experienced a swift surge of satisfaction. He had
accomplished in two months what might have
taken a less determined man triple that time to
achieve. But then, he had the advantage of the
duke's considerable resources at his command, and
he had not stinted in using them.

By the end of August, Lathrop would have his
castle. Unfortunately, the duke would find it patently meaningless had he failed in the interim to
win his chosen duchess.

The clatter of hooves on the cobblestones came
as if in answer to that final, brooding thought.
Conscious of a quickening of his pulse, Carmichael turned.

She had come, and for once without a horde of
younger Powells to lend her countenance. Oakes
would be disappointed. His former sergeant-major
had developed an unexpected fondness for giving
piggyback rides and tea parties to giggling young
girls and grubby schoolboys.

Carmichael frowned, wondering if Lucy's mama
knew she had come unchaperoned.

Lucy, spotting her quarry, waved and trotted up
to him. "Phillip. How glad I am to see you. I hope

I have not come too early. Isn't it a magnificent morning! Have you been riding? I thought I saw one of the lads leading El Guerrero toward the stables."

The corners of Carmichael's lips twitched in bemusement at this medley of observations uttered with hardly a breath between them. "As a matter of fact, I have only just ridden in."

Lucy's eyes sparkled, green with excitement. "And now you are about to ride out again. Hurry and send for El Guerrero to be brought back. I shan't dismount. There isn't time."

"I have no doubt." Carmichael, resting his hand on the cantle, gazed quizzically up at her. "Pardon my curiosity. Time for what?"

"To reach our destination while the fish are still biting. Early morning or evening just before dusk is always best. At noon it is too warm, and the trout stay close to the bottom. Hurry, now. And do not say you will not come, for I warn you I do not intend to take no for an answer."

"Naturally I should not dream of disappointing you. Only allow me a moment to fetch a pole and a few things."

"That will not be at all necessary. I have arranged everything." She laughed, eager as a child to have him away. "Now, please do come along. I want to show you something— a secret, very special place. I promise you will not be disappointed."

Carmichael, gazing up into flushed cheeks and laughing eyes, did not doubt her for a moment. If it were a desert, barren and lifeless, to which she was taking him, she would have transformed it with her sparkling vitality.

Signaling to a boy, he called for his horse to be brought around.

By turns mysterious and teasing, Lucy led Carmichael along the clifftops, away from the castle and the road leading down to Greensward. Indeed, she seemed anxious to avoid coming into view of the manor as she worked her way back along the curve of headland, careful to keep the ridge between them and the Elizabethan house below, until at last they came to the craggy lip of a ravine.

Without warning, Wind Star plunged over the edge into what might once have been a trail but which had long since been lost in dense vegetation. Carmichael cursed, certain to see horse and rider hurtle to their deaths down the steep side of the slope. Obviously the mare had gone that way before. She picked her way down the precipitous descent with a sure-footed ease that Carmichael must have found reassuring. Stern-faced but silent, he followed after the girl, who sat her horse with a maddening lack of concern, even going so far as to turn and gaze smilingly back at him over her shoulder. Grimly, he vowed he would throttle her gladly if ever they reached the bottom alive.

Thickly wooded with elms, beech, and ash, it was a marvelously wild and lonely place to which she had brought him. Clouds of mist, like steam, rose from the floor of the ravine, and he could hear, clearly above the rustle of leaves and branches in the breeze, the sound of rushing water somewhere below. In addition to birdsong and the flash of wings, Carmichael saw deer sign and glimpsed in a thicket of furze the wary eyes of a fox. Gradually he felt ease from his chest the pressure that had been engendered by the sight of Lucy's heedless disregard for her safety.

"It is not far now," Lucy called over her shoulder, as the mare, reaching a grassy level, snorted and shook her disapproval of the treacherous climb now behind them. Before them stretched a narrow, secluded valley of green meadows, rife with celandine, daisies, and violets. A swift stream, widening into still, deep pools before sudden barricades of boulders, hurried toward the sea, while a steady roar of water announced the presence of a falls somewhere upstream.

Lucy turned her mount toward the sound of the falling water.

"This is where Bancroft Beck ends its journey to the sea," she informed Carmichael as he came abreast of her. "I've never brought anyone here before, except for Francie. The twins never cease to beg and cajole in the hopes that I will show them the secret of the ravine. I haven't, though. I should be in a constant state of anxiety on their account were I ever to do anything so patently foolish."

"Perish the thought," agreed Carmichael, who did not doubt his future was to be plagued with similar anxieties, though not about the twins. "One day I've no doubt they will find it for themselves."

"Yes, I suppose you are right," Lucy reflected soberly. "By then, with any luck, however, they will be old enough to know better than to start a brawl midway down the face of the wall."

"A hideous prospect," Carmichael murmured with sardonic appreciation. "Have you no such qualms concerning your enterprising little sister?"

Lucy, lifting a drooping willow branch out of her way, smiled and shook her head. "You must understand that, while Francie is a little daredevil ready to take on any number of haunted castles, dungeons, or steep ravines, she has absolutely no

interest in fishing. She has never once demonstrated the least inclination to come back to my
secret place— perhaps because on her one and only
visit she came as close as she ever has to an untimely death by drowning."

Carmichael's eyebrows lifted toward his hairline
in sudden and complete understanding. "Ah, the
ill-fated experiment in aquatics. I should have
guessed. And this, I must presume, is the habitat
of a certain legendary fish."

Lucy beamed in approval. "Welcome," she said,
"to the home of Old Slippery. Shall we have lunch?
I feel positively famished."

Carmichael, having dined well on roasted
chicken, boiled eggs, tart cheese, celery sticks, and
thick bread spread with honey, reclined at ease
with his back to the trunk of an elm tree while he
watched Lucy pack the remains of their lunch in
the picnic hamper. Her black beaver riding hat lay
on the grass where she had carelessly discarded it,
and her glorious hair, having just as quickly shed
its combs and pins, fell in a loose riot of curls
down her back.

She was, he decided, perfectly suited to her sur-
roundings, and far more beautiful, even, than her
wild sylvan glen.

It was little wonder that she loved it here. One
could hardly have asked for a more perfect setting.
His gaze lifted to the escarpment over which Bancroft Beck made its sheer plunge of forty feet or
more to the boulder-strewn pool below. He had
seen mountain cataracts in the Americas that
would make this one seem little more than a water-
shoot, but what it lacked in grandeur it more than

made up for in charm. The wide, rippled pool falling away into rapids over moss-covered rocks was soothing rather than breathtaking, and the stolid English oaks and slender ash trees were comfortably familiar.

Smiling in amusement at himself, he smothered a yawn behind his hand. If it was not awe-inspiring here, it was at least conducive to the thought of a long, pleasant nap, and that was a luxury whose value he knew better than most.

"There, it is done," Lucy announced suddenly and quite unnecessarily as she set the basket aside and came to sit down beside him. "You know," she added with an air of innocence, "there really isn't any use in breaking out the poles just yet. I daresay Old Slippery is at the bottom of the deepest part of the pool just now, catching his forty winks while he waits for the heat of the day to pass."

"Is that what you think?" A wry gleam came to Carmichael's eyes as they met hers with perfect understanding.

"Indeed, I am quite certain of it. I have made an extensive study of the old gentleman's habits." She patted her lap, waiting.

Carmichael gave in without a struggle. "Well, in that case." He stretched out his long length on the picnic blanket and settled his head in her lap. Hesitating before dropping his curly-brimmed beaver over his face, he looked up at her, his eyes quizzical. "Where, by the way, are these poles we were about to break out?"

Lucy laughed. "Pray do not worry. I have them. I would not for the world miss seeing you hook Old Slippery."

Carmichael widened his eyes. "Are you so certain of it? What makes you think I can do what you could not?"

"I never said I *could* not," Lucy declared archly. "I had some interference the last time, if you recall. I know you will hook Old Slippery because, Mr. Carmichael, *I* have a secret weapon."

She would not tell him any more than that, but, taking his hat from him, plopped it over his eyes. "Go to sleep, Phillip. I shall wake you when it is time."

It occurred to him that it was highly unlikely any man could fall asleep with his head in so disturbing a proximity to Lucy Powell. It was the last thing he remembered— until he was awakened by the soft brush of a fingertip against his ear.

He stilled, keenly aware of the intimacy of the gesture and of the marvel that he had not slept so well for longer than he cared to remember. He waited, his senses attuned to the fresh clean scent of the girl, to the feel of her body, warm against him. He wondered what thoughts had been running through her lovely head as she sat watching over his slumber.

Then, softly, he heard, "Phillip?"

He felt her bend over him and, in a single swift motion, tipped up his hat.

A startled gasp breathed through her lips, and her eyes widened at finding herself staring so suddenly into his.

"You're awake," she said.

"Am I?" He smiled crookedly. "I thought I might be dreaming."

A becoming tinge of color flooded her cheeks. She drew back. "I could pinch you if you like," she suggested, her defenses going up along with a marvelously skeptical eyebrow. Could it be that the sworn spinster had at last been given to see that her dearest friend might not be quite so indifferent to her as she persisted in believing him to be? The devil, he thought. It was all he could do not to kiss her.

He sat up and, climbing easily to his feet, offered her a helping hand. She took it without quite meeting his eyes. Carmichael smiled faintly to himself, wondering what she had to feel guilty about.

"Now, about those fishing poles," he said, pleased with what he had accomplished but not fool enough to rush his fences.

Lucy, berating herself for a fool to even think Carmichael had been manifesting an unsettling awareness of her as a woman, came close, in her distraction, to losing her footing as she navigated the rocky ledge behind the curtain of falling water. It was only his way of teasing her, she little doubted. And, besides, it was a trifle late to be considering the dangers of being isolated in a lonely ravine with a man about whom, when one came right down to it, she knew very little.

Carmichael, she reminded herself, was a gentleman and her friend. She trusted him implicitly. He would never do anything to take advantage of their situation. Indeed, why should he? The terrible truth was, she very much feared it was not Carmichael she needed to worry about but her own unnerving reaction to having passed an entire hour with him asleep and in what could only be termed an intimate proximity.

Had she known beforehand the peculiar sensations to which she would be prey, she undoubtedly would have entertained second thoughts before inviting him to lay his head in her lap. As it was, she had given in to sympathy and an irresistible impulse. After all, she could hardly have failed to note upon first setting eyes on him that morning that he had not the look of a man who had just risen from a night's restful repose. Indeed, he had appeared hollow-eyed and quite worn to the nub, rather as if he had not been to bed at all. It had immediately occurred to her that he was working far too hard, the blame for which she laid squarely at the duke's door.

Later, upon seeing Carmichael succumb to a yawn, it had seemed only natural, in the circumstances, to insist he lie down.

Faith, what a mistake that had been! No matter how she tried not to have done, she could not but be utterly fascinated by the long, lean masculine length of him. In sleep he had seemed so oddly vulnerable— Carmichael, who had never once the entire time she had known him relaxed his formidable defenses in her presence. Nor was that all or the worst of it. The very weight of his head on her lap had worked havoc on her sensibilities. She had found she could not take her eyes off the firm, sensitive mouth, not even when she had discovered, to her horror, that she could not but wonder what it would be like to be kissed by those lips. It had been a moment of sublime revelation when she realized she wanted nothing more than to have him awaken and do that very thing. Nor had it been in the least convincing to tell herself she wished it solely in the spirit of literary research.

On the contrary, she very much feared she was not only of a wanton nature but quite utterly and hopelessly shameless. She, Lucille Emily Powell, who had always prided herself on her ability to

tell right from wrong, had committed a most un-
forgivable breach of conduct. She had not only
availed herself of another's private correspondence but she had opened and read it as well!

It did not excuse her in the least that the letter
had slipped harmlessly out of his pocket as he
slept, for the act of giving into temptation was not
all or the worst of her transgressions. After having
read what was never meant for her to read she
had succumbed to an even greater ignominy. She
had not scrupled to search his coat pockets for a
certain piece of jewelry described in the letter.
That she had found it— a gold locket with, inside
it, the miniature of the missive's author— gave her
no satisfaction. Indeed, she had been a deal hap-
pier had she never been made to lay eyes on it at
all. Roxanne, for that was the correspondent's
name, was not only possessed of a beauty of the
sort to rival even that of Patience Merriweather,
but she was clearly the object of Carmichael's un-
requited love as well.

Roxanne, having written of her undying affection
for her dearest Phillip, had ended with the expressed wish that he would come to her wedding.

What a strange pang she had suffered at the
thought of the beautiful Roxanne in Phillip's
arms! No doubt the fickle young beauty had cast
him off because of his questionable parentage,
Lucy speculated darkly, her heart going out in
sympathy to Carmichael. Indeed, it came to her
that she would gladly have healed his heart if only
it were in her power to have done. She, however,
would have made a poor second to the incomparable Roxanne.

* * *

The cave behind the waterfall remained just as it had been the last time she had visited it. The rods, wrapped in oilskin, reclined where she had left them on a narrow shelf at the back of the shallow depression. The metal box, also wrapped in oilskin, was there as well, with her tackle quite intact, as were her fishing creel and net.

With Carmichael's help, she gathered everything up and they proceeded back the way they had come. If she could not heal the hurt Roxanne had inflicted, she reflected, she might at least provide him a temporary diversion.

Once more on the grassy bank, Lucy set about with the ease of long practice to set up the poles, while Carmichael watched with bemused interest. In the manner of a true connoisseur of the sport, Lucy would not allow anyone else to do what only she could do best.

It was midafternoon and there was the first sign of storm clouds beginning to gather when Lucy stood back from her task.

"I am about to show you the one and only thing that has ever fooled Old Slippery into striking," she announced, turning to Carmichael with the assumed air of one about to unveil a masterpiece. "I do not hesitate to boast that it is my own invention and that I have jealously guarded it from my incorrigibly nosy little brothers, who would not qualm at stealing my design and using it for their own purposes."

"You intrigue me, Miss Powell," replied Carmichael with proper gravity, belied by the gleam of amusement in the look he bent upon her.

"I do wish you will treat this with the seriousness that it deserves," Lucy admonished, awarding him a moue of displeasure. "This, Mr. Carmichael," she said, dangling the end of the fishing line before him with a flourish, "is my very own Lathrop Fly. No one other than myself has ever laid eyes on it, let alone used it. You have the privilege of being the first."

"Then naturally I am honored," replied Carmichael, enchanted, no doubt, to find himself staring into the large, protruding green eyes of what gave every appearance of being a black, hirsute fly approximately the size of the tip of his little finger. "A lovely creature. Did I hear you say it bears the distinguished name of Lathrop?"

Lucy choked on a gurgle of laughter. "You know I did, just as you are perfectly aware it is not in the least lovely," she retorted. "Beauty, however, is in the eye of the beholder, and this representative of *Diptera Tabanidae,* as it happens, is practically irresistible to our quarry."

"A fish of indisputable taste, it would seem," murmured Carmichael, accepting the pole Lucy held out to him. "May I suggest that we do not keep him waiting?"

Lucy, explaining that this was to be his fishing expedition, left the second pole beside the picnic basket and directed him to take position behind a low stand of willows.

"We may not be able to see Old Slippery," she whispered in Carmichael's ear, "but you may be sure he will spot us if we are not careful. Fortunately, your green riding coat should prove excellent camouflage. Have you any experience in fly casting?"

"It may surprise you to learn that I am not entirely a novice," Carmichael replied whimsically. "I used to fish quite a lot as a boy."

"No, did you?" murmured Lucy, who had never

heard him reveal anything of his boyhood before. "What else did you do as a boy?"

Carmichael flicked his wrist, sending the Lathrop Fly whipping out over the water, then immediately snaked it back again. "All the things most boys do," he answered and cast again.

Lucy grimaced, resigned to the fact that he did not intend to further enlighten her, and settled back to watch him play out his line, sending the fly farther upstream and letting it float down again with the current.

Carmichael might be a trifle rusty, but there was no denying he knew what he was about. With each cast of the fly he grew better, more sure of himself. He played the fly, making it appear to buzz the water several times before allowing it to land and float tantalizingly with the current.

After a time he changed locations and began again, tantalizing and tempting the pond's reluctant inhabitants.

There were fish there in numbers. Lucy could see them, green shadows hovering against the current or a silver flash through the shallows; none, however, the size of Old Slippery. It was obvious the fish were not biting.

It was hardly a novel experience for a fisherman of Lucy's experience. There had been days like this before. She simply had not wanted this to be one of them. She was trying to console herself with the old fisherman's adage that there would always come another day, though she knew perfectly well it was hardly likely there could ever be another like this one with Carmichael, when everything seemed suddenly to happen at once.

The sun vanished behind a cloud, and the first raindrops spattered the ground. Lucy glanced skyward. Carmichael cast. The Lathrop Fly snaked out over the pool— and disappeared into the monstrous mouth of Old Slippery, who launched himself out of the water. There was a tremendous plop and a splash, and Old Slippery vanished beneath the surface.

Lucy heard herself cry, "You've got him! Good God, you've got him! For heaven's sake, set the hook!"

Carmichael, with the never quite forgotten instinct of the fisherman, set the hook with a jerk, then held on, letting the fish play out the line.

"That's right, make him tire himself out," Lucy called, and held her breath, well aware that hooking a fish like Old Slippery was a long ways from landing it.

Carmichael, stepping clear of his cover, braced his weight against the straining pole and bent the pole back, reeling in the line before letting the tip down again. The line cut through the water, back and forth, carried by the great trout's desperate flight. Each time Carmichael bent the pole back, reeling in and letting the pole down again, he worked Old Slippery ever closer to the bank.

It was soon to be over. Old Slippery was a magnificent fighter, but he was no match for the man. The fish was visibly tiring.

And then Old Slippery did the unexpected.

Lucy, reaching for the net, saw it all out of the corner of her eye— Carmichael, digging in his heels and pulling against the pole; the sudden slackening of the line as the fish darted toward him; Carmichael, thrown off balance and scrambling for a footing. Lucy started up. Carmichael's boot slipped on the wet, grassy bank. The line went taut. Lucy froze in horror. Then suddenly it was over.

Carmichael toppled forward, full-length into the pool.

He came up, streaming mud and water, his hand still gripping the pole from which the line trailed, limp and tangled, minus the Lathrop Fly and minus the fish. Lucy clapped a hand to her mouth as, slowly, he waded toward her, out onto the bank.

Lucy stared at him, unable to speak. He stood over her, his hair plastered to his forehead, his eyes exceedingly grim. At last Lucy reached out to pluck futilely at his ruined neckcloth, hanging in a bedraggled heap. In another moment she knew, to her horror, that she was going to laugh. By God, she could not help herself.

"Are-are you all right?"

The question was too obvious to require an answer. Carmichael elevated a single expressive brow. And then at last their eyes met and held for a single breathless moment. Lucy choked, and they both burst into helpless peals of laughter.

It was several moments before either was in any condition to realize it had started to rain in earnest.

"The cave," Carmichael gasped. Snatching up the blanket and basket, he pulled her toward the falls. "There's no sense in both of us getting a drenching."

Slipping and sliding on the wet bank, they made for the only shelter available to them.

"By God, he was a fighter!" Carmichael exclaimed some moments later as they huddled behind the white curtain of water.

"He is everything I promised he would be," Lucy agreed, secretly both disappointed and relieved that Old Slippery had slipped the hook again.

"As was your magnificent Lathrop Fly." Carmichael looked down at her. "I'm sorry that I lost it."

Lucy shrugged. "I can make another." She felt a shiver shake his powerful frame and exclaimed in quick concern, "You're cold, Phillip. You should take off those wet things."

Carmichael gazed at her askance. "A charming idea. It does occur to me, however, that it might put something of a damper on polite conversation. Or are you accustomed to keeping company with gentlemen attired as nature made them?"

"I wish you will not be absurd." Lucy blushed. "Oh, very well. But you might at least take off your coat and shirt. Here, let me help you."

She was already reaching to undo the gilt buttons on his riding coat; and, bemused, no doubt, by her apparent resolve to disrobe him, Carmichael let her. Indeed, he was most peculiarly silent as, having finished that part of the task, Lucy next attempted to pull the coat off his back. She ceased when it became awkwardly apparent that the operation was impossible from her present position, facing him.

"Phillip." She lifted her head to look up at him and found, in the close proximity of the ledge upon which they stood, that her lips were within inches of his. Even worse, however, and considerably more distracting, his eyes stared into hers with a light, piercing flame. She swallowed, her heart starting most inexplicably to pound. Indeed, she had never felt anything like what she felt at that moment. It was rather as if time had come to a standstill, leaving her feeling absurdly as if she waited on the edge of a precipice. Wondering abstractly if her arms were about to betray her by climbing of their own accord around his neck, she swayed irresistibly toward him.

The moment was over as swiftly as it had come. Unbelievably, she saw the shutter drop in place over Carmichael's stern features. Abruptly he pulled away.

Lucy blinked, wondering if she had only imagined that he had been on the point of kissing her. Certainly *she* had been on the point of making a momentously prodigious discovery, one that she was not at all certain she wanted to make.

Dazed, she watched him shrug out of his coat, then hand it to her to hold. Unfortunately, it slipped out of what proved to be suddenly nerveless fingers.

Carmichael, cursing himself for having come within a heartbeat of taking advantage of Lucy's innocence, went abruptly still at the sound of her low, startled gasp. His glance flew to her face.

His shirt, soaked through, clung to him in sodden transparency, and her gaze was fixed with horrified disbelief on a point midway between the ribs on his right side beneath the arm— at the disfiguration of a scar, terrible to behold.

"Good God," she breathed, lifting huge eyes to his. "How close I must have come to losing you!"

Nine

"Oh, hell and the devil confound it!" Lucy said wrathfully, having just jabbed her finger for the third time with the darning needle.

"If I were you, I should quit before I found myself permanently disabled," commented Francie, who was sprawled on her belly on the floor, while she thumbed desultorily through an outdated copy of *La Belle Assemblee*. "I fail to see why you have set yourself to mend all those old stockings anyway. Nobody is likely to ever wear them again."

"It is called penance," Lucy answered, pressing the wounded member to her lips. *"Damn* Phillip Carmichael," she added, not hesitating to lay the blame for her clumsiness at the door of the one she most deemed responsible. "May the devil fly away with him!"

"I beg your pardon." Francie shoved aside the fashion magazine and sat up to scrutinize her sister with sudden keen-eyed interest. "Whatever would you wish that for? You can hardly blame Phillip because you pricked your finger."

"Oh, can I not?" Lucy retorted crossly. "That's how much you know. I daresay I can blame Phillip Carmichael for any number of things. I shall, in fact, very probably end up a candidate for Bedlam or the penal colonies, whichever comes first, and it will be all because of Phillip Carmichael."

"Lucy, for heaven's sake," exclaimed Francie, in the manner of one faced with a troubling anomaly. "Are you listening to yourself? If I did not know better, I'd say you had completely lost your reason."

"I shouldn't be at all surprised," admitted Lucy wryly. "I appear to be suffering all the classic symptoms. The fact is that awake or asleep, I am become impossibly obsessed with Philip Carmichael. At night he haunts my dreams, and during the day he preys upon my thoughts, until my temper has become hopelessly frayed. I have no appetite for food, and sleep eludes me, very often until the wee hours of the morning. Even worse, I cannot write. Oh, I wish I had never set eyes on him that day in Lathrop Tower! Faith, you cannot know the depths of depravity to which I have lately sunk because of him."

"No, but I should like to," said Francie, intrigued at the novel idea of her oldest sister, sunk in a morass of moral turpitude.

"Indeed, I can see you are all eagerness," Lucy retorted in exceedingly dry tones. "Well, and why should I not tell you? I have thought about it ad nauseum, and I am still no closer to making any sense of it. It might help me were I to discuss it with someone. But you must swear on your honor never to reveal a word of what I shall tell you."

"I'll swear it on whatever you like," replied Francie, scrambling to her knees. "Besides, who the deuce would I tell?"

"Francie," declared Lucy reproachfully, "your language. Mama would have a fit if she heard you."

"She would go into an apoplexy if she heard yours. Cut line, Lucy. I'm on your side, remember? Don't be afraid to open the budget."

Lucy spread wide her hands in a helpless gesture. "It is not that exactly. It's . . . Faith, I hardly know where to begin. There are so many things. The dueling pistols, our visit to the dungeons, Phillip's stubborn insistence that I should make Lathrop a perfect duchess. You already know most of that. I suppose I could begin with last Tuesday, when I took Phillip to my secret place."

No doubt her peculiar malady had seen its inception on that fateful afternoon when Old Slippery had given Carmichael the slip, she began. Certainly, that had been the beginning of her penance. The thought of Carmichael pining for his Incomparable was proving a far more effectual punishment for her invasion of his privacy than even a mountain of mending could have done. She had come to think of the mysterious Roxanne as a raven-haired enchantress with the blue beguiling eyes of a siren, and she had cast her spell over Carmichael.

But who was Roxanne? And what penance? Francie felt compelled to interject. While she could not but be more than a little impressed at the sight of Lucy's fiercely flashing eyes and clenched fists at the mere mention of the mysterious Roxanne, she was having the very devil of a time following her sister's greatly abbreviated narrative.

Lucy, thus reprimanded, back-tracked, relating all the events of her fishing expedition with Carmichael, leading up to and including the discovery of Roxanne's letter and the locket.

"Lucy, you *didn't*," squealed Francie, when Lucy

came to the part about searching Carmichael's pockets.

"It was only one pocket." Lucy gave an impatient gesture of the hand. "Naturally I am not proud of it, but, having read the letter, I had to see what she looked like, did I not?"

"But of course you did," Francie declared. "It is what I should have done in your place. I simply find it difficult to believe *you* could have done it. And then what happened? Is that when Phillip woke up?"

"No, not then. I managed to get everything safely put back before I awakened him. After that I showed him to the cave."

Lucy quickly related the incident of Old Slippery's near capture and subsequent escape in hilarious detail, which left both girls gasping for breath.

"Poor Phillip. I must say he took it better than I should have done," said Lucy, sobering as she came to the final part of her narrative. "You must understand he was soaking wet, and it was not in the least like the day you decided to try your hand at swimming because it was so hot that you could not bear it. He was trying very hard not to show it, but I could see that he was cold. And so I insisted he must—"

"—take his wet things off! Lucy, you did, didn't you? I know you so well. You suggested he take his clothes off."

"Well, it would be the sensible thing, would it not?" Lucy said defensively as her cheeks flooded with color. "Naturally, however, Phillip objected. In the end he would only agree to removing his coat. And that is when I saw it."

Lucy shuddered anew with remembered shock

and horror. The white linen shirt, soaked through so that it clung to the skin, had been rendered wholly transparent. The terrible wound, with its hideously puckered scar, had been plainly visible, its tale of infection and pain all too apparent. How greatly he must have suffered!

In typical fashion Carmichael had been maddeningly evasive, dismissing the entire matter with a shrug and the cynical remark that the scar was only one of his many souvenirs of the war.

"I have not been so fortunate," Lucy confessed to her sister. "I have been able to think of little else in the three days since I saw it for myself. Oh, Francie, you cannot imagine the thoughts that have gone through my head."

The wound, on his right side, for example, had seemed to hold a dread fascination for her. Indeed, it had called hauntingly to mind the afternoon in the duke's study when Carmichael had instructed her in the finer points of dueling. The particularities of the stance, with the right side presented to the opponent, the arm bent to afford the maximum protection— until, that was, the arm was extended straight out from the body when the actual shot was fired, leaving the right side unprotected— she could not banish from her mind.

Francie stared at Lucy, her eyes round with comprehension. "Faith, Lucy. You think he was shot in a duel."

"It would seem to conform with a wound like Phillip's," Lucy reluctantly agreed. "And it might explain a lot of things. For example, why Phillip was compelled to resign his commission when he must obviously have been a valuable asset to Wellington. And why he refuses to talk about himself,

and most especially anything concerning what he
did on the Peninsula."

"Well, that *could* be it. Or we might be jumping
to conclusions," Francie temporized with a hint of
regret. "Oakes did boast that Phillip had never met
his equal with pistols or swords, or had you forgotten?"

Lucy smiled mirthlessly. "I am not likely to forget anything about that day at Lathrop. Just because Phillip was wounded, it does not necessarily
follow that he met his match. The shots could have
been fired simultaneously, with both men hitting
their targets. Only, what if Phillip's hit dead center?"

"A duel to the death," pronounced Francie in
awed accents. "Oh, but this is simply marvelous! I
could love Phillip myself. First the dungeons and
now this. It is simply too fabulous to contemplate."

"It is no such thing," Lucy uttered in quelling
accents. "It is dreadful, if it is true. It would have
been enough to end what must otherwise have
been a brilliant career. And, worse, it must nearly
have put a period to his existence. Blast the man!"
Slamming down the sock she had been mending,
she came to her feet. "How dare he risk his life
on anything so foolish as the field of honor! And
how much worse if it was for a woman who in the
end jilted him for another."

Francie drew in a sharp breath. "You mean Roxanne?" she said. "But, Lucy . . . !"

"No, do you not see?" Lucy interrupted. "The
first time I saw him I could sense that he had
suffered. It was written all over his face. You saw
how pale he was, the lines about his mouth. He
gave every manifestation of one suffering the effects of an exquisite anguish."

"Yes, but . . ."

"And now there can be little doubt that I was right." Lucy, oblivious to her sister's repeated attempts to interject herself into the conversation, began to pace fitfully about the room. "Oh, it is all so clear to me now— Carmichael, lying wounded nearly to death for a woman who could not wait to get herself betrothed to another. Is it any wonder that he is bitter, or that he cannot bear to talk about his past? And then she had the unmitigated gall to send him a letter begging him to attend her wedding! For that alone she should have been taken out and horsewhipped. Indeed, I cannot think of a punishment dire enough for one who can only be as heartless as she is beautiful."

Francie, who had never seen her usually most sensible of sisters in what could only be described as a murderous state, was stricken with a sudden dawning sense of enlightenment. "Lucy," she exclaimed, "by all that is marvelous. You are not going mad. You have only fallen in love! Admit it: You have lost your heart to Phillip Carmichael!"

Lucy stared aghast at Francie. "I wish you will not be absurd. I have done no such thing."

"Well, if you have not, you are giving a very good imitation of it. In fact, I should say your case is far more desperate than Florence's."

Whatever Lucy might have said in reply to that outrageous remark was interrupted by Josephine, who had come to remind Francie that they were expected in the schoolroom.

Lucy, grateful to be left alone, sank down on the chair to gather her thoughts, or at least her composure, in the wake of Francie's unsettling pronouncement.

It was all perfectly absurd, of course, she told

herself. She was not in love with anyone, and most certainly not with Carmichael. And yet she could not deny that she had been prey to a whole new and bewildering array of emotions of late, all of them stemming from those moments spent in the cave with Carmichael.

Indeed, if she were to be perfectly honest with herself, she could not deny that her first reaction to Carmichael's wound, one of shock and the realization of how close Carmichael had come to death, had in itself been a revelation. There was only one conclusion possible to one of an analytical mind: She could not have experienced so poignant an anguish if her heart were not a good deal involved.

That was a most disconcerting discovery for one who had not since she was very young considered any future other than that of a spinster pursuing the career of which she had always dreamed. Even if she could have engaged Carmichael's affections, which was highly questionable, she was not sure she would want to. It would only complicate matters that she had thought comfortably settled.

Even less appealing was the notion of falling victim to a love that was wholly one-sided. Pining away of a broken heart was fine in a Gothic novel of love and romance, but living it in reality would seem to her to leave a great deal to be desired.

Faith, how could such a thing have happened? She was plain, unexceptional Lucille Emily Powell, hardly the sort to find herself suddenly in the role of romantic heroine. She could not hold a candle to the raven-haired Roxanne, who was, at least in appearance, everything to be desired by a man, like Carmichael, possessed of an exceedingly passionate nature. She could not hope to replace her in Carmichael's affections. And it would certainly never do to allow Carmichael to perceive the hopelessness of her situation. He had suffered enough without being made to feel responsible for her affliction. The very thought of such an eventuality filled her with revulsion. Good God, he would very likely feel obligated to offer for her out of some misplaced sense of honor, and that she could not countenance!

Hell and the devil confound it! What in blazes was she to do? Nothing she had ever read could have prepared her for the eventuality of finding herself victim of an all-consuming love. She was not in the least suited for it. Indeed, she was far too practical-minded.

If she were in danger of losing her heart to Carmichael, then she must simply place a closer guard around it. It was only a matter of a few short weeks before Lathrop must surely put in his appearance, and then, whether she liked it or not, Carmichael would vanish from her life forever. Until that time she must just keep her distance, for her sake as well as for his.

The decision having been made, she should have experienced a measure of comfort. How absurd, then, that she should have had, instead, a dreadful hollow feeling invade the pit of her stomach. Indeed, if she did not know better, she would suppose she was on the point of succumbing to a fit of the vapors.

"Oh, the devil fly away with him!" she uttered and, hurtling her darning, sock and all, across the room, dropped her face in her hands and wept for no good reason at all except that she felt like it.

* * *

Lucy's vow to hold herself aloof from Carmichael's sphere of influence was to prove far more difficult to keep than she could possibly have imagined. Indeed, it was not until she had resolved to banish him from her heart and mind that she began to discover how indelibly he had become imprinted upon both of those unruly faculties. It was not enough that he continued to invade her dreams, both sleeping and awake, but now, whenever she tried to lose herself in her writing, images of him invariably obtruded into her thoughts so that every hero, bandit, or villain turned out to be disconcertingly like Carmichael. With the result that she spent almost as much time scratching things out as she did writing them.

Nor was that all or the worst of it. It seemed that Carmichael, without her previously being aware of it, had made himself an indispensable part of her family, even going so far as to engage her father in regular intellectual discussions of the earl's beloved antique books and to instruct her twin brothers in the manly art of fisticuffs. William had taken to aping Carmichael in his dress, his speech, and his mannerisms. Francie had requested his advice on how best to break Jester to the saddle. And while Florence made every effort to win his attentions, Josephine showed every sign of one suffering an acute case of hero worship. Furthermore, having made a conquest of Lady Emmaline, he had become a regular guest at their table.

Carmichael was, for all practical purposes, maddeningly inescapable, and the more Lucy was thrust into his company, the nearer he came to battering down her already tenuous defenses.

One morning, little more than a se'ennight after

the day of her momentous decision, Lucy sat down early for breakfast, thinking to avoid any and all company that might, no matter how inadvertently, bring Carmichael to mind. She had just spent a fruitless hour revising yet again a chapter she had already rewritten no fewer than six times, thanks to Carmichael's intrusion in her creative processes. He had appeared in the guise of the coachman, then again as Lord Maplethorpe, the archplotter, and had even demonstrated a marked tendency to reveal himself in the character of Brother Jessop, the monk. It really was too infuriating, the way he was always popping up, not only in the pages of her manuscript but in the flesh as well.

No sooner had that thought crossed her mind than a light step and a faint perception of movement glimpsed out of the corner of her eye alerted her to the presence of someone else in the room.

She knew before she glanced up that it was Carmichael.

The sudden leap of her heart at sight of the tall masculine figure lounging easily in the doorway was not only disconcerting, but all too revealing. It was useless to pretend that her pulse had not quickened or that her blood did not sing in her veins at his nearness. Indeed, she was ruefully aware that her face must instantly have lit up with a glow of happiness that, no matter how quickly doused, must certainly have been perfectly obvious to anyone but a blind man. It was all so patently unfair! Against the devastating effects of his slow, lazy smile, she seemed utterly defenseless!

"The devil!" she blurted before she could stop herself.

Carmichael, regarding her in no little bemusement, elevated an odiously sardonic eyebrow. "So you declared me on one other, particularly memorable occasion. I thought, however, I had disabused you of such a notion."

Lucy choked on an unwitting burble of laughter. "I wish you will not be absurd," she replied. "You know very well I was not referring either to your character or your identity, but to your unexpected appearance."

"You relieve my mind," drawled the captain whimsically. "I confess I had come to entertain the hope that I might eventually cease to have an unsettling effect on you."

Lucy gazed at him askance, wondering what the deuce he had meant by that cryptic utterance. "You startled me," she retorted. "Which is hardly surprising. It is a trifle early for callers, even for those who are encouraged to think of themselves as part of the family and, as such, to run tame about the place. What, pray, are you doing here at this uncivilized hour of the morning?"

Carmichael, reminded of his privileged status, strolled past Lucy to avail himself of a cup of coffee. "As it happens, I am here at Will's suggestion. He has offered to accompany me on my rounds of the duke's tenants. He will, I trust, be down directly."

"Yes, I should suppose he will," Lucy agreed, acutely aware of Carmichael's leisurely progress back to the table. She hoped her brother would put in his appearance rather sooner than later.

Taking a place across from her, Carmichael settled back in the chair, his long legs, crossed at the ankles, stretched out before him. Lucy, feeling his eyes on her, pretended to go on with her breakfast in spite of the fact that she had quite lost her appetite for turbot.

"You have not been to the castle for the past several days to see how the work progresses," he observed after a moment.

Lucy colored. "No. I have been busy, working on a new story." She drew a breath and smiled brightly. "Florence tells me the parlor is completed, along with several of the upstairs rooms. She reports that the transformation is truly remarkable." At last she found the courage to look at him. "Is it true you have managed to lay to rest all the ghosts at Lathrop Castle?" she asked, trying for a touch of humor and succeeding, to her horror, in sounding like an absurd, simpering schoolgirl.

She was rewarded with a distinct hardening of Carmichael's lean, chiseled jaw. "Is that what you think I have been doing? Laying ghosts to rest?"

"Well, and haven't you?" Thinking to brazen her way through, she gave a gay facsimile of a laugh. "I daresay it must be true, else Flo would not set foot across the threshold. I do hope you have not chased them all away. Lathrop without its ghosts would not be at all the same."

"Then you may rest assured." Carmichael's voice sounded peculiarly grim. "The ghosts of Lathrop Castle are well and thriving. You may take my word for it."

Lucy made a show of spreading her toast with butter. "You cannot know how relieved I am to hear it," she said, thinking she would surely choke if she had to eat even so much as a bite. "You may be sure I shall not enlighten Florence. Not now, when she is looking forward to helping you pick out the fabrics for the upholstery and drapes. I am afraid she does not look upon the notion of disembodied spirits with the same fondness as

Francie and I do. A shame, is it not? Just think what she is missing."

"I haven't the least idea what she might be missing," replied Carmichael acerbically. "I, however, seem to be missing the point. Do you not think it is time you told me why you are doing your best to avoid me?"

Startled, Lucy stiffened. Guardedly, she lifted her eyes to his. "I'm sure I don't know what you mean. I told you I have been busy."

"Writing your story." Carmichael's lip curled ironically.

"Yes," Lucy insisted. "Writing my story."

Carmichael visibly relaxed. A faint smile, vaguely reminiscent of that of a wolf's who has just spotted a motherless lamb, hovered about the handsome lips.

"I have never had the privilege of reading your stories," he observed after a moment. "Why is that? I wonder. At least we used to discuss them on occasion. Tell me about this project that consumes all your time. Does it concern the fair Evalina?"

Lucy shook her head. "No, this is a different one." She hesitated, tempted. She missed talking to Carmichael more than she could ever have thought possible. But then, it was just one of the things she would have to learn to live without, she reminded herself. On the other hand, it might be the very opportunity she had been looking for to have a few things about Carmichael clarified. Certainly it would not hurt to try. "I am working on a new heroine," she ventured, poking casually at her food with her fork. "Perhaps you could help me with some of the details."

Carmichael's eyes narrowed ever so slightly on

her face. It was, however, the only sign of emotion on that maddeningly unreadable countenance. "I should naturally be delighted to try. Tell me something about her."

"Well, she is an Incomparable, of course."

"Naturally." Carmichael studied her speculatively. "One of your blue-eyed innocents? Or an Irish beauty perhaps, with hair the color of flame and eyes the grey-green of the moors in the mist."

Lucy flushed. "I wish you will not be nonsensical. Her eyes are blue, and she has hair the color of ravens' wings. Her heart, however, is false."

"A beauty with a heart of jade." Carmichael's lip curled ever so slightly. "I am familiar with the type. No doubt the hero is hopelessly taken with her."

"Oh, hopelessly, indeed. No doubt you will recognize him as well. He is tall, like you, and broodingly handsome, with an impenetrable air of mystery about him."

"And how not?" Carmichael's expression was distinctly sardonic. "It is the mystery that makes him appealing."

"Quite irresistible, in fact," Lucy admitted. "Except to our heroine, who, as it turns out, is really the villain."

"Because she does not love him."

"No, because she pretends to love him, when, in fact, she is already in love with someone else." If she had been hoping for a reaction from Carmichael at this crucial part of the scenario, she was to be disappointed. She could detect no change in him, except, perhaps, that he had become even more impenetrable than before and that his eyes glittered between slitted eyelids with an odd, piercing intensity that made it absurdly difficult for

Lucy to think coherently. She forced herself to con-
centrate. "And this is where I need your help. The
Incomparable lures him into fighting a duel over
her, a duel in which, though he kills his man, he
himself is most dreadfully wounded."

"He is, in fact, brought nearly to the brink of
death," suggested Carmichael without the flicker
of an eye.

"Indeed," Lucy nodded. "He suffers most
dreadfully."

"Why?"

Lucy blinked. *"Why?"*

"Why does he fight the duel? And with whom?"

"But that is just it. I don't know," Lucy answered. "That is the very thing with which I hoped
you could help me."

"I see; it is the motivating factors that have
eluded you. But it is obvious, is it not?" His eyes
held her peculiarly spellbound. "The villainess is
neither false nor heartless."

Surprised, Lucy caught her breath. "No. Is she
not?"

Carmichael smiled mockingly. "On the contrary,
she is, like all true heroines, a beautiful young innocent— an heiress, in fact, in love with a youth
who is both worthy and courageous."

Lucy frowned, baffled by this new turn of events.
"But then, if she is not the villain, who is?"

"A nobleman, both powerful and dissolute, who
desires her for her beauty and her innocence,
which he seeks to corrupt. Knowing her heart already belongs to another, he plots to dispose of
his rival in a duel."

"Can he be so certain of winning?" Lucy asked,
her blood running suddenly cold.

"There is little doubt of it. He is a noted swordsman and a crack shot, and he has the advantage of experience. He has not scrupled on three previous occasions to kill his man."

Lucy's stomach turned suddenly queasy. "Good God, a professional duelist."

Carmichael shrugged a careless shoulder. "In a manner of speaking. He is a cold-blooded killer against an untried youth. The outcome is most certainly predictable. Which is why the young beauty, upon learning of the villain's insidious plot, has no choice but to implore the help of someone clearly more suited to the task. She begs your hero to intercede on the youth's behalf."

"And our hero agrees to it? Why?" Lucy queried, sensing they had come at last to the crux of the matter. "If it is so dangerous."

"If he *is* a hero, how not? You cannot think he could turn her away?"

Lucy slowly shook her head. "No, I suppose not. It would not be in his nature to do so." Feeling her heart absurdly heavy, she lowered her eyes to the exceedingly unappetizing food on her plate. "He must love her very much then."

"He has watched over her all her life. And she has always looked to him for protection. He can only be grateful she has had the sense to bring the matter before him before it is too late."

"Yes, of course," Lucy said with a hint of bitterness. "He would naturally do anything to preserve her happiness, even take the place of another in a duel to the death in order to save the life of the man she loves." At last Lucy lifted searching eyes to his. "And what will be his reward for his noble sacrifice? Will he be forced into exile for what he has done?"

Unbelievably, Carmichael laughed. "Where is the

sacrifice, noble or otherwise? He is alive, and he has lost nothing that he will not do better without. As for his future— " His eyes looked straight into hers. "— That is entirely in your hands, surely."

Lucy started. "Mine?" she demanded incredulously.

"Whose else? It is your story, after all, is it not?"

Lucy stared at him. His smile, she noted, was odiously mocking, but whether he mocked her or himself she could not be certain.

"Yes, of course," she said, bitter with disappointment. "No doubt I should thank you. You have been most helpful." Abruptly she shoved back her chair. "Now, I really must ask you to excuse me. I feel sure Will will be down directly."

She had risen and was halfway around the corner of the table when Carmichael came to his feet. "Lucy." With his hand on her arm, he stopped her. "Lucy, I— "

There was the sound of a step at their back. And then Will's, "Ah, Phillip. You are here. I'm sorry if I am a trifle late."

Lucy lifted her eyes to Carmichael's, waiting.

For a moment their eyes locked; then Phillip's hand dropped. "I shall hope to see you again at Lathrop," he said, the shutter dropping in place. "I should like to think we are still friends."

"And why should you not," Lucy answered with only a hint of irony. "Whatever we are, it would seem nothing has changed between us."

Turning, she made her escape. What a fool she had been to imagine she might if only for a few minutes break through the barrier he so carefully maintained between them. Obviously he would never believe in her enough to confide in her, in spite of the fact that she had done everything to let him know that he might. And why should he? She meant little or nothing to him, and no doubt he would forget her as soon as he was gone from Lathrop. She did not stop until she had reached her attic room under the eaves, where she fell immediately to pacing.

A plague on Carmichael! How dare he tease her so! Indeed, she was quite sure she had never before met anyone more infuriatingly evasive. Talking to him was like trying to converse with the Sphinx— or the devil. She might have known she would get nothing but riddles from him.

Even so, she could not deny that, riddle or reality, she had never heard anything that had affected her quite like Carmichael's story about Roxanne. And it *was* about Roxanne; she did not doubt it for a moment.

She felt cold with reaction. It was all so much more complicated than she had imagined it to be. Roxanne was not only beautiful but good and innocent, and he had been willing to give his life to ensure her happiness. Not even the lost Lord of Lathrop's hopeless passion for Patience Merriweather could possibly compare with Carmichael's selfless love for Roxanne!

The thought was not one conducive to comfort. Indeed, not only was Lucy stricken with a slow, rending pang somewhere in the vicinity of her breastbone, but she was quite certain she had never in her life entertained so great a dislike for anyone as she did for the incomparable Roxanne.

It was only when she found herself contemplating the merits of a Roxanne confined to a nunnery, preferably in the farthest reaches of Outer Mongolia, that she was brought to a sudden standstill in the middle of the room.

Good God, she was clearly losing her mind. Indeed, she doubted not that she would go stark raving mad if she did not cease to dwell on Carmichael. Certainly it did not help to remain in her room mooning over him, she thought, chagrined to realize she had allowed the morning to slip entirely away from her.

Going to the window, she thrust the sashes wide and breathed deeply, grateful for the cool breeze against her heated cheeks. There must be any number of things she could do to occupy herself. If nothing else, she could go for a gallop on Wind Star. Surely the fresh air and sunshine would go a long way to clearing her head.

Immediately she discarded the notion upon sighting Carmichael and her brother before the stables. Curse the luck! It was clear from the way Will was running his hands down his gelding's left foreleg that the horse had turned up lame, which undoubtedly accounted for their early return. It looked as if she would be confined for a while longer in her room if she wished to avoid running into Carmichael. Having turned the animals over to one of the grooms, they were already on their way to the house.

She watched them, bemused to see how great a transformation acquaintanceship with Carmichael had worked on her brother. Having discarded his cossacks and high-padded Jean de Bry coats, he had adopted the same quiet elegance in fashion that distinguished Carmichael. Nor was that all: He gave every indication of having spent no little time practicing the older man's easy supple grace in both mannerisms and walk, until Will very nearly had it down to perfection. Obviously, Carmichael had exercised what could only be accounted a good influence over the youth. A shame he would not be around to similarly shape the twins into at least the semblance of civilized gentility.

Hardly had that thought crossed her mind than Timothy and Tom, bolting out of the house with Florence in hot pursuit, had the misfortune to hurtle straight into Will and Carmichael. Lucy, from her upstairs window, was able to glean very little from the resulting exchange of words, save only that apparently a certain Bilston enameled inkwell that had been used to sit on their papa's desk had suffered most certain annihilation with detrimental results to the claret-colored Ushak rug that ornamented the study floor.

The next instant, Will, grasping each of the twins by an ear, conducted them into the house, leaving Florence in the sole company of Carmichael.

Thinking that now was her chance to escape the house unnoticed, Lucy snatched up her writing box and fled down the servants' stairs. Moments later she slipped out the side door and, stealing through the rose garden, made for the entrance to the maze of holly, which a previous earl had had constructed for the entertainment of his new young countess, who had not been at all certain she could tolerate a life of rustication.

Lucy, like all the other Powells, had long since familiarized herself with the key turnings. She was just congratulating herself on having executed a successful escape from her eagle-eyed family and was thinking to spend the entire afternoon in the seclusion of the seldom-visited maze when she stepped through the final gap in the hedge into the center of the labyrinth— and was met with the sight of Florence, gazing up at Carmichael with every manifestation of one in the throes of a sublime illumination.

Ten

Lucy, taking in the scene in a single sweeping glance, froze suddenly in her tracks.

If Florence wore an expression of one in the grips of sublime illumination, Carmichael's might more nearly have been described as that of a man in need of divine intervention. Neither noticed Lucy step carefully back behind the hedge, where she could peek around the corner at the scene being enacted before her.

"It would seem we have been misled by your brothers," observed Carmichael dispassionately. Studying Florence with unreadable eyes, he withdrew the Sevres snuffbox from his pocket and, flicking open the lid with his thumb, drew forth a pinch of his favorite mixture. "Obviously your sister is not here," he said and, inhaling the snuff, brushed an imaginary speck from his sleeve before returning the box to his pocket.

"No," agreed Florence, who could not have sounded less surprised at the discovery. "Phillip," she ventured, lowering the thick veil of her eyelashes over her eyes. "I have a confession to make. I-I knew we would not find Lucy."

Faith, did she not think that was as plain as a pikestaff? The naive little minx, fumed Lucy.

"I realize it was wrong to deceive you," continued Florence, "but you cannot know how long I have waited to be alone with you."

"I daresay you cannot be blamed for thinking me obtuse," observed Carmichael in exceedingly dry tones. "In light of our present circumstances, I can only marvel at my own lackwittedness."

Florence gave a gay trill of laughter. Lucy closed her eyes in a grimace. "Oh, Phillip, you are roasting me. We both know you are not in the least bit a slow-top. I daresay you have known all along how I feel about you."

"I think it is safe to say that I have at times been given an inkling of it," agreed Carmichael reminiscently. "Certainly you have done your best to enlighten me. If we are not, however, to enlighten your parents to it, I suggest we should return to the house before we are missed."

"But I don't care if we are missed," Florence returned with a pout. Clearly things were not going quite the way she had planned them. Twining the end of a bright green ribbon at the neck of her bodice around one finger, she glanced coyly up at her tall companion. "Phillip, don't you like me at least a little?"

"Whether I like you or not has very little to say to the matter," Carmichael grimly assured her. "A fact that you, my child, are in grave danger of discovering for yourself."

Florence's face flooded with color. "I am *not* a child. And I will not be treated like one." Crossing her arms over her outraged bosom, she turned her back on him with a flounce. "Furthermore, I have no intention of showing you the way out of here until I have made you see me for what I am."

Carmichael's eyebrow arched a bare fraction of an inch. "Then, my dear, I suggest you do so at once. You may be sure there is nothing wrong with my eyesight. I see you very well as you are."

"Then you must see that I have lost my heart to you." Florence came around with a look of entreaty. "Surely that must mean something to you?"

Lucy, torn between pity and dismay at Florence's extremely unwise stratagem, started forward with the intention of putting an end to it before things got any further out of hand. She was stopped by Carmichael's response, which, in the circumstances, was not quite what she had expected.

After only the minutest of hesitations, during which he presumably digested this startling information, he grasped Flo's hand and, with every manifestation of a man moved by an overriding emotion, carried it to his lips. "But, my sweet Florence, it makes all the difference," he declared, gazing at her over her knuckles. "What a blind fool I have been not to realize before what a treasure was mine for the taking."

"Phillip!" gasped the object of his ardor, blanching at the suddenness of his reaction. "Then you do care a-a little?"

"Can you doubt it, my dove?" murmured Carmichael with uplifted eyebrows. "Now that I know how you feel about me, I shall not have any peace until I have made you mine." Pausing briefly, he reflected, "A pity you did not think to take greater care in your dress."

"My dress?" echoed Florence blankly. "What has my dress to do with it?" Then, with a darkling expression, "Are you saying you take exception to my gown?"

"On the contrary," replied Carmichael of the exquisite creation of sprigged muslin. Trimmed in green ribbon, it was in the first stare of fashion.

"It could not be more breathtaking, but I cannot think it is entirely suitable for a lengthy journey. However, I am afraid it cannot be helped. The house is far too risky, even if there were time for you to change."

"Too risky?" Florence drew back in sudden alarm. "Phillip, what are you talking about? What journey?"

"Why, our wedding journey, of course," Carmichael coolly informed her. "My foolish little dove, you did not think I should allow you to be ruined by this afternoon's rendezvous? We shall leave at once for the Scottish border. But first we shall stop at the castle for my curricle and pair."

"Your curricle?" echoed Florence in fading accents. "But, Phillip, I cannot think this is at all necessary."

"My sweet innocent, naturally you could not be expected to have thought it all out," Carmichael drawled with the practiced air of one experienced in stealing off with any number of schoolroom misses. "You must, of course, feel some trepidation at riding neck or nothing in a curricle, but you have nothing to fear in it. I am no mere whipster. And a coach and four, after all, is clearly out of the question if we are not to be overtaken by the earl and your older brother."

"The earl and-and . . ." Florence appeared on the point of swooning.

"I fear it is unavoidable," Carmichael regretfully informed her. "They are not likely to look with approval on an elopement, and you are underage. The last thing I should wish is to have to engage in a shooting match with either of my future in-laws. But what would you? If you insist on the coach, I shall naturally take that risk. Fortunately,

I am a crack shot. The odds are better than even that they shall sustain nothing worse than a trifling wound to the arm or the shoulder."

Lucy, who had long since gone from palpitations of horror to stifled paroxysms of mirth as she witnessed Carmichael's outrageous performance, was further treated to the sound of a horror-stricken gasp from her sister. *She* no longer demonstrated the least inclination to fall to a faint.

"You-you monster!" she gasped, drawing herself up to her full five feet three-inches in height. "Shoot Papa and Will? Oh, I would shoot you myself before I allowed such a thing! I'm afraid I have entirely misjudged you, Mr. Carmichael. You are not at all the noble gentleman I had imagined. Far from wishing to elope with you, I hope never to have to lay eyes on you again!"

Succumbing to a strangled sob, Florence bolted. Fortunately, she was too blinded by tears to catch sight of Lucy, who had only just enough presence of mind to duck into the nearest blind alley.

The same could not be said of Carmichael, whose vision was not in the least impaired.

"You may come out," he announced, "when you have quite recovered yourself, Lucy Powell."

The effect of his command, voiced in tones clearly meant to brook no denial, was to render Lucy instantly sober. Pausing only long enough to set her writing box on the ground, she presented herself before an exceedingly grim-faced Carmichael.

"Very well, Phillip," she murmured with quiet dignity, "I am here. How long have you been aware of my presence?"

"Long enough to realize you must have overheard everything."

"As a matter of fact, I did," Lucy readily confessed.

"And— ?"

A wondrously warm light sprang to Lucy's eyes. "And I can only be grateful that *you* were the object of my sister's first infatuation with an older man." Smiling, she extended her hand. "Thank you, dear friend, for letting her down in such a manner as to leave her pride intact."

Carmichael's lips twisted wryly. "I should have trusted you to see through my little charade," he said, closing strong fingers about her smaller ones. "I am afraid, however, that the earl and Lady Emmaline may not be depended upon to view it in a similar light."

"You needn't worry." Lucy laughed, setting her eyes to dancing. "I shall explain everything to Mama. You may be sure she will understand and apprise the Earl of what was, after all, a kindness. They will be as grateful to you as am I, I promise you."

"Yes, no doubt," Carmichael replied strangely. Lucy, glancing up into the stern features, was made suddenly and uncomfortably aware that he was staring at her with a singular brooding intensity.

"Phillip? What is it?" she faltered, feeling her heart inexplicably lurch.

Carmichael appeared to shake himself out of what gave every manifestation of being less than rewarding thoughts.

"Nothing." Taking her arm, he turned her toward the gap in the foliage. "Come, let us be gone from here. I've had enough of labyrinths to last me."

Carmichael, brooding and taciturn, did not encourage conversation; and Lucy, troubled by the suddenness of the change in him, led the way wordlessly through the turnings. The silence stretched, an almost palpable thing, between them until at last they came to the opening in the hedge.

Lucy stood blinking in the glare of sunlight, keenly aware of Carmichael's unsettling presence.

"You will come in for refreshment, won't you?" she ventured, vaguely nettled at his exceedingly odd behavior.

A wry gleam of a smile flickered briefly about Carmichael's lips. "Somehow I cannot think that would be at all advisable. Besides, my horse is waiting." At last he looked at her. "Lucy—" Whatever he had been about to say froze on his lips at sight of her.

She could not know what a glorious picture she made with the sunlight glinting red sparks in her hair. She knew only that her knees had started to tremble in a most ridiculous manner and she felt peculiarly light-headed. She stood, frozen to the spot, as Carmichael reached slowly up to crush one of her curls in his hand. He held it for a moment; then, releasing it in his palm, watched it spring back as if it had a life of its own. Only then did he look into her eyes, a long searching look that unaccountably took her breath away.

The next instant the mask dropped in place, leaving his face inscrutable again. Deliberately he straightened. "I shall take my leave of you here," he said curtly. "No doubt it would be better if you did not accompany me."

"If that is what you wish, Phillip," Lucy answered, a frown starting in her eyes. "I suppose it would be better if Florence did not see us together."

"Quite so." Carmichael smiled mirthlessly and lifted his hooded gaze to the castle brooding in the distance. "Perhaps it would be better if no one saw us together for the time being."

Startled, Lucy stared at him. "But, why? I told you I should make everything clear to Lady Emmaline and the earl."

"It is not because of Florence," Carmichael answered shortly. "It is you, Lucy."

"Me?" Lucy felt her heart skip a beat.

Carmichael's laugh rang harshly. "You really haven't the least idea of what I am talking about, do you?" His eyes probed her face. "No, why should you?" he said, and looked away. "I have written to inform the duke that his castle will be ready for him by the end of next week."

"So soon?" murmured Lucy, turning away to hide her dismay. "I had thought there was a great deal left to be done."

"And so there is. I have rendered the castle inhabitable. It is for the duke and his new bride to make of it what they will."

Lucy went suddenly quite still, an odd sort of sick feeling in the pit of her stomach. "And you think that will be me."

"It is my sincerest hope—for both of us," he had the unmitigated gall to answer her.

Lucy caught her lip between her teeth. She had the insane urge to laugh at the irony of it all. But then, he had never made any secret of the fact that he considered it his duty to persuade her to the duke's cause. And his heart, after all, belonged to Roxanne.

From somewhere she found the wit to answer him. "Then I am afraid you will only be disappointed." Lifting her head, she made herself turn and face him. "I told you," she said lightly, forcing a smile to her lips. "I shall only marry a man whom I can love, and I know now for certain that that can never be the duke."

"Then you are either green or a fool!" he declared with a savagery that quite took her off her guard. "You cannot possibly know that you and the duke will not suit. You may be certain that if circumstances had not made Phillip Carmichael what he is— a mockery, a man without substance— he would not hesitate to do all in his power to make you his. And you may be equally certain the duke will feel no differently. At the very least it would be a pity if you did not give him that chance. Dammit, Lucy! You were never meant to live your life as a spinster, any more than was your Irish great-grandmama."

Lucy felt herself bridle with resentment at the injustice of his attack. Indeed, she was shaking all over. "There are worse things than being a spinster," she retorted witheringly, stung more than she could possibly have imagined by his harshness. How dare he judge her! "At least I have the courage to stand by my convictions, something which you apparently lack." Lucy was hard put not to flinch at the cold leap of fury in his eyes. Indeed, she wished she might snatch the words back. Instead, she grasped her hands tightly together before her in the vain hope of regaining her composure. "I think perhaps you should go now, Phillip," she said, feeling herself dangerously close to disgracing herself in his presence. "Before I say something we shall both regret."

For a moment he looked at her, his eyes, steely points, boring into hers. Then, abruptly, a curtain fell over the hard features, leaving behind a bleak coldness in the remarkable orbs. "No doubt you are in the right of it," he murmured with a chilling lack of emotion in marked contrast to his earlier harshness. "It occurs to me that Phillip Carmichael has stayed overlong." Ironically he inclined his head. "Goodbye, Lucy Powell."

He said it in a manner that struck Lucy as most poignantly final. Her hand went out to him in unwitting supplication, but he had already turned on his heel and was stalking away with long, swift strides, leaving Lucy prey to a host of unsettling sensations.

"Hell and the devil confound it!" she exploded when he had vanished around the corner of the house. Indeed, she was quite certain she wished him without remorse to the devil. She might be plain and a throwback to her Irish great-grandmama, but she was not without feelings. How dare he treat her with a total disregard for the effects it might have on her sensibilities!

Furiously, she swung round on her heel and fled blindly back into the labyrinth. Fully cognizant of the fact that she was in no state to encounter any of her numerous family, she wandered aimlessly through the hedge-bordered alleyways until the turmoil within her breast had quieted enough to allow her to think in a more coherent fashion.

Only then did it come to her that she was behaving in a most idiotic manner, not at all in keeping with one who was normally accounted a sensible female. Nor did it excuse her in the least that it was all due to the odiously erratic Carmichael. He was like a chameleon, forever changing before her very eyes, until she could not be certain she knew him at all.

One thing was for certain: Any attempts she had

made to secure her heart from him had failed miserably. Indeed, she was ruefully aware that her most ardent wish as he had held her, spellbound and helpless beneath his gaze, was that he would take her in his arms and kiss her.

Hellfire and damnation! There was no use in denying it: She was hopelessly, shamelessly, in love with a man who not only could not return her affection, but wished nothing more than that she would wed someone else!

The days following Florence's ill-considered confrontation with Carmichael in the labyrinth marked a change back to the previous even tenor of life at Greensward. Florence, save for treating her younger siblings with an air of saintly forbearance and Lucy with the aspect of one who had gained through suffering a greater enlightenment, seemed for the most part to have come through her disillusionment in love without any lasting ill-effects.

The same could not be said of Lucy, who could no more stop herself from hoping every minute of every day to see Carmichael appear on her doorstep than she could prevent herself from breathing. Not even launching herself, however, into a fury of housecleaning, which prompted a harried Mrs. Ivy, the housekeeper, and her staff of maids to complain piteously to Lady Emmaline that "the poor dear was out to drive them all to an early grave," could assuage the bitter certainty that she would never see Carmichael again.

Carmichael had ceased to come to Greensward. And Lucy, telling herself that it was better so, would not allow herself to go to Lathrop, no matter how greatly she might wish to have done.

She could not be altered in her decision, not even when the rumors began to reach Greensward that Carmichael had apparently embarked on a road to dissolution and self-destruction.

Bevan Fahey had seen him more than once. In the dead of night it was, said the gameskeeper to Lucy, his old eyes knowing. The captain, draped all in a cloak of black, his hair, the color of ravens' wings, streaming in the wind. And those bloody eyes of his all aglitter in the moonlight. "He come thundering out of the night, he did, on his great black stallion, Miss Lucy. He were riding for all the world as if the devil hisself were after him."

Nor was that all to reach Lucy's ears in the succeeding days. Mary Higgens, who had been hired on as an upstairs maid at Lathrop, had told her father, the earl's head groom, that Mr. Carmichael, may God bless him, had taken to wandering the castle corridors when the work was done and the laborers had gone to home. She herself had overheard the captain shout something fierce at Mr. Oakes. "Told him to leave him be, he did. Said if he wanted to go to the devil in a handbasket, it wasn't no one's business but his own." Mr. Oakes had come out of the duke's study, his poor scarred face looking older than what it had any right to be. Muttering to himself, he was, something about the captain drinking himself to an early grave and all because of a female. "My Mary says Mr. Carmichael is a brooding, tormented man, Miss Lucy," Higgens had reported with a somber shake of the head. "Belike he's searching for something, the way he's always prowling the castle at night."

Lucy was plagued enough without the additional

worry over Carmichael's exceedingly odd behavior. Exhausting herself by attacking with a vengeance every cobweb, dust mote, and carpet stain in the manor might fill her days, but it did little to alleviate the lonely hours of the night, when she lay awake, too weary to sleep and too despondent to write. For the first time she was given to understand just exactly what it might mean to suffer an exquisite anguish, and she was quite certain that, save for those wishful of having a house devoid of the smallest speck of dirt or for one who was in need of trimming off excess poundage, she really could not recommend it.

Even her mama had at last been moved to take her to task, warning her that she was wearing herself perilously near a sharp decline. And if that was not enough to convince her to resume her normal habit of eating on occasion, perhaps the necessity of standing for hours on a stool in naught but her underthings while she was fitted for an entire new wardrobe to replace the gowns that now hung shapelessly on her altered frame would, the countess admonished her daughter one afternoon in the Summer Room.

"Surely this has gone on long enough, Lucy. Do you not think you should at least make an effort to see Phillip?" Lady Emmaline went on to suggest in her inimitably gentle manner, "You might at least talk to him. What could it possibly hurt?"

"It could not possibly help, Mama. I have been foolish enough to fall in love with him." Lucy's eyes flashed green sparks out of stormy grey mists at the memory of their last encounter. "He, on the other hand, has made it perfectly clear that he has not the least interest in me. Except, perhaps, to persuade me I could do no better than marry the Duke of Lathrop," she added bitterly. At last she turned from the window out of which she had been blindly staring and dropped to her knees beside the countess's chair. "Oh, Mama, how could this possibly have happened? I have always been accounted a wholly sensible female. I have known from the very beginning that there could be nothing but friendship between us, and still I now find myself prey to every extreme in emotions to which I once thought myself safely immune. Why? Was it like this with you and Papa?"

"I believe I did not suffer as you and Florence have," admitted Lady Emmaline, smiling reminiscently. "There was a time, however, when your father was away to school at Oxford, that I learned what it was to know the agony of doubt. Of course he was not your father then, and we were only two very young people very much in love. He was used to write at least once every fortnight; consequently, when I went the whole month before Christmas his second year without receiving a word, I quite naturally began to assume the worst. You may imagine my chagrin when he came home for the holidays with his writing arm in a sling."

"I remember," Lucy said, grinning in shared amusement. "It was the time he broke his arm in a cricket match. It is one of his favorite stories about his school days."

"It was a shame I wasted all that time imagining all sorts of things. And all because I was too proud to go to his mama and ask how William went on," reflected Lady Emmaline. "I have learned since that it is far better to go straight to the heart of the matter than to torture oneself with unfounded doubts and suspicions."

Lucy, suppressing a sigh, came to her feet to drop

a buss on her mama's cheek. "Thank you, dearest," she murmured around a lump in her throat. "I promise I shall take your counsel into consideration, though I cannot see that your experience is at all comparable to mine. Papa, after all, has always loved you, and Phillip . . . well, Phillip has made it clear that he can never feel that way about me."

"On the other hand, my dearest Lucy, some things may not be at all as they seem to be," said the countess with an air of inscrutability. "*I* should not be so quick to judge Phillip harshly."

There was not the opportunity to question Mama any further on the subject as the twins, in concert with Francie and Josephine, burst into the room at that crucial moment with the news that a letter had come for Bancroft from the duke and that another had arrived for Lucy from a Mr. Tobias Pendergraft, Number 10 Savile Place, London.

"A letter for Lucy?" inquired the earl, entering in the wake of the excited delegation of Powells. "From a Mr. Who?"

"Pendergraft, Papa," Timothy explained. "See? Timmons is fetching them. He would not let us have more than a peek."

"A peek at what?" queried Florence, summoned from the garden by all the clamor.

"Lucy has received a letter from London," Josephine informed her with an air of importance. "And Papa has one from the Duke of Lathrop. Timmons is bringing them now."

"Ah, yes, Timmons. Excellent. Let us have them, then," said the earl to the aged butler, who had made his entrance carrying a silver salver bearing the marvelously mysterious correspondence. "Well, well, and so it is a Mr. Pendergraft. And it is addressed to Miss Lucille Emily Powell. Come,

child, take it. Let us hear what this Mr. Pendergraft has to say."

"Oh, but, Papa," Lucy groaned, in a sudden
quake of anticipation mingled with dread. "Must
I read it before everyone?"

"And how not? It is not every day that a daughter of this house receives a letter from London.
There are no secrets beneath this roof."

Lucy, giving in to the inevitable, picked up the
folded missive and, with fingers that trembled
slightly, broke the seal of wax.

The words, *delightfully narrated tale of adventure
and romance* fairly leaped out at her, along with
such phrases as "pleased to offer you" and "shall
be looking forward to your next literary endeavor"
before the importunate cries of her siblings demanding that she read out loud penetrated her
reeling mind.

"Good Lord," she breathed, sinking weakly
down on the edge of the sofa next to the countess.
"I am to be a published author. Mr. Pendergraft
has offered me the sum of five pounds for *The
Lady in Waiting, or the Skeleton in the Castle Dungeon!*
Indeed, he expresses a keen interest in *The Lord
of Lathrop, or the Watcher in the Tower* and any of
my future endeavors. He likes my writing and believes I have a true talent for it. Oh, I cannot believe it. Indeed, I cannot think at all coherently.
Someone read it for me, I beg you."

Francie, who was not loath to comply, took the
letter from her sister's nerveless fingers and read
the missive out loud in its entirety.

"I say," remarked the earl, clearly as dazed as
his eldest daughter by the news. Taking out his
reading glasses, he clipped them on the bridge of

his nose. "Here, Francine, let me see that. Are you sure there is not some mistake?"

"Of course there is no mistake," smiled Lady Emmaline, hugging Lucy to her. "Why, my dear, I could not be more pleased for you. It is not everyone who can realize a lifelong ambition."

"Oh, but this is simply too marvelous. I always knew you could do it, Lucy," Francie declared, giving an impromptu pirouette before dropping into a grand curtsey before her elder sister. "I shall be the sister of a famous novelist, and together we shall travel to any number of exotic places."

"Yes, that is all very well for you to say," said Florence, beaming with quiet pleasure for Lucy. "First, however, you will have to graduate from the schoolroom."

It was at this juncture that Josephine presented herself before Lucy, her delicate features pinched and pale. "You are not really going to leave us, are you, Lucy?" she asked. "Please do say you are not."

"I am not going anywhere, little goose," declared Lucy, wrapping the child in her arms and drawing her down on the sofa beside her. "If ever I were to go traveling to distant places, you may be sure I should wait until you were grown up enough to go with me."

"But who is Lucinda Evalina?" demanded Tom, doing his best to peer over his papa's shoulder at the momentous letter.

"Apparently it is your sister Lucy," the earl supplied. "It is not uncommon for authors to employ a nom de plume. There is the well known M. B. Drapier, a pseudonym employed by Jonathan Swift upon occasion. And Isaac Bickerstaff, of course, who everyone knows was Sir Richard Steele. And . . ."

"And now there is Lucinda Evalina," pronounced Timothy, who knew all too well that the earl was quite capable of supplying an entire catalogue of examples. "Egad, Lucy. Was that the best you could come up with? It sounds dreadfully foreign."

"That's because it is foreign, stoopid," said Tom, feigning a punch to his brother's midriff. "It's supposed to be."

"Fat lot you know about it," Timothy instantly bridled, blocking the punch. "Or maybe you've taken to reading girls' stories."

"If either of you should ever take to reading anything, I should only be pleased, Timothy," remarked their papa, sapiently eyeing over the rims of his spectacles his twin progeny, who were even then squaring off, presumably with the intent of drawing one another's cork. "As it happens Tom is quite right. Obviously, Lucy chose her name for its exotic flavor."

"Well, I think it is lovely," commented the countess, smoothing troubled waters. "Perhaps we should celebrate Lucy's wonderful news with tea."

It was at that point that Will, striding in after just having returned from a visit to one of the outlying farms, demanded to know what all the uproar was about, and everything had had to be gone over all over again. With the result that the second missive, from the duke, was all but forgotten. Indeed, it was not until the tea tray had been brought in, the dishes filled and handed all around, and a toast proposed in Lucy's honor and drunk, that Josephine shyly pointed out the oversight.

"Ah, quite right, my dear," rumbled the earl. "In all the excitement I forgot all about it. Well, then, let us see with what news His Grace has chosen to favor us."

Lucy, who thought she knew very well what His Grace had written, was hardly surprised when the earl informed them that the duke, in the company of Lady Barrington, had undertaken the journey to Lathrop and might be expected to arrive no later than the morrow, at which time they would be pleased to call on the earl and his countess at their earliest possible convenience. Lucy, after all, had been expecting just such a missive.

Nevertheless, the news gave her no pleasure. On the contrary, in the wake of the triumph occasioned by Mr. Pendergraft's letter, the certainty of the duke's imminent arrival hit her rather like a pitcher of ice-cold water.

As soon as she gracefully could, she slipped away from the others and fled to her room. Not even re-reading Mr. Pendergraft's letter to reassure herself that she had not been dreaming, however, served to calm her restless spirits. Plagued with the fidgets and unable to bear being confined within four walls, she hastily changed into her riding habit and stole out of the house to the stables.

Minutes later, mounted on Wind Star and wishing to avoid any encounters with her siblings or anyone else, for that matter, she headed the mare along the trail that climbed out of the valley to a lonely stretch of moors overlooking the sea and was soon out of sight of Greensward.

She rode with a fearless disregard of the rugged trail, glorying in the feel of the wind and the sun against her face— and, coming around a bend in the trail, was nearly ridden down by Carmichael on his big, rangy stallion.

Eleven

It was Carmichael as she had never seen him before. His neckcloth missing, he wore his shirt open at the throat, and his coat was rumpled as if he had only recently slept in it. Furthermore, the lean jaw was covered with the distinct shadow of a beard, his hair was decidedly more disheveled than was strictly acceptable, even for the Windswept, and the lines about his mouth seemed harsher, more pronounced than she remembered.

"You!" Lucy blurted, reining in her mare.

"Even so," murmured Carmichael, sweeping her a bow from the back of the stallion. "You astonish me, Miss Powell. I had not thought to see my lady beyond the walls of her impregnable fortress."

"And I had not thought to see you in such an altered state," Lucy retorted, stung by his sarcasm. "Have you been ill, Phillip? You look perfectly dreadful."

"How kind in you to point it out," Carmichael replied, his slow, lazy drawl edged with irony. "I had come to believe I was beneath your notice."

Lucy, feeling a blush invade her cheeks, hastily averted her face. "How can you say so?" she managed in a stifled voice. "We are friends, are we not?"

"I was fool enough to believe so— once," he answered, maddeningly cool. "Lately I have not been so sure. But then, it little signifies. If ever you were concerned, you need be no longer. I shall be leaving Lathrop in the morning."

Lucy felt her heart suddenly heavy beneath her breast. "Leaving? But why? Where—?"

The stallion edged closer, crowding the mare to the side of the trail. Carmichael, however, appeared not to notice.

He shrugged, maddeningly indifferent. "I have not decided where. One place is as good as another. As to why, surely you must know the answer to that. Lathrop is arriving on the morrow. You will no doubt pardon me if I choose not to remain witness to his wooing. You will forget me soon enough, while I, methinks, shall not be so fortunate."

Lucy's eyes flew to the pale, lean countenance. "You are mistaken, Phillip. I cannot forget you— ever. Though I shall soon be wishing to if you do not cease to tease me so."

Carmichael uttered a short bark of laughter. "Wish it or not, my lady. When you are chatelaine of Lathrop Castle I shall be less than a fading memory."

At last Lucy's temper flared. "I wish you will cease to be absurd. I cannot see why you persist in marrying me off to the duke when I have repeatedly told you I have no intention of marrying anyone. And do not call me 'your lady.' I am Lucy to my friends."

His gaze shot to hers. "If I had my wish, you would be 'Your Grace' before another month is out. And Phillip Carmichael would be as if he had never been."

"Well, *I* do not wish it," Lucy declared, alarmed

at the strangeness of this new mood of his. "Do you hate Lathrop so much that you cannot bear to be near him?"

"Hate him?" He laughed. "It would be like hating myself, and it is true I have lately found little to like and much to loathe in Phillip Carmichael. It is long past the time a period was put to his existence."

Never had Lucy felt such fear as struck her then. "Good God, what are you saying?" she cried, kneeing her mount closer to Carmichael's. "Stop it this minute! I will not listen to you talk of putting an end to your life. Indeed, why should you? Can you have loved her so much that you cannot find the courage to go on living without her?"

"Have I been in love, then?" queried Carmichael, his expression most peculiarly whimsical.

Lucy paled. Good God, in the throes of his exquisite anguish he was losing his very grip on reality! "You know you have," she prodded. "You love Roxanne."

"Ah, Roxanne, is it?" A gleam of something like enlightenment flickered behind the hooded eyes. "I suppose it is true. One might say that I have a certain affection for her."

"But of course you have," Lucy applauded his attempt to gain a hold on his flagging memory. "It is unfortunate that she loves another, Phillip, but you must not allow this cruel twist of fate to ruin your life."

"She loves another, does she?" Carmichael's lip curled sardonically. "It is true I have not been lucky in love of recent date. No doubt you will pardon my curiosity. I cannot but wonder what you can know of it."

Lucy flushed with remembered guilt. "I know

Roxanne is pledged to marry another. I-I read the letter she wrote swearing her undying affection. Oh, how greatly you must have suffered, and yet, still, it need not mean you cannot find consolation."

"Does it not?" Carmichael returned, an odd glitter in the look he bent upon her. "And where, pray tell, do you suggest I find this consolation?"

"In me," Lucy said. "If only you can be made to see it." There; she had said it, and now there was no turning back again, she realized, marveling at her own brazenness.

"In you?" At last it appeared she had pierced Carmichael's formidable defenses. His hand tightened on the reins, and the stallion bolted a step, snorting, before Carmichael pulled him up again. "Would you sacrifice yourself for me, then?" he demanded, his eyes steely points of flame, boring into hers. "Why, Lucy?"

Lucy swallowed dryly. "Because I am your friend. Because I care what happens to you even if you do not. Phillip, I know I can never be to you what she has been."

A wry gleam of a smile flickered briefly about Carmichael's lips. "No, I daresay *that* you could never be."

His words brought a fresh wave of color to her cheeks. "Still," she made herself continue, determined that she would not show craven even in the face of so pointed an acknowledgment of her own shortcomings, "I believe I can make you forget your pain in time. I can help you to go on with your life. I know I can, Phillip, if only you will give me the chance."

"Are you so certain?" Deliberately he reined his mount nearer hers until his knee brushed Lucy's.

"Oh, yes, Phillip. If nothing else, I should make you laugh. You said it, after all. A man would never be bored with me for his wife."

"Yes, so I did, and yet—" Leaning out of the saddle, he pulled her ruthlessly to his chest. "You tempt me, Lucy, as no other woman ever could. And still I wonder—"

He did not finish whatever he was about to say, and Lucy, held powerless in his embrace, could only stare, her heart pounding madly, as he lowered his head toward hers.

She was not sure what to expect at the touch of his lips to hers, but certainly it was not to feel a shock course through the length of her body or to feel her head, suddenly giddy, start to spin. Nor should she have expected to be struck suddenly and most unaccountably with a slow-mounting fever, like a hot wind that scattered her thoughts and rendered her delirious.

When at last he released her she was left trembling and weak, her senses reeling. With a sigh, she let her head loll back against his shoulder, placed conveniently for that very purpose. At last, slowly, she opened her eyes to him.

A faint smile twitched at Carmichael's lips at sight of her dazed and dreamy look. But Lucy, in the grips of a momentously prodigious discovery, was too stunned to see it. Faith, it was true— everything she had ever read or imagined about the first embrace between lovers. She could not doubt the evidence of her own senses. His was the sort of kiss she had always dreamed about, the kind one only experienced with one's own true love.

From the very beginning— indeed, long before fate had brought them together— she had been destined to love Phillip Carmichael. But somehow the equation was incomplete: Phillip Carmichael loved another!

She sustained a sharp pang of loss when at last he put her from him, and a resurgence of fear as she watched him. His face was as maddeningly inscrutable as ever as he gazed broodingly out over the moors curtained in mist.

"Tomorrow you will meet Lathrop," he said with a strange remoteness that made her wish to shake him. At last he looked at her. "After that, if you are still of a mind to offer me consolation, come to me in the tower room."

It was on her lips to ask why the tower room, but the mocking light in his eyes robbed her of speech. It was obvious he did not believe she would do as he asked.

"I will be there, Phillip," she answered, her eyes afraid for him. "Promise me you will do nothing foolish before then."

"You have my word." He lifted the reins. "Tomorrow at sunset, Lucy. I shall be waiting. Pray do not be late."

Lucy, stricken with fear for him, was, nevertheless, filled with a strange exultation as she watched him send his mount plunging down the trail. It was in her power to save him. No matter what he believed, nothing could keep her from her assignation in the tower, and most certainly not the Duke of Lathrop!

If turmoil was the normal state for the inhabitants of Greensward, it was chaos that reigned on this morning of the duke's scheduled arrival, Lucy noted, as she hurried upstairs to change her gown. Florence, apparently having abandoned her saintly fortitude, had been moved to fling a tortoiseshell brush at Timothy's head for nothing more onerous

than that he had dared to burst into her room
without knocking just at the moment that she had
decided that her morning gown of lemon yellow
shagreen made her complexion appear sallow. Nor
did it help in the least that he had come at the
behest of their mama to inform her that she was
to cease to try everything on in her wardrobe and
to come directly to the Summer Room to help ar-
range flowers.

And then there had been Josephine's unprecedented rebellion, which had required all of Lucy's
considerable powers of persuasion to put down.
The youngest of the Powells, and normally the
most docile of children, had demonstrated a sudden stubborn streak, declaring that she would not
make her curtsey to the duke no matter if she were
consigned to her room for an entire week on a
diet of nothing but bread and water. It was because
of Lathrop that Carmichael would be leaving and
taking his amiable giant away with him, and the
very thought of such a loss had rendered her in-
consolable. Only the promise that Lucy would do
her best to persuade their parents to allow her at
last to have her very own pony had in some small
measure mollified the weeping child. Lucy had left
her woebegone but willing to at least go through
the motions of a properly brought up young miss.

If that were not enough to try Lucy's patience,
Tom had managed somehow to sneak out of the
house to go fishing in his best coat and trousers,
returning an hour later covered from head to foot
with grass and mud stains, but ecstatic at having
caught a trout nearly as long as his forearm. He
had had to be dumped into a bath and every inch
of him scrubbed, after which there had been no
recourse but to dress him in his second-best

clothes, which were two inches too short in the sleeves and the pantlegs.

Lucy arrived in her room, surprised to discover Clara, her mama's abigail, already there, waiting for her.

"It's about time, miss," pronounced that redoubtable personage, eyeing Lucy's wilted dress and wild mane of hair with distinct disapproval. "Her ladyship sent me to see that you were made presentable, but even Clara Biggerstaff can't work miracles in minutes. Into the tub with you, Miss Lucy. Time's awasting."

Lucy, who could not have cared less how she looked to the Duke of Lathrop, soon found herself at the mercy of one who prided herself on putting out ladies in the first stare of fashion. Somewhat to her surprise, she found that she did not mind in the least being forced to take a chamomile bath or having her hair washed with a concoction of rosemary, basil, and sage and rinsed with chamomile water. In fact, she found it rather refreshing. She was less enamored of being forced to submit to a manicure, while wearing a facial pack made up of crushed cucumbers and oatmeal, or having to listen to Clara wax eloquent about the evils of fresh air and sunshine to the complexion. Indeed, she was quite certain that if she heard one more aspersion on the subject of her lamentable freckles, she would gladly throttle the well-meaning abigail. And when at last she was seated before the mirror, dressed in naught but a dressing gown and her underthings, while Clara, scissors and comb held ominously in hand, studied her from every angle, Lucy was as close as she had ever been to open rebellion. Gritting her teeth and closing her eyes, she braced herself for the first snip of the scissors.

In a surprisingly short time it was finished, and a pile of rebellious red curls lay, vanquished, in a pile on the floor. Cautiously, Lucy opened one eyelid, then, in dawning amazement, the other.

In wonder she stared at a miracle of transformation. Cut in three-inch lengths all over, her hair, relieved of its previous weight, formed a lovely cluster of curls all about her head. Not only was it far more attractive, drawing attention to her fine bone structure, but it was eminently more practicable. Indeed, she wondered why she had not thought to rid herself of the frizzy mass long ago.

"Clara," she breathed, "you are in truth a wizard with hair. I should never have believed it had I not seen it for myself."

"It's well enough, if I do say so myself," replied the abigail, rather grimly turning to business again. "But now we've more important matters to attend. I've taken the privilege of examining your wardrobe, Miss Lucy, and I can only say it's a good thing your mama has given me a free hand to do what I must."

Crossing to the wardrobe, she drew forth a morning dress that had the distinction not only of having come fresh from the seamstress but of being one of Florence's newest acquisitions.

"Oh, but I could not," Lucy declared. "Florence would never forgive me."

"I'm afraid Miss Florence has little to say in the matter," replied Clara, shaking out the skirts of the green jaconet round gown. "Her ladyship's instructions were quite implicit."

Gathering up the skirts, she directed Lucy to stand with her arms up.

* * *

It struck Lucy some few moments later, as she stood staring at her reflection in the looking glass, that perhaps it was not so bad after all, being the throwback to her Irish great-grandmama. If red hair was not all the fashion, at least, cut in the proper style, it could be rather pleasing to the eye. And, in spite of the obvious drawback of a light sprinkle of freckles across the nose, at least her complexion was remarkably creamy and had just the right touch of natural color in the cheeks. No doubt it was due to the muted pine green of her borrowed gown that her eyes appeared to shimmer— grey-green, it was true, but mysterious somehow, and remarkably compelling.

As for the gown itself, it was not too difficult to see that it would hardly have suited Florence's ivory complexion, her blue-violet eyes, or her hair, the color of wheat at harvest time. No doubt, left to her younger sister, it would inevitably have been relegated to hang in the wardrobe, along with any number of other never-to-be-worn dresses. On Lucy, the high-waisted round gown with its low-cut square neck and narrow empire skirt took on a quiet elegance, perfectly suited to her slender build and athletic grace. For the first time in her life she saw herself dressed in the first stare of fashion and realized she was not at all that bad to look upon.

Inevitably it came to her to wish that Carmichael might see her thus. Indeed, it seemed a shame that Clara's Herculean efforts should be wasted on the duke.

No sooner had that thought entered her mind than Clara, who had been standing to one side critically examining the results of her work, gave a gentle cough. "It's time, miss," she said, not unkindly. "There's no sense in putting it off any longer."

"No." Drawing a breath, Lucy turned from the mirror. "I suppose there is not. I might as well let the others see the fruits of your labors. You have indeed worked wonders."

"It's what I draw my wages for, miss. Still, I'm glad you're pleased."

Lucy smiled wryly and, squaring her shoulders, turned and let herself out the door.

Expecting the entire family of Powells to be gathered, ready and waiting, for the duke's arrival, Lucy was no little surprised when, a few minutes later, she arrived in the Summer Room to find the earl and Lady Emmaline, along with Will, its sole inhabitants.

"But where is everyone?" she exclaimed. "Pray do not tell me the twins have bolted or that the girls cannot decide on what to wear at this late date."

"You may be sure it is no such thing," smiled the countess, holding out her hands to her daughter. "Your father and I have decided it would be best not to overwhelm His Grace by subjecting him to the lot of us all at once. How lovely you look! Come, my dear, let us see you."

"I say, Lucy," exclaimed Will, "you look splendid."

"And how not," observed the earl, as if there had never been any question that his eldest was a beauty of the first water, "when she is the spitting image of my Irish grandmama. She, if you must know, was accounted a great beauty in her day."

"No, was she, Papa?" queried Lucy, startled at such a revelation.

"But I told you, Lucy, time and again," Lady Emmaline gently chided her. "She turned heads wherever she went—just as you will."

Any further discussion of Lucy's Irish great-grandmama was curtailed by the hollow clang of the front door knocker.

"By Jove," remarked the earl, drawing forth and examining his pocket watch, "His Grace is punctual. I'll say that for him."

Lucy, now that the long-awaited moment was at hand, felt a strange, steely calm descend over her; rather, she thought whimsically, like the calm before the storm. For the first time it came to her to wonder what he would be like, the duke who had come all the way to the North Yorks to court a bride upon whom he had never laid eyes. She pictured a tall, graceful figure, not unlike that of one other who had been indelibly etched in her mind and heart. Indeed, if it were true that all the Windholm men bore a remarkable likeness, it would be surprising if he did not resemble Phillip.

She got no further than that in her reflections as Timmons appeared at that moment in the doorway. Her breath caught as the butler intoned, "Lady Barrington and His Grace, the Duke of Lathrop." Bowing, Timmons stepped aside to allow the small, plump figure of a woman, well past middle age and becomingly gowned in a rose silk morning dress, her implausibly blond curls topped by an attractive winged mobcap of white crepe, sweep into the room, her arms outstretched.

"Emmaline, how good to see you," she ex-

claimed, offering her rouged cheek to the countess. "And Bancroft. Faith, how long has it been?"

"Two years or better, I shouldn't wonder," replied the earl, bowing over the plump hand that
had been offered him. "I must say you are looking
as lovely as ever, Lucille."

"And you are a flatterer, but I shan't cavil. At
my age one does not look a gift horse in the
mouth. And this must be Will. Faith, I should
hardly have known him. And Lucy. Heavens, it
cannot be you."

"Indeed it is, Aunt Lucille," said Lucy, the hon-
orary title coming to her lips from long practice.
"Have I changed so much?"

"You, my dear, have become everything I knew
you would," Lady Barrington answered, her
shrewd eyes growing a trifle misty. "Indeed, everything that I assured Patrick you would be. Come
now, and let me introduce you. I have waited long
enough for the moment when I should bring the
two of you together."

In all the flurry of Lady Barrington's entrance,
Lucy had spared the tall form limned in the doorway only the most cursory of glances. Now, she
experienced a small flutter of nervous anticipation
as her godmother drew her forward.

"Patrick, dear boy, come here that I may present
to you the Earl of Bancroft, his countess, Lady Emmaline, young William, who is Viscount Lethridge,
and Miss Powell, my goddaughter. Dearest
friends— His Grace, Patrick Windholm, Duke of
Lathrop."

Lucy froze, the blood draining from her face, as
the tall figure of the duke stepped into the full
wash of sunlight streaming through the windows.
Indeed, it seemed that His Grace had a most un-

natural effect on everyone of the assembled company with the exception of Lady Barrington, who stood smiling in anticipation, and the countess, who, after only the briefest of pauses, stepped forward, her hand graciously extended.

"Your Grace," murmured Lady Emmaline, "you are welcome, as always. I can only wonder what has kept you away from us these past several days. You must know that you have been missed."

A faint smile, distinctly ironic, flickered briefly across the handsome countenance. "Lady Emmaline." Taking her hand in his, Lathrop carried it to his lips. "It would seem you are as perceptive as you are gracious. I esteem it a distinct honor to be numbered among your acquaintances."

It was at this juncture that Bancroft, who had been standing in frozen immobility, apparently recovered his powers of vocalization. *"Harumm!"* he interjected, vigorously clearing his throat.

"Quite so, my dear," murmured Lady Emmaline, smiling with complete understanding. "I am sure I could not have expressed it better."

"I beg your pardon?" queried Lady Barrington, who was staring from one to the other with every manifestation of one in the midst of previously unsuspected Bedlamites. "I am afraid nothing you have said makes the least little sense. I haven't the slightest idea what any of you are talking about."

"Naturally you would be somewhat confused," sympathized Lady Emmaline. "I am not sure I understand everything myself."

"Perhaps it would help if His Grace explained that, far from being a stranger, he has become almost a member of this household," Lucy stated coldly.

"A member of the household?" Lady Barrington sank down somewhat weakly on the sofa. "On the contrary, my dear, it would seem to help very little at all."

"But then, Aunt Lucille," drawled Lathrop, his eyes never leaving Lucy's, "you must surely have guessed that we are all already acquainted. You did wonder, did you not, where I have spent my summer, and why I contracted to meet you at York. Did it not occur to you it was because I was already in the north of England?"

It was only then that Will, having come to a momentous realization, stepped forward, his face expressive of a curious mixture of bewilderment and utter certainty.

"Good God," he ejaculated, reaching for and vigorously pumping the duke's hand. "It's Phillip!"

Twelve

Lucy, quite certain that she had never in her life experienced an hour more dreadful than the one she had just spent in the company of the Duke of Lathrop, fled at the very first opportunity to her bedroom.

Once there, in the safe haven of her room, she flung herself across the bed and waited for the tears to come. That they did not was no doubt due to the fact that she was seething inside with an anger the likes of which she had never felt before. Indeed, she had never been so humiliated by anyone as she had been by the odious Duke of Lathrop— or so totally betrayed. Good God, she had confided in him, everything, from the dreams and ambitions she held most dear to her most ardent beliefs and fondest childhood memories. Faith, she had all but declared that she loved him!

Good grief, how he must have laughed when she had offered herself to him like some sort of consolation prize in exchange for the love he had lost! She writhed on the bed, tormented by the memory. What a fool she had been to imagine for one moment that he might truly care for a provincial from the wilds of Yorkshire. All along, from the very first moment of that dreadful day in the tower, he had had only one purpose— to secure himself the wife whom, in his supreme arrogance, he had decided upon to fulfill his requirement for a brood mare to bear him the requisite heir. No doubt he had seen her as a challenge, the one woman who, far from being tempted by either his title or his fortune, had preferred to remain independent and a spinster. How *that* must have pricked his pride!

She saw it all so clearly now. What she had assumed to be an overwhelming sense of duty and loyalty to an employer had been nothing more than his own obsessive self-serving interest. All along he had been the Duke of Lathrop, and Phillip Carmichael naught but an invention. How much more had been a contrivance to appeal to her romantic nature? The letter from Roxanne, the supposed duel, the kiss on the hillside? Sickened by the possibilities, she stifled a groan and clutched at her pillow.

Oh, but he was loathsome and vile, and she was quite certain she wished him without remorse to the devil. But that, too, was a lie. The truth was that, no matter how vilely he had deceived her, she could not stop herself from loving him. And that was the greatest irony of all. She had wished for an all-consuming love, had sworn herself to a life of spinsterhood rather than marry without it, and she had been foolish enough to tell Phillip Carmichael. Well, she had gotten her wish, and now she must just find some way to live with it.

With a groan, she sank back against the pillows. Good God, she had lost herself. Indeed, she did not know how she could ever show herself outside her door.

The gentle rap on that oaken barrier came like a mockery of her own despair. Hastily she sat up.

"Yes, who is it?" she called, and straightened her dress and her hair.

The door opened, and Lady Emmaline quietly let herself in.

"Lucy," she exclaimed softly, crossing to the bed, "my poor dear. I came as soon as I could. I have just left Lady Barrington, whom I have persuaded to lie down for a short rest until she is in some measure recovered. For you must know she sustained a terrible shock to discover the manner in which her nephew had deceived her goddaughter."

Lucy smiled, albeit a trifle wanly. "Poor Aunt Lucille. The supreme moment for which she had been waiting all these years was not at all what she had expected. She must be dreadfully disappointed."

"She will recover. It is you I am concerned about, my dear. You and Phillip."

"Phillip!" Lucy caught her lip between her teeth to keep from further betraying herself. "You mean His Grace, do you not? Phillip never existed."

"You could not be more mistaken if that is what you think." Seating herself on the bed beside Lucy, Lady Emmaline took Lucy's hand in hers. "He has explained everything to your father and me. Can you not see that he conceived this charade because you left him little other choice in the matter?"

"*I* left him no choice!" Lucy exclaimed indignantly. "Good heavens, Mama. Now is it to be my fault?"

"Well, you will admit, will you not, that you never overlooked an opportunity to impress on him the fact that you were opposed to his suit?"

Lucy colored at the undeniable truth of it. Still that did not excuse the duke's deplorable deception. "I am still opposed to it. And at least *I* told the truth," she said stiffly.

"But of course you did," soothed her mama. "If you are to be fair, however, I should think you would try and see it from Phillip's point of view. He liked you from the very first. How else was he to find a way for the two of you to come to know one another? You had vowed to send the duke packing as soon as he showed up on your doorstep. So long as you believed he was coming only to please his aunt, what chance had he to overcome your prejudices against him? He loves you, my dearest Lucy," Lady Emmaline finished eloquently. "Surely you can forgive him this small deception when it was done with the noblest of intentions?"

Lucy, however, was in no mood to forgive him anything. Indeed, she could not see how she could ever bring herself to trust him again. "He might have tried presenting himself under his true colors. It would at least have been honest. As it is, far from forgiving him, I wish only that I may never lay eyes on him again."

Lady Emmaline sighed. "Very well, my dear. I shall not dwell further on it." Rising from the bed, she went to the door, where she paused, her hand on the doorhandle. "Phillip said it would be useless to plead with you." Turning her head, she looked at Lucy. "How well he must have come to know you these past weeks."

When Lady Emmaline was gone Lucy flung herself once more across the bed, grateful to be left to herself again. She was not, however, to be allowed to enjoy her solitude long. Next to come to plead the duke's cause was Florence, who, upon learning the truth of his identity, had had little difficulty in perceiving the stratagem he had employed to cure her of her silly schoolgirl infatuation. Surely a man capable of such a generous act could not be all bad. She had ended by begging Lucy not to fling away her chance at happiness; then, giving Lucy a sisterly hug, she had left her.

Lucy could not but be touched at Flo's eloquent championship of the duke, coupled as it had been with a sincere wish to ease Lucy's pain, but she could not but be relieved to see her go. It did not help to be forced to remember the things she had come to love in Phillip Carmichael. Indeed, if anything, she was left feeling even more miserable than before.

Nor was that the last of her afternoon callers. Francie came to suggest a ride to make Lucy feel better and to add ingenuously, before leaving, that, in spite of everything, it had been terribly clever of Phillip to fool them all into thinking he was a right one when he was really the detestably devious duke. No doubt it would be only as he deserved if he were to succumb to a slow, lingering death just as Lucy's Lord of Lathrop had done over his lost Lucinda.

Lucy had only just managed to quell the urge to fling a pillow after Francie when she heard Timothy outside her door arguing with Tom as to which of them should plead with Lucy to change her mind and marry the duke. "Aw, Lucy," Timothy had entreated from the other side of the closed barrier in response to Lucy's peremptory command for them to take themselves off. "It isn't fair. Phillip was going to teach us how to fence until you drove him away."

They were saved from a throttling at Lucy's hands only by the timely arrival of William, who, after chasing the miscreants away, paused long enough to implore Lucy to reconsider Lathrop's case on the basis of the good he had brought to the valley. "You ought to at least give him a chance, Lucy. It would be a shame if he closed down the castle after all the work he has put into it. After all, he did it all for you. Surely that must account for something."

Half hysterically, Lucy had begun to wonder when her papa would come to exonerate the duke. Perhaps Clara would have something to say on the subject, as well, or Timmons and Mrs. Ivy, and why not Higgens, while they were at it. No doubt they were all in favor of Lathrop.

It was Josephine, however, who stole into Lucy's room as the sun slanted heavily through the windows and, tiptoeing to the bedside, whispered Lucy's name.

"Lucy? Are you asleep?"

Stifling a sigh, Lucy rolled over on her side. "Come." Pulling the girl on to the bed beside her, she slipped an arm around her waist. "Now, tell me why you think I should marry Lathrop."

Josephine turned her head on the pillow to look with startled wonder into her sister's eyes. "How did you know?" she whispered.

Lucy shrugged, smiling. "Perhaps I am a mind reader. Now, tell me. What did you come to say?"

Josephine snuggled closer. "Lucy. Do you remember that day in the tower when you read us the *Lord of Lathrop?* Do you remember what you said?"

"I said that I should never marry, and I have not changed my mind, dearest. Why do you ask?"

"Because . . ." Josephine exhaled a long breath. "Lucy, you were wrong when you said no man could ever lose his heart to you. Phillip did. I know it. It is the only thing that makes any sense. Why else would he go to so much trouble if he was not terribly, hopelessly in love with you?"

Lucy stared into her sister's eyes. "I don't know, darling," she said after a moment. "And that is what troubles me most of all."

Lucy did not know how long she lay beside Josephine, slowly stroking the child's hair, until at last the little girl drifted off to sleep. She only knew that she could not bear another moment alone with her doubts. Nor was she in the least enamored at the thought of enduring another curtain lecture from her well-intentioned family. Noiselessly, she stole from the bed.

It was no doubt inevitable that she was drawn to the castle as the last rays of the sun cast deep shadows across the valley. She rode with her eyes on the tower, her heart telling her he would be there, waiting, and her mind chiding her for a silly, romantic fool.

The bailey was steeped in shadows and a mist was rolling in over the moors from the sea when she passed through the castle gates. The muffled clatter of the mare's hooves against the cobblestones echoed eerily through the empty courtyard. She had half expected a stable lad or a groom to appear to take her mount, but none came, and she dismounted, unaided, before the tower door.

The castle brooded in the approaching dusk, lifeless and seemingly empty, and she suffered a chill of apprehension. She was too late. Lathrop, already convinced that she would not come, had closed down the castle and left.

She dropped the reins to the ground and made herself go into the stairwell. Feeling her way in the gloom, she climbed, her steps quickening as she came at last to the darkened room at the top.

"Phillip!" Her heart nearly failed her as a figure loomed out of the deeper shadows. She gasped, "You are here. I-I thought when no one came for my horse that you— " She stopped, blushing furiously.

"I gave the staff the evening off. Except for Oakes, the castle is empty." A glow of light spilled out of the darkness so that Lathrop seemed to leap out at her. It was Phillip, and yet not Phillip. The dearly beloved features were the same, but the eyes were different— clearer, somehow, unguarded, the eyes of a stranger. Deliberately he set the dark lantern, the sort used by mariners for signaling, on the window ledge before turning back to her. "I thought it more appropriate this way. It offers a certain symmetry, don't you think?"

"It is the way it was that first time." She smiled crookedly. "I hope you do not expect me to powder my hair with dust. I may feel like a ghost of my former self these days, but I am in no mood to emulate one."

"You have cut your hair. When I saw you today I thought perhaps a cruel trick had been played on me. I was no longer Carmichael, but the duke; and you were not Lucy, but a haughty young woman of fashion who had somehow taken her place. Ironic was it not?"

"It was despicable," Lucy retorted, the spell broken by his allusion to the charade he had played. "How could you do it? We were friends. I trusted you."

In the light of the lantern she could not mistake the hard leap of muscle along the lean line of his jaw. "Indeed, you trusted me. Enough to confide in me your singular views regarding marriage with a duke. Should we have been friends if I had been Lathrop, the wealthy nobleman in need of a wife to set up his nursery? You will pardon me if it did not seem so to me at the time. The opportunity presented itself for me to be someone else, and I took it. Pray do not ask me to regret what came of it, for I cannot."

"You deceived me, Your Grace," Lucy accused him.

"And do not think I have not been made to pay for it." He loomed over her, suddenly very large and very dangerous somehow. Stifling a gasp, Lucy moved back a step and then another— and came up hard against the tower room wall. "I had the misfortune to lose my heart to you, here, in this very tower, Miss Powell," growled Lathrop, following her. "And I have wanted you so that I have been driven nearly mad by it and the certainty that you could never forgive my deception. Surely that is punishment enough even for you."

"It was all a lie," Lucy flung back at him, refusing to give in to the happiness that, like a dart, had pierced her heart at his confession. "Everything, from the very beginning. Do you deny Roxanne was a lie? And the duel? Even your name, Your Grace."

"Roxanne, Miss Powell, is my sister. I killed the man who plotted to abduct her. That part was all true. Even if my father had not met an untimely demise in a carriage accident, leaving me the title, my military career would have been at an end because of that bloody duel. As for my name— " Lucy flinched as his hands came up against the wall on either side of her, effectively trapping her where she was. "My name is Patrick Phillip Carmichael

Windholm. Carmichael was my mother's maiden name, in case you are interested."

"I am not in the least interested, Your Grace," Lucy lied glibly. "Carmichael never really existed, and that is the only thing that I find pertinent."

"Do not push me too far, Lucy," Lathrop warned, exceedingly grim. "Phillip Carmichael may have been a fabrication, but he was nearer to the truth than the duke you invented. You may be sure I have no intention of abandoning my duchess in the country in order to pursue my pleasures in London."

Lucy, afraid to snatch at the happiness that he would seem to be offering her and wanting to prolong the moment before she gave into him, lowered her eyes to hide the gleam of joy in their depths.

"Still, if he was a lie," she said, "then how can I trust anything I have thought or felt about him these past weeks? Surely you see my dilemma. How can I know that it is Lathrop to whom I would pledge my heart and not Phillip Carmichael?"

That traitorous organ nearly failed her at the sudden fierce leap of Lathrop's eyes. "If you wish to have me court you as the duke, I shall," he drawled in a steely edged voice that sent chills down her back. "Only do not put it off for too long, my love. I want you, Lucy. More than I could ever have thought possible. But more than that, I need you, as I have never needed anyone or anything in my life before."

Lucy felt her knees go suddenly all weak and trembly. At last he had said them, the words that she had been longing to hear. Still, it was not enough. Indeed, she very much feared she was utterly shameless. It gave her such pleasure to tease him. Deliberately she lifted her eyes to his.

"That is all very well for you to say, Your Grace," she replied, surprised that her voice should sound cool and unruffled when inside she was feeling something quite different. "I, however, do not know yet who it is who professes to love me. Indeed, I know of only one way to be sure. I require a kiss, Your Grace. It is all I ask of you. And then I— "

She was not allowed to finish what she had been about to say, as with a growl, Carmichael, or Lathrop perhaps, crushed her ruthlessly to his chest. Nothing she had ever imagined before— indeed, nothing she had ever read before— could have prepared her for what happened next.

Lathrop's mouth closed over hers in a kiss of such passionate tenderness that fire was ignited in her veins. And if that were not all or enough, she felt the room start to spin and her knees threatened all at once to buckle beneath her. With a groan, she wrapped her arms around his neck, presumably to keep from falling. And when at last he released her it was all she could do merely to cling to him.

"I must know, Lucy," Lathrop whispered, his voice husky with lingering passion. "I love you and I want you for my wife."

"But I told you, Your Grace," Lucy murmured dreamily. "I intend to remain a spinster and write tales of Gothic horror, mystery, and romance. Indeed, if you must know, I am on the point of becoming a published author, and it is in a great measure thanks to you. Mr. Pendergraft was most impressed with my realistic account of a duel and my detailed description of a dungeon. Perhaps you would be interested to learn that I have called it

Lady in Waiting, or the Skeleton in the Castle Dungeon."

"The devil you did, and why do you think I went to such pains to instruct you in the fine art of dueling?"

"Because you thought it might in some way be useful to me, my lord duke?" queried Lucy, not in the least intimidated by the fierce, burning light in his eyes.

"Because I wished to demonstrate that you might discover a great deal to inspire you— married to a duke, my impossible love."

"Then, Your Grace," murmured Lucy, who was quite sure she had never felt more inspired than she did at that very moment, "I think perhaps I had better marry you. Because it is quite true, you know. A kiss does leave one trembling and weak— " smiling, she lifted her face to his "— when, that is, it is with the one man whom one is destined to love. Oh, yes, Patrick Phillip Carmichael Windholm— my dearest lord duke. Unlike Patience Merriweather, who was obviously never a true romantic heroine, I will most gladly marry you."

About the Author

Sara Blayne lives with her family in Portales, New Mexico. She is the author of five Zebra regency romances: *Passion's Lady, Duel of the Heart, A Nobleman's Bride, An Elusive Guardian,* and *An Easter Courtship.* Sara is currently working on a Valentine's Day novella, *Cupid's Arrow,* which will be a part of *Valentine Love* (to be published in January 1996). Sara is also working on a historical regency romance, which Zebra Books will be publishing in September 1996. Sara loves to hear from her readers, and you may write to her c/o Zebra Books, 850 Third Avenue, New York, NY 10022. Please include a self-addressed stamped envelope if you wish a response.

ELEGANT LOVE STILL FLOURISHES —
Wrap yourself in a Zebra Regency Romance.

A MATCHMAKER'S MATCH   (3783, $3.50/$4.50)
by Nina Porter

To save herself from a loveless marriage, Lady Psyche Veringham pretends to be a bluestocking. Resigned to spinsterhood at twenty-three, Psyche sets her keen mind to snaring a husband for her young charge, Amanda. She sets her cap for long-time bachelor, Justin St. James. This man of the world has had his fill of frothy-headed debutantes and turns the tables on Psyche. Can a bluestocking and a man about town find true love?

FIRES IN THE SNOW   (3809, $3.99/$4.99)
by Janis Laden

Because of an unhappy occurrence, Diana Ruskin knew that a secure marriage was not in her future. She was content to assist her physician father and follow in his footsteps . . . until now. After meeting Adam, Duke of Marchmaine, Diana's precise world is shattered. She would simply have to avoid the temptation of his gentle touch and stunning physique — and by doing so break her own heart!

FIRST SEASON   (3810, $3.50/$4.50)
by Anne Baldwin

When country heiress Laetitia Biddle arrives in London for the Season, she harbors dreams of triumph and applause. Instead, she becomes the laughingstock of drawing rooms and ballrooms, alike. This headstrong miss blames the rakish Lord Wakeford for her miserable debut, and she vows to rise above her many faux pas. Vowing to become an Original, Letty proves that she's more than a match for this eligible, seasoned Lord.

AN UNCOMMON INTRIGUE   (3701, $3.99/$4.99)
by Georgina Devon

Miss Mary Elizabeth Sinclair was rather startled when the British Home Office employed her as a spy. Posing as "Tasha," an exotic fortune-teller, she expected to encounter unforeseen dangers. However, nothing could have prepared her for Lord Eric Stewart, her dashing and infuriating partner. Giving her heart to this haughty rogue would be the most reckless hazard of all.

A MADDENING MINX   (3702, $3.50/$4.50)
by Mary Kingsley

After a curricle accident, Miss Sarah Chadwick is literally thrust into the arms of Philip Thornton. While other women shy away from Thornton's eyepatch and aloof exterior, Sarah finds herself drawn to discover why this man is physically and emotionally scarred.

Available wherever paperbacks are sold, or order direct from the Publisher. Send cover price plus 50¢ per copy for mailing and handling to Penguin USA, P.O. Box 999, c/o Dept. 17109, Bergenfield, NJ 07621. Residents of New York and Tennessee must include sales tax. DO NOT SEND CASH.

Taylor-made Romance from Zebra Books

WHISPERED KISSES   (0-8217-3830-5, $4.99/$5.99)
Beautiful Texas heiress Laura Leigh Webster never imagined
that her biggest worry on her African safari would be the handsome Jace Elliot, her tour guide. Laura's guardian, Lord Chadwick Hamilton, warns her of Jace's dangerous past; she simply
cannot resist the lure of his strong arms and the passion of his
Whispered Kisses.

KISS OF THE NIGHT WIND   (0-8217-5279-0, $5.99/$6.99)
Carrie Sue Strover thought she was leaving trouble behind her
when she deserted her brother's outlaw gang to live her life as
schoolmarm Carolyn Starns. On her journey, her stagecoach
was attacked and she was rescued by handsome T.J. Rogue. T.J.
plots to have Carrie lead him to her brother's cohorts who murdered his family. T.J., however, soon succumbs to the beautiful
runaway's charms and loving caresses.

FORTUNE'S FLAMES   (0-8217-3825-9, $4.99/$5.99)
Impatient to begin her journey back home to New Orleans,
beautiful Maren James was furious when Captain Hawk delayed
the voyage by searching for stowaways. Impatience gave way
to uncontrollable desire once the handsome captain searched
her cabin. He was looking for illegal passengers; what he found
was wild passion with a woman he knew was unlike all those
he had known before!

PASSIONS WILD AND FREE   (0-8217-5275-8, $5.99/$6.99)
After seeing her family and home destroyed by the cruel and
hateful Epson gang, Randee Hollis swore revenge. She knew
she found the perfect man to help her—gunslinger Marsh
Logan. Not only strong and brave, Marsh had the ebony hair
and light blue eyes to make Randee forget her hate and seek
the love and passion that only he could give her.

*Available wherever paperbacks are sold, or order direct from the
Publisher. Send cover price plus 50¢ per copy for mailing and
handling to Penguin USA, P.O. Box 999, c/o Dept. 17109,
Bergenfield, NJ 07621. Residents of New York and Tennessee
must include sales tax. DO NOT SEND CASH.*

TODAY'S HOTTEST READS
ARE TOMORROW'S SUPERSTARS

VICTORY'S WOMAN   (4484, $4.50)
by Gretchen Genet
Andrew—the carefree soldier who sought glory on the battlefield, and returned a shattered man . . . Niall—the legandary frontiersman and a former Shawnee captive, tormented by his past . . . Roger—the troubled youth, who would rise up to claim a shocking legacy . . . and Clarice—the passionate beauty bound by one man, and hopelessly in love with another. Set against the backdrop of the American revolution, three men fight for their heritage—and one woman is destined to change all their lives forever!

FORBIDDEN   (4488, $4.99)
by Jo Beverley
While fleeing from her brothers, who are attempting to sell her into a loveless marriage, Serena Riverton accepts a carriage ride from a stranger—who is the handsomest man she has ever seen. Lord Middlethorpe, himself, is actually contemplating marriage to a dull daughter of the aristocracy, when he encounters the breathtaking Serena. She arouses him as no woman ever has. And after a night of thrilling intimacy—a forbidden liaison—Serena must choose between a lady's place and a woman's passion!

WINDS OF DESTINY   (4489, $4.99)
by Victoria Thompson
Becky Tate is a half-breed outcast—branded by her Comanche heritage. Then she meets a rugged stranger who awakens her heart to the magic and mystery of passion. Hiding a desperate past, Texas Ranger Clint Masterson has ridden into cattle country to bring peace to a divided land. But a greater battle rages inside him when he dares to desire the beautiful Becky!

WILDEST HEART   (4456, $4.99)
by Virginia Brown
Maggie Malone had come to cattle country to forge her future as a healer. Now she was faced by Devon Conrad, an outlaw wounded body and soul by his shadowy past . . . whose eyes blazed with fury even as his burning caress sent her spiraling with desire. They came together in a Texas town about to explode in sin and scandal. Danger was their destiny—and there was nothing they wouldn't dare for love!